Sanibel Moonlight

A Shellseeker Beach Novel
Book Seven

HOPE
HOLLOWAY

Hope Holloway

Shellseeker Beach Book 7

Sanibel Moonlight

Copyright © 2022 Hope Holloway

This novel is a work of fiction. Any references to historical events, real people, or real locales are used fictitiously. Other names, characters, places, and incidents are the product of the author's imagination, and any resemblance to actual events or locales or persons, living or dead, is coincidental. All rights to reproduction of this work are reserved. No part of this publication may be reproduced, stored in or introduced into a retrieval system, or transmitted, in any form, or by any means (electronic, mechanical, photocopying, recording, or otherwise) without prior written permission from the copyright owner. Thank you for respecting the copyright. For permission or information on foreign, audio, or other rights, contact the author, hopehollowayauthor@gmail.com.

Cover designed by Sarah Brown (http://www.sarahdesigns.co/)

Introduction to Shellseeker Beach

Come to Shellseeker Beach and fall in love with a cast of unforgettable characters who face life's challenges with humor, heart, and hope. For lovers of riveting and inspirational sagas about sisters, secrets, romance, mothers, and daughters...and the moments that make life worth living.

For release dates, excerpts, news, and more, sign up to receive Hope Holloway's newsletter! Or visit www. hopeholloway.com and follow Hope on Facebook and BookBub!

A Personal Message From The Author

As I reviewed the final proofs of this manuscript, Hurricane Ian blew into the southwest coast of Florida, taking lives, flattening communities, and utterly destroying the piece of paradise known as Sanibel Island. Like millions of others, I am in profound mourning for the loss, having visited so many times, with strong friendships developed in the process of researching and writing this series.

Like many of you and all the residents, the loss of Sanibel as we know it hurts in a way that is difficult to describe.

I want readers to know that a portion of the proceeds from the sale of this book and the entire Shellseeker Beach series is being donated directly to Sanibel Island relief efforts. My goal is to raise at least $10,000, but I hope it can be more. Obviously, it won't be enough, but I thank you for buying this book in digital, paperback, or reading it in Kindle Unlimited. Every dollar will help.

In many ways, Sanibel Island itself has become a character in this series, as embedded into the stories as any of the people I've created. This book includes many landmarks and real places, and some might no longer be there. The lighthouse is still standing, thank God, but as I write this, we still don't have a full picture of damage to the island.

I hope you will put aside reality, enjoy the story, and remember this is fiction. In my world, Sanibel Island remains a glorious, unique, and blessed place full of lovely people who are grateful to live there. That may not be the case today, but it will be the case again someday. Someday soon, I hope.

We are all—residents, guests, and lovers of the island —Sanibel Strong.

All the best,

Hope Holloway

Chapter One

Asia

How could she smile? How could Asia Turner do anything but collapse and cry right now when her entire life just blew up in her face?

But she felt her lips rise as her whole body relaxed into Dane Whitney's capable and reassuring embrace, his whispered words giving her the hope she so desperately needed.

"No guts, no glory, Dane," she repeated as she dropped an item of clothing she was about to frantically throw into a suitcase. "I hope you're right about that."

He eased back, searching her face, his hazel eyes narrowed with concern.

"There's no chance this was just a...mistake or coincidence?" he asked, holding out the toy folding fan they'd just found on the doorstep. "We don't know our neighbors in this townhouse complex yet. I saw a little girl in the parking lot last week with her mother. Is it possible she dropped this?"

"I wish," she muttered, forcing herself to look at the paper and plastic, her heart falling as she saw the outline of a red dragon on a black background. "That is Spencer Keaton's calling card."

Her stomach roiled as she said his name out loud for the first time in a long time. Maybe since the day she stood in an office in London and asked to see the man she thought was her committed boyfriend, her six-weeks-pregnant body vibrating with excitement over her big announcement. But on that rainy day in England, Asia was the one who got a life-changing surprise.

"Mr. Keaton's out for two weeks on his honeymoon, ma'am. Can someone else help you?"

Spencer's admin's British accent still echoed in her head, a year and a half later.

"But...a folding fan?" Dane asked. "Why? Because he makes you hot?"

She almost laughed at that. What Spencer Keaton made her was furious and heartbroken. And maybe a little scared.

"Not at all. Every time he gave me a gift, it had an Asian theme—he thought I'd like that, because my name is Asia." She shuddered. "I just can't believe he found me."

"Could he know where your parents live? Did you ever mention to him that Roz and George lived on Sanibel? Does he know their names?"

She felt her eyes widen as his questions helped her brain re-engage after the shock of finding the fan a few minutes ago. She and Dane had just returned home after a spectacular night of playing songs they'd written together during an open mic night at Little Blues, high on life and each other.

The success of the night, the euphoria of both of

them getting a songwriting contract, and, oh, the chemistry that rocked their bodies as they returned to the apartment they'd recently rented as "platonic" roommates...*all* of it had disappeared in a flash when she'd spotted the folding fan left on her doorstep.

"I don't know if Spencer could or would seek out my parents," she said. "When we were dating, I'm sure I mentioned that Roz and George lived in Florida, but I'm not sure I ever said Sanibel Island." Panic slid up to her throat as she realized Dane wasn't asking about her parents. He was thinking of Zane. Little Zee, as she called her six-month-old baby, was right now spending the night at Roz and George's house.

"I better call my mother." She moved away, looking around for her phone. "She can wake Zee and..." No, no, that wouldn't work. "But I have to tell my mother—"

"Asia." He reached for her and guided her to the bed so she could sit. "You can call her in a minute, but we have to put together a plan to deal with this guy."

"A plan? I don't even know what he wants. I told you, he doesn't know he even *has* a child." Her voice cracked as she dropped onto the edge of her bed. "Unless...oh, God, *how* did he find me?" Then she moaned with realization. "Of course. The application for this townhouse. I bet our names and addresses went on a database. I've been so careful, but we couldn't get this place without giving them all kinds of information that probably got sold like new renters' data always does."

"Hang on a second," he said as he sat next to her.

"Please tell me more about this...Spencer? Is that his name?"

She flinched at the name, one she purposely had never mentioned, even when she'd confessed her past to Dane. "I already told you everything," she said.

"All I know is that you were in a fairly long relationship with a guy who lived in London and visited the States monthly," Dane replied. "You learned you were pregnant, and then flew across the Atlantic to surprise him with what you thought would be happy news. Right?"

She shrugged. "I wasn't sure how he'd react, but *I* was happy."

"But when you got there, you found out he was on his honeymoon."

With a grunt, she dropped her head back and looked at the ceiling, reliving the shame. "And I stood there like the world's biggest chump, managed not to cry, and left the building."

"But you never actually told him you were pregnant, right?"

"Nope. I ghosted him, quit my job, and never talked to him again. What else do you do when you find out the man you were dating just married someone else, and you're pregnant with his child?"

He rubbed her back as her voice grew taut with an old pain.

"So then, what makes you think he found out about Zee?" he asked. "Maybe he's just come to tell you he's sorry and close that chapter of his life?"

Silently, she stared straight ahead. "I have dreaded this day for a year and a half, Dane. I was so careful to never put my name or address anywhere official so he couldn't find me...or his son."

"Well, you can't live in this world anonymously," he said. "You must have known he'd find you at some point."

"I seriously hoped he'd quit looking and just forget I existed."

"But if he *did* find out you had a baby, he'd know it was his."

She swallowed hard, hearing something in Dane's voice that pressed on her chest.

"I know it was wrong," she said softly. "I know a man has a right to know he fathered a child, but he broke my heart and cheated and married another woman when he told me he loved me. Don't judge me."

"I'm not," he assured her, hugging her a little closer. "I swear I'm not, Asia."

"Then what are you thinking?" she asked, surprised at how very much it mattered to her.

"I'm thinking...a lot of things. Why leave the fan, and not a note? Or why not wait for you? Or find your phone number and call you? This..." He gestured toward the fan on the bed. "This silent message is disturbing. Is he creepy?"

"He wasn't, but then I found out I didn't know him at all, beyond his resume and quite outstanding recommendations. Remember, my recruiting firm—the one I was working for at the time—had placed him in a high-level position in London for a company headquartered in Columbus, where I lived."

"So he's British?"

"No, no. American. But we only got to know each other after he got that job, so our relationship was always long-distance. The kind that leaves a lot of room for... lying. Which, evidently, he did plenty of."

Dane nodded. "Well, he's a married man, and I'm sure he knows you figured that out by now." He shook his head, his eyes narrowed as he thought about it. "I'm just trying to put myself into his shoes and imagine what's motivating him to show up here and leave...that."

"You? In his shoes?" she scoffed. "They won't fit."

"So he's a bruiser and I should be scared?" he asked with a soft laugh.

"I meant they won't fit metaphorically. He's...not you. He's not kind and not gentle and not logical, but ruled by emotion and, yeah, he's kind of a control freak. He has to get his way, and always figures out how to do that."

"So we have to figure out what his 'way' is, as far as you're concerned."

She closed her eyes. "I don't ever want to see him again. Ever. He hurt me so..." She tried to breathe. "He *wrecked* me."

"Asia." He grunted. "I'm so sorry on behalf of all men."

"You are not *all* men, Dane." This time she put her hand on his cheek, inching closer to him. "And I was just about to show you that when that...that...that...*bad memory* stepped into our very, very new romance."

"Oh, it's a romance now?" His lips lifted in a smile. "No more homeless souls who moved in together to save money and sanity?"

Once again, she found herself smiling. How did he do that? "Yeah, I think it is a romance. Or was." Her smile faded. "You are free to go back to a platonic friendship with me now, just as roommates. I wouldn't blame you a bit."

"After I marched up to your room with my whole 'we can do anything together' speech?"

She sighed again, thinking of how she'd bolted and left him in shock by the front door, running up to her room in a panic. But Dane didn't panic, and she should know that by now. He thought things through with magnificent sense and a truly good heart.

"Thank you for that, Dane," she whispered. "It would have been very easy to just let me take off to my mother's, to get the baby, to run away..."

"No. You're not running anywhere, and neither am I." He took her hand. "You're stuck with me, Asia Turner. I don't run, but I do like to figure everything out and approach a problem with a logical plan. Pros and cons, you know."

"I'm afraid there's no 'pro' where he's concerned."

"Still, we can be methodical and logical."

She smiled. "I always forget you're a computer guy. I think of you as a musician."

"Aw, Aje. You'd be the only person in the world to call me a musician first and a software engineer second, so thank you. And, don't forget, bartender now, too. But this logical guy really needs to know how this man found you and what he wants."

"How is easy," she said. "When we applied for the townhouse, we got in a database and he found me."

"But why is he *looking* for you if he met and married someone else?" he asked. "Does he think he has a chance?"

She rolled her eyes. "He's a lot of things, but not stupid."

"Then maybe he found out you had a baby, through mutual friends or business

acquaintances, and when he did the math, he knew the sperm bank story you told everyone was a lie."

She considered that possibility. "We didn't have a lot of mutual friends. He didn't live in Columbus. We recruited him from a job in Oklahoma City, and during our whole year-plus relationship, he lived in London but came to town once a month. We really didn't have any people in common."

"Even the company where you worked? His business was your client, right?"

"Yes, but there wasn't overlap. And even if he met someone I knew, I'd joked about having a baby on my own for years when I had a string of bad luck in the dating department. That's why it was so easy to say I'd made the decision to do exactly that, and friends and family didn't question it. So he'd probably believe it unless he knew Zane's *exact* age, to the month. Then he could, as you say, do the math."

"Well, he's here now," Dane said. "So he's bound to find out one way or the other."

The magnitude of that made her whole body sink with defeat. "Am I obligated to let him meet Zee? Spend time with him? Have custody? What's the law?"

"We can ask Claire," he said, referring to his aunt, an attorney. "And while we're at it, we can ask Miles for help, too."

"Miles Anderson? What can he do?"

"He's a private investigator. He might be able to find out more about this guy than you actually know. Information is power, Asia." He eased her closer. "Plus, I've learned one thing about living in Shellseeker Beach, Florida."

"Which is…?"

"No one is alone in any crisis, big or small."

She stared at him, thinking about that. Her mother was the only person besides Dane to know the truth, including her own father, and anyone who was in their close circle at Shellseeker Beach, all of them like family to her.

"Do you want me to tell everyone?" she asked.

"I don't *want* you to do anything, Asia. Everything is your call."

Another thing she adored about this man. He managed to offer support without taking her independence. "Thank you."

"And if you don't want to stay here at the townhouse because he knows you live here, maybe we can stay with my mother."

"We? You're not obligated—"

"You're not going to be here alone all day if I go to work at Little Blues," he interjected, not giving her a chance to offer an out. "People need to know this guy's around and looking for you. You'll be safer that way, and so will Zee. And we can—"

"Dane."

"What?"

She looked hard at him, shaking her head. "I can't believe you're real."

He looked confused, an expression she didn't see often on this bona fide genius.

"I can't believe how much you care," she whispered. "You just got dragged into this with a woman you haven't known for two months. Instead of asking a bunch of questions or making me feel like garbage for the dumpster fire that was my past, you jump right into how to help me."

He smiled. "Is it a huge surprise to you that I have a crush on you the size of that Gulf of Mexico out there?"

"Not a huge surprise," she admitted on a laugh. "I've known you liked me since..."

"Since the moment you walked on the beach and my sister accused me of drooling over you."

"Sounds like Livvie." She made a face as a new realization dawned. "Oh, do I have to tell her, too?"

"Asia, what are you ashamed of? I mean, I understand why you told people you had a baby on your own, but you didn't do anything wrong. He wasn't married when you were in a relationship with him. He cheated on you, not the other way around."

"It's just so embarrassing. I was dumb, then I lied about it, I just..." She squeezed her eyes shut as the whole thing hit her hard again. "I want him to go away. I don't want this."

"Maybe he will," Dane said. "Maybe he'll see that you're happy and in a relationship—even if it is only about five hours old—and that you're surrounded by friends and family."

"What if he wants Zee?"

"He can't have him, period, end of story," Dane said matter-of-factly, the words and his tone giving her such a rush of affection, she almost kissed him.

But she didn't, because her brain was already thinking...custody battle. Oh, that could be long, ugly, expensive, and uncertain.

She refused to go there yet. Instead, she looked at the man next to her, and let herself lean into him, physically and emotionally.

"You are such a good man, Dane. You know darn well where our little make-out session in the parking lot was about to lead." She tipped her head toward the bed. "Your first night up here."

"In the queen's bedroom." He gave her a light peck on the lips. "We'll get there, Aje. But not until we have this sorted out, and you're at ease, and Zee is safe. You'll never sleep if we stay here. So we can crash at my mother's beach house, or wake your mother—"

"I'll go to my parents' house," she said, knowing instinctively it was the right—if difficult—thing to do.

"My mother sleeps light when she's babysitting little Zee. And I want my baby next to me all night."

"And he will be." He pushed up from the bed. "Pack what you need and I'll take you there."

"You can stay there, too," she added. "My mom will make up the couch in the den."

He shook his head. "I'm going to stay downstairs in my bedroom. If this clown shows up here, I'll...deal with him."

"Dane." She squeezed his hand. "Thank you."

He brought their joined fingers to his lips, never taking his eyes from her. "You don't have to thank me," he said. "I'd do anything for you."

She let her eyes shutter, gut-punched by how much she cared for him, and how long she'd needed someone who loved her unconditionally. If this ruined everything, it would...well, ruin everything.

"So, uh, what does this Spencer character look like?" he asked. "And what's his last name again?"

"Keaton. His name is Spencer Keaton and he's... good-looking."

"Not sure I'd know that if I saw it. Like Superman or something?"

"Just a big, square-jawed, dark-haired Caucasian man. Kind of..." She wiped a hand from shoulder to shoulder. "Well-built."

Dane snorted a laugh. "Great. So some big, brawny, handsome dude might show up and I'll—"

"You'll outsmart him," she finished for him. "You're a thousand times the man he is, Dane."

"Thanks." He stood and tugged her hand. "We'll get through this," he said, easing her into a warm embrace. "I promise you."

She hugged him back, holding him for a long time, praying he was right.

Chapter Two

Eliza

O f the many things Eliza Whitney loved about living on Sanibel Island, the unusual geography was strangely way at the top. Unlike most barrier islands that acted as a perimeter around the coast of Florida, Sanibel stretched from east to west, like God had reached down and tipped the piece of paradise on its side. And surely He'd done that so the island could boast of glorious sunsets *and* sunrises, and a bounty of seashells unlike any other place on Earth.

To celebrate all of that, Eliza rarely missed an opportunity to walk the beach morning and evening. During those walks, she looked up at the glorious colors of the sky and down to search the sand for treasures. And many mornings, she also looked to her side to see the familiar face of her sister, who frequently joined her for a sunrise stroll on Shellseeker Beach.

During that hour, the sisters who'd spent most of their lives unaware that each other existed made up for a lot of lost time.

They shared stories about their pasts, discussed their lives in excruciating detail, exchanged secrets and revelations, helped each other through life's little trials, and opened up their hearts to each other.

Today was no different, although it was an unusually chilly March morning, and Eliza and Claire wore cotton pullovers and comfy sweats instead of their usual T-shirts and shorts.

"So this is winter on Sanibel Island," Claire said, tugging at her sleeves. "I honestly didn't know it ever got cold."

"Not exactly cold, but Teddy said this is just about the closest we'll ever get to a snow day. Also, she said it'll go back up to seventy tomorrow."

"The beauty of a short winter," Claire cracked.

"But that's a good thing, because we can't keep Shellseeker Cottages full of guests and tourists if it's not hot and sunny." Eliza glanced toward one of the colorful cottages at the end of a boardwalk. "Although I had a cancellation in Slipper Snail this week. I'll fill it soon, even with this chilly weather."

Claire didn't answer, but she hugged herself and moved her gaze to the distant horizon, quiet, as she often was.

"You cold, Claire?" Eliza asked. "I'd think the temp in the fifties would be nothing to a New Yorker like you."

"Not a New Yorker for long," Claire said, lifting her brows. "I got an offer on my apartment and I think I'm going to take it."

"Really?" Eliza punched the air with a victory fist. "It's almost official that you live here."

"*Almost* being the operative word," Claire said, glancing down at the sand, then bending over it. "Oh, I thought that was a Junonia," she said, picking up a broken shell. "I've yet to find even a piece of one. I'm beginning to think that seashell is folklore."

"You can buy one for twenty bucks in Sanibel Treasures," Eliza joked, but her smile faded as she replayed her sister's last comment. "But what do you mean 'almost' is an operative word? That sounds kind of...squishy."

"Oh, I'm not squishy. It's my, uh, partner? Is that what I should call DJ?"

Eliza eyed her, knowing her sister didn't just spew words to fill the air. Claire was the more pensive of the two, and when she had something to say, it was always worth listening to.

"I'd call DJ the father of your only child, for starters," Eliza said.

"Kind of a stretch to call twenty-six-year-old Noah Hutchins a child," Claire said.

"Or you could call DJ the man you are currently living with," Eliza suggested. When Claire didn't answer, she added, "The object of your affection? Maybe main squeeze? Or we could go very classic and just say boyfriend. What feels right?"

Claire looked out at the horizon again, still silent.

"Or doesn't anything feel right at the moment?" Eliza asked softly.

On a sigh, her sister closed her eyes. "You always know me, don't you?"

"Well, that's easy today, since you're as transparent as the water. What's going on with you?" Eliza pressed.

Claire shrugged. "Like I said, things are squishy."

"And you, my lawyer sister, don't really like squishy, do you?"

She looked down and rubbed her toe into the sand. "I like that kind of squishy," she said. "But not..." She tapped her chest. "This kind."

"What do you mean?" Eliza asked, true concern growing. "Is everything all right with you and DJ?"

"I don't know," she said. "I honestly do not know, and that's always been my problem with DJ from the day he showed up in Shellseeker Beach after I reunited with Noah. I never know what he's thinking or feeling."

"Do you ask?"

"Yes, I do. And his responses vary from, 'I'm thinking how pretty you are' to, 'Feelings aren't made to describe, they're made to have' or some quote from a philosophy book that he and Noah are reading." She gave a bitter-sweet smile. "And then Sophia flounces into the room, causes drama, and my questions are forgotten. No, scratch that. *I'm* forgotten."

Eliza studied Claire's expression, considering the sheer amount of information her sister had just shared.

She was used to honesty—they'd promised each other nothing but when they met less than a year ago—but Claire was rarely this raw in her candor. Her lifetime career as an attorney gave her tremendous skill at diplo-macy and well-chosen words, saving the ones that slice for the most important moments in life.

Which this just might be.

"This sounds serious," Eliza said on a whisper that got caught on a strong breeze from the Gulf. "Want to sit?" She gestured toward the gazebo that stood high on a rise of sand, tucked into the palms and sea oats that lined the shore.

The lacy structure had been the setting for long conversations and revelations for both of them in the past, plus the place where Eliza's daughter and Claire's mother each recently married the men of their dreams.

"The honesty house?" Claire laughed. "Not sure I'm ready for that."

"Come on." Eliza took her hand. "It won't be as chilly up there and you only have to be as honest as you want. Although, it's me, so..."

"So, in other words, spill," Claire finished for her, running her hand through her messy long hair as they walked toward the empty gazebo. "All right."

A minute later, they were sitting side by side on one of the benches that lined the gazebo perimeter, peering out at the water, both quiet while Claire collected her thoughts.

"I guess the problem *is* Sophia," she finally said. "Or at least it feels like she rocked the boat that was previously cruising along okay."

Sophia Fortunato, DJ's seventeen-year-old daughter, had blown into town from California not long ago, after one fight too many with her mother and a break-up with her boyfriend. The plan was that she'd take some classes at the local high school to get her diploma, and she even worked part-time at the Cottages, helping with house-keeping.

Claire let out a sigh. "Ever since she got here, the vibe —if I may use that ridiculous word—has changed in our house."

Eliza snorted. "Teddy loves that word. But how has it changed?"

"Well, she shifted the center, you know? There were three of us, all virtual strangers, but we made it work for us. There was me, single for almost my entire life, a woman who lived alone and worked constantly, certain she was destined to do that to the end. And then, suddenly, I became a mother and a...well, not wife, but partner."

"That made you happy," Eliza reminded her.

"Very much so. And it made DJ happy to pick up where we left off two and a half decades ago, despite what I think is a constant tug of the family and life he left behind in California. Still, he's a live-in-the-moment kind of guy." She laughed softly. "I guess that's an understatement, but he seemed pretty content with things."

"And Noah is beyond content," Eliza said, thinking of the constant smile worn by the young man that college-aged Claire had given up for adoption.

"Oh, yes, he is, and understandably so. I mean, the poor kid's adoptive parents died in 9/11, and he was raised in foster homes. Now he has a real family again—his *real* biological parents—and a happy and healthy rela-tionship with Katie Bettencourt to boot."

"It's all been so good for the three of you," Eliza mused. "Did Sophia really wreck all that apart?"

"It's almost like she's trying to," Claire said.

"Ouch." Eliza had worried when Claire and DJ had opened their home to his daughter, but she thought the little ad hoc family had been so strong. "Is she affecting your ability to study for the bar? I know you were disappointed when that office space on the mainland fell through."

"Yes," she agreed. "I could have used that escape, but I study during the day and she's not there much. I like the study station I have set up at home and have so much more flexibility this way. But when she *is* home? Whoa. She's a force to be reckoned with."

"How much power can one teenage girl have?"

Claire rolled her eyes with a snort. "Don't underestimate the drama mama, as Noah calls her."

"And is she really having an impact on your relationship with DJ?" Eliza asked, sensing that somehow Claire's current state of "squishy" had more to do with the father than the daughter.

Claire shrugged. "Well, for one thing, he spoils her, and I don't think that's smart, but she's not my daughter. I mean, I get spoiling a kid after a divorce, but don't you have to draw the line somewhere?"

"I guess it depends on what he's spoiling her with," Eliza said. "Is it his time or his money or his attention?"

"All of the above," Claire said. "Which is probably fine, but I don't know, because I've never had a family before, Eliza. I haven't raised children or even had siblings around, and you know my childhood was far from traditional. I don't know what's right and wrong with a seventeen-year-old girl, nor do I know how much say I have in things. She's not my daughter, so even if I had any experience, I have no place to say a word."

"Well, she's living in your home and upsetting your apple cart, so you certainly have a right to say much more than a word," Eliza said. "Someone has to."

Claire nodded, considering that.

"You should talk to DJ, Claire," Eliza said softly. "Tell him what's bothering you. You can't have a relationship if you're not honest."

"You're right." She blew out a breath. "I will talk to him. I thought we'd have more time these weeks while my mother and Buck are off on a honeymoon, but DJ's been so busy negotiating the deal to buy Luigi's pizza parlor. He's there all the time."

"They've been talking for quite a while. Are they any closer to a deal?"

"Closer?" Claire gave a wry chuckle. "You get two Italian pizza makers together and they talk dough—and not the kind that will be exchanged if and when DJ buys that restaurant. Flour, crust, mouthfeel, and yeast starters. That's *all* they really care about."

Eliza searched her sister's face. "Is there any other reason you don't talk to him?"

"Yeah," Claire admitted with a crack in her voice. "And I guess because I'm in the honesty house, I should tell you."

Eliza took her hand. "You can tell me anything, Claire."

"I'm scared, Eliza. I'm so scared to lose this, because I've never had it before."

"This, meaning...love?" Eliza asked, not sure what her sister meant.

"Meaning a real family," Claire replied on a whispery breath. "A man at home, a son in the picture, his lovely girlfriend who's going to be a dream daughter-in-law, and she has a little girl who makes me a grandmother. It all feels so...fulfilling."

"I get that, Claire. I really do."

"I'm well into my forties and I've never had a family life," she continued, the dam broken now, along with the tear ducts. "Even as a child, I had no siblings and Camille and Dutch had the world's weirdest marriage. This is like a dream of...of normalcy for me. I am so scared it's going to go up in smoke and I'll lose it all as quickly as I found it."

"You'll never lose me," Eliza assured her. "But I truly understand how new and wonderful this is for you. I do."

"I know you do." Claire leaned into her. "And now, enough about me, please. I'm done talking about myself. Tell me more about last night at Little Blues. I can't believe Dane and Asia did so well at the open mic that they got a songwriting deal!"

"It was amazing. Talk about a happy couple. Who would have thought those two would hit it off?" Eliza beamed, thinking about her son and his new lady love.

"And I think he had a nice talk with Miles and all that whitewater is behind us."

"That's it, then," Claire said with a knowing look. "That's it with Miles."

"What's *it* with Miles?" Eliza asked.

"You have passed your one-year-as-a-widow mark, your son has reconciled with the fact that Miles is the man in your life, you're settled into running Shellseeker Cottages with Teddy, and...what else has stopped you from having a full-blown relationship with Miles Anderson?"

"I guess it depends on what you mean by full-blown."

"I mean the whole enchilada, Eliza. Love, marriage, commitment..." She gave a soft elbow nudge. "The good thing."

Eliza laughed at the euphemism, but her smile wavered. "Yeah, no, not yet."

"And you're hesitant, because...?"

"Fear. Uncertainty. The fact that he wants forever, and I did that once."

"You did marry once," Claire agreed. "And it was wonderful, but Ben is gone and you are ready to move on."

"Can't argue that," Eliza said. "Miles is an amazing, kind, funny, charming, fantastic man who's been nothing but adoring, attentive, and patient since the day we met."

Claire stared at her. "What is the *but* I don't want to hear?"

"*But* he wants something I can't give him."

"Eliza. You're fifty-four years old. You can spend the night with a man and no one will judge."

"It's not that," Eliza said quickly, then made a face. "Although it kind of is. I was so young when I met and married Ben. He was, you know, my only one. I do feel like there has to be a real commitment before that happens."

Claire lifted a brow. "Pretty sure Miles would run into this gazebo and be the next guy to say, 'I do' under these ancient beams if you gave him half a chance."

"Oh, he would," Eliza said on a laugh. "He never hides the fact that he's in this for the long haul."

"And?"

"And I could do a long haul, but not...marriage." She punctuated that with a tight smile. "I don't know how to explain it, Claire, but when I took the vows with Ben, I meant *forever*."

"You do remember there's a line in those vows that says, "Til death do us part."' She softened her words by touching Eliza's arm. "Not both your deaths, Eliza. Just one."

Eliza stared at her for a long time, feeling the turmoil rise in her chest. "It still doesn't seem right," she admitted.

"Is it possible," Claire leaned closer as she spoke slowly, "that you're not sure about how you really feel about Miles? That your reluctance to go the next step—either at the altar or in the bedroom—has less to do with your late husband, Ben, and more to do with Eliza?"

Eliza considered the question, long and hard. "Maybe," she finally admitted.

"Do you love Miles?"

She bit her lip. "I think I do. He's essentially flawless, you know."

"But love isn't just appreciating a lack of flaws. It's... deeper. It's..." Claire laughed. "I'm not sure I know what it is, but you have to love the flaws, too."

"If he had any," Eliza cracked, but her smile wavered. "The thing is, I don't know life on Sanibel Island without Miles. I met him days after I got here, and I was still deep in the throes of grief."

"Maybe..." Claire wrinkled her nose as if she didn't want to say the rest but knew she had to. "You should try a little time apart and see how that feels."

"We did spend a few distant weeks when Dane first arrived, and it didn't do anything but make me want to see him more."

"Then you have your answer."

She sighed deeply. "Can a person have two...ones?" she asked on a whisper. At Claire's baffled look, she added, "I mean, the expression is, 'He's *The One.*' Not, '*The Second One.*'"

"You're asking a woman who hasn't had the first 'One' yet."

For a moment, Eliza forgot her personal issues and thought only of her sister. "Oh, Claire. DJ's not The One?"

"I don't know anymore," she confessed on a whisper. "I just don't. But I'll talk to him. I promise."

They looked at each other for a long time, silent, thinking, and as deeply connected as sisters could be.

"No answers today," Eliza said. "Just a lot of questions."

Claire put her arm around Eliza and snuggled them closer. "No one I'd rather ask them with, though."

"Amen, sister." Eliza added a smile. "Wow, I love having a sister."

Chapter Three

Noah

As he did every morning when the sun peeked over the horizon, Noah Hutchins jumped in his car and drove to the apartment complex where Katie and Harper Bettencourt, his two favorite girls on the face of the Earth, would be rising and getting ready for the day.

He knew that even on a chilly day like this, when the two beachfront businesses where he worked might be a little slower than usual, he had a long day ahead of him.

So before it truly started, he'd have coffee and some breakfast with the girls, then they'd all get into his car and take Harper to kindergarten. Then he and Katie would head to Shellseeker Beach, where he would split his time between the tea hut and the rental cabana, and Katie would spend the day cleaning and beautifying the cottages at the small resort.

In the late afternoon, after sneaking in lunch with Katie, he'd head home to help his father make dough for the next pop-up pizza event they held several times a week at Shellseeker Cottages.

And in the evenings, he'd work on his novel. Well, he'd *try*.

But coffee with Katie and pancakes with Harper was always the best part of the day.

It was a decent life—except for one thing. His dream of writing a novel was so far on the back burner, it wasn't even warm anymore. What could he cut out of his life to make room to pursue his most fervent passion?

Right now, nothing.

Before he could go down the rabbit hole of how he wanted to change his routine, Harper swung the apartment door open and jumped into his arms. He certainly couldn't cut out time with this precious girl or her mother.

"Noah!" Her blond hair swung over tiny shoulders. "Chocolate chip or blueberry? Mommy wants to know *now*."

"Now?"

"Mixing batter," Katie called from the kitchen. "Pick your poison."

He smiled just hearing her voice. "What's your pleasure, Doodlebug?" he asked the squirmy five-year-old in his arms.

She just gave him a dead-on "are you kidding" look that cracked him up.

"I'm thinking chocolate chip, Katie," he called back as he lowered Harper to the ground.

"You're thinkin' right, buster," Harper teased, then spun—twice, because one pirouette was never enough—and danced into the apartment, which already smelled like coffee, bacon, and pure joy.

"Morning," he greeted Katie, who was stirring yellow pancake batter in a bowl at the counter.

"Hey." She looked up and blue eyes that matched the five-year-old version that had met him at the door warmed with affection. "You look bright-eyed and bushy-tailed today, Noah."

"So many jobs, so little time." He rounded the peninsula-style counter and planted a kiss on soft, sweet lips, resisting the urge to pull her in and make it deeper, but only because Harper had scampered onto a barstool and watched their every move.

"You *are* a man with three jobs," Katie noted, stealing another peck before turning her attention back to the pancakes.

Four jobs, if he counted writing, which was certainly not a job.

"But the cabana and tea hut might not be slammed in this cold weather," she said, then lifted a dripping wooden spoon to point at Harper. "Which reminds me, kiddo. Long pants today, and a light jacket. Otherwise you'll be freezing on the playground."

"Hardly freezing," Noah said, but Katie shot him a look he instantly read. "But that's the right call," he added, turning to Harper. "Long pants and a parka, I say. Boots, too, and some snowshoes."

She giggled. "What are snowshoes?"

"Tennis rackets for your feet," Noah told her with a bop to the nose.

"Harper, go get your school clothes on while I finish these and we'll have breakfast with Noah."

"'Kay!" She slid off the stool and started to run, then froze. "But I need green, Mommy! We're all supposed to wear green today for St. Patrick's Day!"

Katie's jaw loosened. "And you were going to tell me this when?"

"I forgot." She looked sheepish, and so dang cute it nearly ripped Noah's heart out.

"Do you have anything green, Doodlebug?" Noah asked.

Before she could answer, Katie huffed out a frustrated breath. "Couldn't they have put a note in your backpack last week so I could have remembered? I could have grabbed a green T-shirt when we were in Walmart on the mainland the other day."

"I can wear my reindeer sweater!" Harper said, bouncing on her toes with the idea. "It's got lots of green and it's really warm."

"It's also got lots of Christmas," Katie said wryly. "Which was three months ago."

"So?" Harper flipped her hands. "I'll be different. You'll see!" With that, she took off, belting out "Rudolph, the Red-Nosed Reindeer."

"Now that is one completely confident little girl," Noah said, pointing in the direction Harper had disappeared. "Kudos to her mom for raising someone who will dare to be different."

She smiled at him. "I love the way you look at life," she said.

"Well, I love the way you look, period." He pulled her in and took the kiss he'd been wanting since he walked in the door, loving how she tasted like mint and coffee. "Good morning again, gorgeous."

He could feel her smile under his lips. "Hi, yourself." As they broke apart, she gave him one more hug. "Did you get anything written last night?"

"Don't ask. Once Sophia stopped playing music, yakking on the phone, and whatever else she does to make noise, I didn't have a creative thought in my brain." He shook his head as he walked to the coffee pot to pour himself a cup. "I know I always wanted a sister, but *eesh*."

"If by *eesh* you mean high maintenance, low productivity, and constant interruptions? She is all that, and I say that as her boss three days a week."

He gave her a look. "I knew offering her that job when you were slammed with the seasonal rush might mean more work for you, not less."

"Well, she's entertaining," Katie said brightly. "And now that she's taking classes at the high school, she's not working with me quite as much."

"And she has to take summer school classes in order to graduate next fall." He groaned. "I guess she's not going back to California anytime soon."

"Do you want her to?" Katie asked.

He sipped the coffee and rounded the counter to take a stool and watch Katie work. "I like having a family, don't get me wrong, but not only is she the loudest person alive, I don't think she's helping DJ and my mom get any closer."

"Oh, no. And they were doing so well. I was starting to hope that was the next wedding in Shellseeker Beach."

He eyed her over the rim of the mug, tempted to say he wanted *their* wedding to be next, but this wasn't the right time. Not that he wasn't certain about their future—he was. And he believed Katie felt the same way.

But he had to be more established professionally, with a decent amount of money in the bank, before they took that step, so he hadn't proposed and wouldn't until the time was right.

None of his jobs was taking him in that direction, however.

"What is she doing to derail Claire and DJ?" Katie asked as she pulled crispy bacon from the oven where she'd been warming it.

"She just sucks the air out of a room, for one thing. Claire's not the most talkative person. I'm afraid she disappears when Sophia is around. And DJ?" He sipped his coffee again, thinking about the dinner conversation last night when all his father and Sophia talked about was California. The redwoods, the weather, the mountains, the Pacific Ocean, and people no one else knew. "Sometimes I don't think he even likes Sanibel Island."

"Well, he likes you. And Claire. And isn't he buying that restaurant soon?"

"I don't know. I think the commitment of running a business like that just goes against everything he stands for now. The man loves his freedom and once you have staff, payroll, inventory, and customers? No more freedom." Noah shrugged, not sure he wanted to get into yet another topic that frustrated him. "He talks a lot, you know."

"Then Sophia comes by it honestly."

"Yeah. It's like there's never any quiet in the house, just the two of them." He took another deep drink of coffee. "I shouldn't complain. I wanted a family more than I wanted my next breath. Now I have one, and I'm going to enjoy it...whether I like it or not."

She laughed at that. "Well, families can be tough, and who knows that better than me?"

He nodded, knowing what she'd been through—leaving home at nineteen, pregnant and alone, and having no contact with her family until her stepsister, Jadyn, hunted her down a few months ago and initiated their reconciliation.

"Sometimes I can't believe that Jadyn actually lives here and we're friends, but things do change in families," she said. "And I talked to my dad for forty-five minutes last night, speaking of family miracles."

"That's great," he said, and meant it. Katie had her own challenges growing up, especially after her mother died when she was not much older than Harper. In fact, Katie and Noah's rocky childhoods were one of the things that had bonded them from the beginning.

She plated the pancakes and kept one eye on him, thinking. "You know, you could write here any evening."

He smiled at her. "Don't tempt me, but I'd never get this book done."

"We can be quiet. Harper goes to bed at eight and I'm not far behind. I don't mind if you work here."

He tipped his head, considering the offer, but it felt

like he'd be invading her home. "I'd be distracted in a totally different way," he admitted.

"Noise cancelling headphones?" she suggested.

"Yeah, I tried the ones Claire got to study for the bar, but I can't write with those things on. I just need two hours, you know? Two hours and I could draft ten pages. But I can't find them."

"They exist in that twenty-four-hour clock."

"Yeah, from four to six in the morning."

She curled a lip. "I still think you'd do better from ten to midnight."

"I would, but those are peak Sophia-talking-to-her-friends-in-California hours."

"Noah, listen to yourself."

"What? It's true."

"What's true is that you have an excuse for every answer. Are you sure you want to write this book? If it's really burning in your heart, I think you'd find a way."

He searched her face, letting the words sink in. Was she right? Was he making excuses? Did he even have what it took to write a novel? Was he—

"Merry Christmas, everyone!" Harper came twirling into the kitchen wearing jeans and quite possibly the ugliest green and white reindeer sweater ever made.

"Harper, you can't..." But Katie's arguments faded out as she laughed at the joy in her daughter's expression. "Well, maybe you can."

"Ms. Kaufman said wear green." Harper climbed onto the stool next to Noah. "I'm wearing green. What is St. Patrick's Day, anyway?"

"'Tis for the wearin' o' the green," Noah said in a thick, fake Irish accent as he put an arm around her. "And you are as bonny a lass as I've ever seen, fair Doodlebug."

She let out a cascade of musical giggles. "What did you say?"

The laughter and chatter continued through breakfast, a rushed cleanup, and the short drive to school, where there were kisses and goodbyes and I love you's before Katie and Noah were alone in the car again.

"So, are you okay?" Katie asked, reaching over the console to take his hand as they drove to Shellseeker Beach.

"I'm fine," he said simply, threading their fingers together. "Life has ups and downs and frustrations, but I have you, and that's all I need."

"And two hours a day to write a novel."

"Which is probably crap anyway."

"Hey!" She squeezed his hand. "You can't say that. Don't put that out in the universe. Just write your lousy first draft. Remember that article I read online by some famous writer? All first drafts are horrible, and someone else said, 'You can't fix a blank page.' So..."

He gave her a smile, loving her for the pep talk, and not wanting her to know it simply wasn't hitting the mark.

"They're not excuses," he finally said. "I know it sounds like that, but I can't walk away from these commitments. Deeley needs me so much now that he's opening another location and we're so busy."

"Teddy wouldn't mind if you stopped working at the tea hut."

He threw her a look. "And let her give away the best homegrown iced hibiscus tea in Florida? She was sitting on a gold mine, just giving away free product, and you know she'd do it again if I weren't there to run the place. Plus, now we've added coffee and other drinks, and the tea hut's booming."

"That leaves helping your dad do the pop-up pizza business."

"Which is also growing more than expected with lots of requests for us to do events around the whole area," he said. "And making pizza is his joy. I love spending that time with him after a lifetime of not even knowing who he was, and him not knowing I even existed. I can't ditch my dad."

He pulled into Shellseeker Cottages' lot and easily found a parking spot at this early hour, switching off the ignition and staring ahead until she put a gentle hand on his arm.

"You're running on a treadmill, Noah. You're keeping everyone else in business so they can follow their passions, but in the process, you're giving up your dreams."

He put his hand over hers, instantly soothed by her touch and her words. But neither made the problem go away.

"Remember, I lived in foster homes for my entire life, Katie. I've never had family, and I wanted that much more than I wanted to write a book. Now I do have it, and if I walk out on these people, who either are or have become family, then I've broken a commitment to them. I won't do that."

"Just another thing I love about you, Noah Hutchins."

He leaned in and kissed her, letting the echo of her words fill his head and heart.

"I'll figure it out," he told her as they parted. "Because I have you by my side and with you, I can do anything. Including write a book that doesn't seem to want to get written."

"I believe in you." She put her hand on his cheek and rubbed her thumb over his lip. "I believe you will write a book—or ten—and you will build the foundation you want and then you will..."

"Spend the rest of my life with you."

She smiled. "Yeah."

He had so much to live for. He just had to figure out how to make it all work.

Chapter Four

Asia

Asia woke wishing it had all been a dream, but as she stared out at the morning skies from her parents' guest room, she had to face reality. Spencer Keaton was back in her life and she was going to have to deal with it.

Turning over, she lifted her head to peek into the Pack-n-Play where Zane George Turner had slept next to her all night. She sucked in a breath at the sight of the empty playpen, but that inhale included a whiff of coffee, so she knew exactly where Zee was. In the protective arms of her mother, who had no doubt tiptoed in here without waking Asia to get the baby and give him a bottle of pre-pumped breast milk.

She groaned, a part of her so tired of Roz Turner's overbearing style. Asia's breasts hurt and she'd wanted to nurse little Zee this morning, but nope. Her *smother* had different ideas.

But it was that very *smother* who, last night, had asked virtually no questions. For Roz, that was a small miracle. And so was the fact that she'd kept Asia's secret from her own husband.

Asia's heart rolled around at the thought of

confessing to George Turner that she'd been spineless and lied. That would be the hardest thing, and the first.

Last night, on the way over here with Dane, Asia had texted her mother with just enough information to let her know what was going on. If she'd been shocked or worried or thrown in any way, Roz was too much of a cool cucumber to let on. Instead, she got out of bed, met Asia at the door with a hug and a cup of tea, then sent her off to the guest room, where Zee was sound asleep.

All Roz said after a question or two was that they'd talk tomorrow, and she'd thanked Dane with a warm embrace and offered him a place to stay, too. But Dane was adamant that he'd stay at their townhouse, ready to face whatever came at them.

With that thought, Asia grabbed her phone to see that Dane had texted about half an hour earlier.

Dane Whitney: *All quiet on the western front. Hope you slept like a baby and next to one. Be over in a bit.*

Good heavens, that man was a find. And they'd come so close...well, he was right. Their romance would wait until this was all cleared up and fixed and finished.

But would her entanglement with Spencer *ever* be finished? Truly, that was all she wanted in the world, but had no idea how to go about making that happen.

Tying on a robe she'd left here when she moved out more than a month ago, Asia headed downstairs, saying a prayer of thanks when she saw her parents' bedroom door still closed.

Sleep, Dad. Sleep longer. I'm not ready to tell you my truth yet.

She heard her mother humming and chattering to the baby in the kitchen, and she followed the sound and that delicious aroma of coffee.

Roz was at the kitchen table, holding Zee in her arms, a bottle at his lips, all managed with one capable hand. With her other, she carefully sipped a coffee without dropping a molecule on the baby or his blanket.

Regardless of her mother's impressive balancing act, Asia waited until Roz set the cup down on the table before saying anything.

"Hey, there," she finally whispered. "Morning."

"Hey, baby." Roz turned and lifted her brows. "How are you feeling?"

"Sleep eludes me." She walked to the coffee pot and reached for her favorite mug on the counter, realizing just then that her mother always put it out for her, like a little gift every morning that Asia was in this house. "You know, I don't give you quite enough credit for being awesome, Mom."

As she poured the coffee, she waited a beat, expecting a typical Roz Turner wisecrack, like, "Oh, Zane, did you hear that? I did something right for a change." But when her mother didn't say a word, Asia turned to find those dark, dark eyes pinned on her and misty with tears.

"You okay?" Asia asked.

"Just worried about you," she answered with uncharacteristic softness in her voice. "And wishing you'd never moved into that townhouse."

"Because then maybe Spencer wouldn't have found me?" she guessed, adding a splash of cream to the coffee before coming to the table. "At least maybe not for a long time."

Before she sat down, she leaned over to gaze at her baby's little brown curls, his skin exactly the color of the cream-kissed coffee in her cup. He bore almost no resemblance to Spencer, a fact that had always pleased her. Maybe she could lie to him and tell him he wasn't the father? Maybe she—

"What are you going to tell Dad?" her mother asked.

"I'm going to tell him the truth," Asia replied, taking a seat. "The same thing I'm going to tell everyone." *Including Spencer,* she thought wryly, knowing that lying to him was the wrong thing to do on every imaginable level. Also, a DNA test would reveal the truth.

"Everyone?" Roz asked. "Like Teddy and Eliza and...everyone?"

She swallowed. "My lies have caught up with me. And, honestly, the only good thing about him showing up is that I can stop lying."

Her mother nodded with understanding, looking down at Zee's tiny hands as they fussed with the bottle. "I knew this day would come," Roz said with a sigh of resignation.

"The 'tell the truth' day, or the 'dang, he found me' day?"

"Neither." She eased the nearly empty bottle out from between Zee's lips. "The 'it's time for real food' day, since this little guy has sucked down this bottle and wants five more."

"I can nurse him." Asia reached for the baby. "I'd like to, actually."

But her mother lifted a brow high into her forehead. "Or I can make pure organic baby food from scratch, Asia. Can we do that today?"

Asia searched her mother's face, a familiar feeling rising up. The need to wrest control from her mother, to call the shots, to be the mother—all the things that made her want to move out of here in the first place. But she tamped that feeling down, not wanting to argue, not today.

"Sure. What did you have in mind?"

"We can start simple. How about a mashed banana?" She pointed to the fruit bowl. "Or I have some vegetables. We could cook and smoosh them up real good."

"I like the banana." She pushed up to get what she'd need to mash a banana, loving the normalcy of the moment. She did not want to discuss Spencer, and somehow, her mother understood that.

She got a small bowl and fork, bringing it to the table as Roz selected the perfect banana, ripe enough to be soft, but not brown. Asia forked it into mush and looked up, smiling while Roz got a burp from Zee and then put him into the bouncy seat on the table.

"Okay, grab your phone, Mama," Asia said in a sing-song voice. "Zee's about to get his first taste of real food."

"Well, I don't want to miss that!" George Turner's voice boomed from the hall one second before he walked

---

in, wearing his signature striped pajamas and a blinding smile.

Was Dad ever not happy? Guess she was about to find out.

"Asia!" He went straight to her and planted a kiss on her hair. "Mom told me you'd slipped in here last night with big news. What is it?"

For a moment, she just stared up at him, taking in his ebony eyes and shiny dome, the face of a man she loved right down to the last strand of DNA.

Would he be hurt by this?

Dumb question. *How* hurt would he be? That was the real question that poked at her chest like the tines of the fork she held.

"I knew things would go well for Dane at that open mic thing last night," he said, oblivious to her inner turmoil. "The boy's got real talent, which is a darn good thing, since he quit that impressive techie job to pursue music."

"Oh, yeah, that." She had completely forgotten that the record company executive in attendance had loved the songs she and Dane had co-written, and that they had been on an indescribable cloud.

"Oh, yeah, that?" George repeated with a snort. "Didn't you sell songs? That seems like pretty major stuff, there, missy. Congratulations."

She dug for that joy, but it seemed distant and lost. "You're right, Dad. They bought the two songs that we performed, and we actually got a contract to write more for Palm Valley Records," she said, forcing brightness. "Cool, huh?"

"That's amazing, honey!" He reached down and hugged her. "All those years of writing poetry has paid off!"

She laughed lightly, warmed by the knowledge that her father had always loved her poems. Roz thought they were "cute," but George had a more sensitive soul than his wife.

Did that mean he'd be more sensitive and upset by the fact that she'd lied to him about the real conception of his very own grandson?

"How did it happen? Did they just hear those two songs, or did you play more? What was the executive like? When did—"

"George, let the poor girl tell you in her own time," Roz said, pushing up. "I'll get you a cup of coffee and you sit here and brace yourself for the big moment when Zee has his first bite of solid food."

He gave a secret eyeroll—one that George and Asia had shared over a lifetime of being husband and daughter of Roz the Control Freak—and followed the order, settling his sizeable frame in one of the chairs.

"Tell me everything, Asia. Every detail. I want to hear how it happened. Do you think you'll give up your career to be a songwriter now?"

"It's more of a side hustle for me," she said. "I'm in a supporting role for Dane. The music comes from his heart, and so do the ideas for the songs. I just string some lyrics together."

"Now don't sell yourself short, young lady." He accepted the coffee Roz brought him with a smile, then looked back at Asia. "What song did you perform? That one called 'Guts and Glory' that I've heard you sing when you don't think anyone's around? It's so pretty."

She nodded, wanting to answer and make small talk and just have coffee with her parents at the kitchen table, but she didn't trust her voice. Her throat was tight with tears, because...this man cared so much for her. He loved her. He adored her. He'd worshipped her since she was Zee's age.

And she hadn't trusted him enough to tell him the truth. She didn't trust herself, so she'd lied. From fear and shame and guilt.

It all suddenly hit her so hard that tears sprang to her eyes.

"Honey! What's wrong?" He leaned over the table and put one of his mighty hands on her arm. "What is it?"

"Daddy," she whispered, using the childish name because it felt right. "I'm sorry. I'm so, so sorry."

"Asia! What are you sorry about?"

"I...I have to tell you something. It's about...the baby."

He drew back an inch, searching her face. "That you know his father and he wasn't a...semen demon baby?"

Her jaw loosened. "How...what...when..."

"George!" Roz gasped, smacking her hands against her chest in shock.

He gave a hearty laugh, the sound so unexpected that Asia almost choked.

"Baby girl, you're *not* the best liar," he said. "I figured it out when we were up in Ohio before the baby was born."

"How?" she asked, stunned by the news.

"I don't know. I guess I just know you so well, honey. I knew you wouldn't go to some...bank to get a baby."

"Why didn't you say something to me?" Asia asked.

"Or *me*?" Roz demanded of George. "You knew I knew?"

"When are you two going to give me some credit for having a brain?" he joked, looking from one shocked face to the other. "Anyway, I figured you girls would tell me when the time was right. Is it?"

Asia looked across the table, a tear dribbling down her cheek. "It is now. Dad, I love you."

Zee kicked and made a little squawk.

"So does my baby," she added.

He smiled and picked up the phone. "You tell me all this business later. Let's get some pictures of my grandson now."

Roz handed her a tiny spoon. "You should do the first bite, Asia."

She accepted it with a smile. "Thank you for being the best parents in the world," she whispered, and never meant anything more.

ONCE THE DETAILS had been openly discussed with her way-too-amazing parents, Dane came to get Asia and take her to Shellseeker Beach. That way, they could talk quietly to Teddy and Eliza, who had become the main artery for the friends and family who frequently gathered there.

It was a start, and with Dane by her side, and Zee in her arms, Asia knew it was the right next step. Eliza would of course bring in Miles Anderson, and Asia agreed the man's people-finding skills could be invaluable. At the very least, he could find out what flight Spencer had arrived on and if he had a return ticket.

She sure hoped so.

"Oh." As they pulled into the parking lot, Asia spied a car she recognized and the very familiar silhouette of a woman leaning into the back, no doubt unlatching a child from a car seat. "Livvie's here?"

"My sister is always here," Dane said, sliding the car into an empty spot a few feet away. "She doesn't go into her store to work until the afternoon, so she spends most mornings with my mom and Teddy. Bash plays on the beach and Livvie gets treated like pregnant royalty."

Normally, Asia would have smiled at that, but seeing her close friend here added a new twist to the day of reckoning she knew she had to have. She opened her door slowly.

It was one thing to tell the truth to Dane's mother and Teddy, but Olivia Whitney—now Olivia Whitney-Deeley—had become a dear friend over the past several months.

The two women, close in age, had shared a multitude of personal insights and stories. And not once, not one single time, had Olivia questioned the sperm bank story.

Shame crawled up Asia's chest and settled like a lump in her throat.

"Oh, hey, you guys!" Olivia called the minute she straightened and saw them. "Look who's here, Bash." She held her toddler, Sebastian, with one hand and waved with the other. "I didn't know you two were going to be here this morning."

Dane paused in the act of climbing out of the driver's seat and turned to Asia. "Are you okay?" he asked softly, putting a hand on her arm.

Would she ever get used to how caring he was? How attentive to her shifting moods? "Just wallowing in guilt and fear, nothing serious."

"Asia."

"It might hurt Livvie's feelings that I never confided in her."

"I doubt that," he said. "But if you want, why don't I take Zee to the beach house first? I'm sure Bash will come with us, and you two can have a moment to talk privately."

Her shoulders sank with the sheer weight of her gratitude. "Why are you so perfect?"

He just laughed, his hazel eyes warm and, as always, locked on her. "So far from perfect, Aje. But do you like that plan?"

"Will you tell them?"

"My mom and Teddy?"

She nodded. "That way, when I get up there, they will have already reacted. And I'll tell Livvie."

"Consider it done."

Without giving it one second of thought, she leaned over the console and kissed him on the mouth.

"Eww, Bash. Look. They're kissing."

Asia and Dane both laughed into the kiss, breaking apart to look at Olivia and the little boy who was staring into the car through Asia's open door.

"Eww, Uncle Dane."

"Mind your own, kiddo." He pointed to the little boy. "How would you like to haul little Zee up to the house to see Eliza and Teddy while your mommy and Asia talk?"

"Yes!" He hopped around like Dane had offered him a trip to Disneyland.

Behind him, Olivia leaned down to look into the car at Asia. "All good?" she asked, no doubt surprised by Dane's request.

"Yep. We're good. I just need to, um, tell you something important."

Olivia's brow flicked up and she glanced from Asia to Dane. "Oookay."

She backed up so Asia could get out and they chatted about the weather and kids and nothing of import while Dane helped get the baby out and made sure he was secure in the carrier.

"Come on, Bash," Dane said once they were ready to go. "Let's roll."

"Let's roll!" Bash repeated, toddling ahead.

As they took off, Asia watched how Dane's hands clasped the carrier as if he had been given responsibility for the crown jewels. She didn't realize she'd sighed out loud at that thought, but Olivia elbowed her.

"I'm starting to think you've got a crush on him as bad as the one he's got on you."

"Badder," Asia confessed, affection for the man welling up in her.

"Is that what you wanted to tell me? That you and my brother are an official thing? Because I saw you two last night at Little Blues after the record company guy left. I swear, my eyebrows got singed from all the sparks flying around."

Asia gave a nervous laugh, trying to think of the best way to say what she had to say. She couldn't help wondering how it would be received, especially considering that Olivia was Dane's sister, and Dane was...in this with Asia.

Well, she couldn't put it off any longer.

"Your brother is a king among men," she started by saying.

"Debatable, but okay. You like him, I got it." Olivia narrowed her gray-blue eyes. "Why am I sensing there's more to this?"

"Because there is." Asia reached for her, guiding her away from a group of tourists unpacking an SUV for a day at the beach. "Liv, I have a confession to make and it's kind of big. It's about Zee."

Olivia blinked and looked in the direction where Dane had gone with the baby and Bash. "Is he okay?"

"He's great, he's just not...a sperm bank baby." At Olivia's blank stare, Asia added, "I know who his father is and I...I lied about it. To everyone, except my mother. But everyone else. Including you, and you're my friend, and I hate that I did that."

"Asia. Wow." She let out a breath and reached out both arms, pulling Asia in for a hug. "You poor thing, carrying around a secret like that."

"You're not mad?" She drew back. "I feel like you've been so honest and I...wasn't."

She shook her head. "I'm not mad. Did this come out because of Dane? You wanted to come clean with him?"

"Not exactly." She shuttered her eyes. "This came out because Zee's biological father has shown up on Sanibel Island and I'm low-key freaking out."

"Whoa. Seriously? What do you mean he 'showed up'? Did you talk to him? Did Dane? What's the story?"

"The story is long, uncomfortable, and kinda ugly," she said with a rueful laugh, leading them toward a bench in the shade. "I'll give you the highlights, but, oh, my gosh, Liv. Thank you for not judging."

"Friends don't judge," she said without hesitation. "But just tell me you're all right."

"I will be, thanks to your brother. He's..."

"A king among men, yeah, yeah, yeah," Livvie joked with an eyeroll as they sat down. "Seriously, he's a rock-solid dude and I'm glad you trust him. Tell me this long, uncomfortable and ugly story."

She did, keeping it to the most salient details, answering Olivia's questions, which, unlike her father's and Dane's, were more focused on Asia's relationship with Spencer.

"Did you know he had this other woman in London?"

she asked. "Did he give off cheater vibes?"

"Not really. But I guess I was kind of blind and... dumb." She laughed softly. "Understatement alert."

"You weren't dumb, Asia. You had a long-distance relationship, so it had to be hard to really know what you were dealing with. But what's he doing here? That's the real question."

"I don't know," she said. "Dane thinks maybe he wants another chance."

"As if," Olivia scoffed. "But what about Zee?"

Asia just shook her head, the pressure in her chest nearly unbearable when she thought about what she was facing.

"Liv, I don't know. But I want to talk to Claire, obviously, to find out what is legally required of me, and Miles, to find out if he can dig anything up about why Spencer might be here. I'm just at a loss. What would you do?"

"I sure wouldn't hide or wait or get myself all stressed out with worry," she said. "I'd stand in my front door and wait for that man to show up and demand all the answers that he owes you. Forget these secret calling cards and silent messages, which are totally disturbing, to be honest."

"I know, you're right, but if he doesn't know I have a baby—"

"You can't hide it forever, Asia, and you know that. That's why you're telling everyone the truth." Olivia put an arm around her shoulders. "You are surrounded by people who love and support you. No one is going to let him take Zee or hurt you or do anything at all. You need to get him to show his face and say what he has to say. If it were me? I'd figure out how to reach him and force the issue."

She sighed, looking out to the horizon, but only seeing Spencer Keaton's face. A face she once loved. But now? Her feelings couldn't be further from love.

"I really never want to see him again, Liv. He broke my heart. I mean, shattered it into a million pieces. What could he possibly say to me that would be worth listening to?"

"I don't know, hon, but if it were me? I'd want to hear it."

She nodded and stood. "I'm going to go face Teddy and Eliza, more people I've lied to. So far, you and my father have been wonderful."

"And they will be, too," Olivia promised. "Remember, Teddy lived with a man who was married to not one but two women at the same time. As scandals go, she sets the bar high."

Asia smiled at that. "But your mother..."

"Not judgey."

"I'm seeing her son. He's now involved in this. Whatever *this* is."

"Hey, Dane needed a little drama in his life. He's a professional songwriter now, and this will inspire his next great hit." Olivia again put a loving arm around Asia and tugged her closer. "We got you, girl."

"I love you, Liv," Asia whispered.

"Back atchya, Mama."

Chapter Five

Eliza

Somehow, some way, the news didn't entirely shock Eliza. Asia made a show of independence, but she didn't quite have the steel nerve it would have taken to head to a sperm bank and conceive a baby alone. Teddy was frustrated that she never got any "vibes" from Asia's aura that she was lying, but then decided it was because Asia was well and truly done with the father of her baby.

But that father obviously wasn't done with her. And whatever his motives, there was one man on Sanibel Island who could find out more about this Spencer Keaton character than anyone.

While Teddy kept baby Zee, Dane and Asia had quickly run back to the townhouse to get some things she'd forgotten for the baby. While driving to Miles's house, Eliza called and briefed him on the situation. They'd been planning to go out on his boat that afternoon, but she knew this issue would probably take priority.

As she parked in his driveway, the front door opened and her favorite dog bounded out of the house with a happy bark and wagging tail.

"Hey, Tinkie." She crouched down to give—and get—

some puppy love, looking over Tinkerbell's black and white head to watch Miles come down the walk at a slightly slower pace than his Boston terrier.

But there was no less love in his expression than Tink had, which always gave her an unexpected jolt of joy. She adored the way Miles made her feel.

"Hey, gorgeous," he said, slowing his step.

"There's my favorite PI. Ready to do some sleuthing?"

He smiled and reached his hand out to her. "I was ready to do some boating with you." As he guided her to a stand, he eased her closer, both of them laughing when Tinkerbell shouldered her way between them as they kissed.

"Boating might have to wait," Eliza said. "This is pretty serious stuff."

He nodded and closed her car door for her, guiding her back to the house with Tinkerbell in the lead. "Using just the guy's name you gave me, I've already run a standard first pass."

"Of course you have," Eliza joked. "You knew my whole history before I even walked up to this front door the first time."

He gestured for her to go in before him. "But I didn't know you were a gorgeous redhead who'd steal my heart and invade my life."

She stopped mid-step. "Have I stolen and invaded?"

"Not nearly enough."

Tinkerbell turned and barked when Eliza didn't

enter, wagging her tail then flattening on the floor to look up with an imploring gaze.

"Just ask Tink," Miles teased.

She laughed and bent over to pet the dog again, then walked into the entry. "So what did you find out already about this perfect stranger? Not that Spencer Keaton sounds perfect," she added. "Far from it."

"Well, I didn't see any red flags on the first standard ID pass I ran. He looks like an upstanding American citizen, the VP of operations for an Ohio-based manufacturing firm's European business. Originally from the Midwest, he last lived in Oklahoma City and now is married, no kids—"

"That he knows of," Eliza muttered.

"Yeah, wow. That's complicated, isn't it?" He ushered her through the entry of his always spotless three-bedroom house, a salt-scented breeze floating in from the open sliding glass doors.

She sighed, as much over the complications of this new turn of events as the pure loveliness of this home. It was quintessential Florida living, from the wide white tile on the floor to the gorgeous fishing boat bobbing at the dock in the back.

She loved this canal-front house. Although it was just a few miles from Shellseeker Beach, it was a completely different atmosphere, but she enjoyed it every bit as much.

"You want coffee?" Miles asked, heading toward the kitchen that opened to a family room.

"When in Rome," she quipped, knowing that caffeine-loving Miles would have a fresh pot brewing.

A few minutes later, she settled at the kitchen counter, sipping a warm cup and discussing the details candidly while they waited for Dane and Asia to arrive.

"You know, I can't help wondering how I'd feel if this had happened to Olivia," she admitted.

"She wouldn't have lied to you, that's for sure."

"Roz knew the truth," Eliza said. "She and Dane are the only two people who did, though. I guess Asia thought that the fewer people who knew, the better her chances of keeping it from the father."

"That had to be rough on her," Miles said. "She's such a tough woman, or appears to be."

"Might be an act." Eliza picked up her cup, thinking. "She comes off as tough because she's always fighting Roz's overbearing mothering style. And from what I picked up in bits and pieces, this Spencer character was overbearing in his own way. She made a comment about how a therapist said being in someone's control was her comfort zone."

Miles made a face. "Poor kid."

"I think letting out the truth is a good thing for her, and I could swear she relaxed more as we talked about it. But there are so many big questions, and that's why they're coming here. Why would the guy show up now? Does he know she had his baby? What kind of person is he? Will he try to take the baby?"

"I don't know the answer to any of that, but you'd be

surprised what I can learn from a person's history. What's her plan? Is she going to seek him out or hide from him?"

Eliza grimaced. "I don't think she's decided. And, I know the guy was a cheater, which is unforgiveable, but he is *still* Zee's biological father. In my opinion—not that I'm supposed to have one—he has a right to know he has a child, and meet that child."

"Plus he has a moral, if not legal, obligation to help her," Miles added.

"I totally agree. And..." Eliza sighed before sharing her deepest thought. "I say this as the mother of the next man in Asia's life, but is having this history and potential landmine fair to Dane?"

"I guess it all depends on what this guy wants and how Asia wants to handle it."

Eliza glanced toward the street when she heard a car pull in. Tinkerbell hopped off the sofa, barking and running to the door so fast, she slid on the tile floor, making them both laugh.

"I guess we'll find out now." Eliza started to stand to get the door, but Miles put a hand on her arm.

"That's it? That's our time today?" He looked genuinely disappointed. "Color me crushed."

"Let's see how it goes with Asia's investigation," she said. "You may want the time to work."

"I might," he agreed. "But it won't take all day. There's still time to take a ride."

"And it's chilly today."

"Great day to be out on the water, but..." His eyes narrowed as he studied her. "Are you blowing me off, E?"

She looked at him, thinking about her conversation with Claire. Would it help give her clarity to see him less? Should she pull back and figure out how she really felt about him?

"No, I just..." She searched his face for a long moment, always honest with him. "I just want to be sure we both have some breathing space."

"The only air I really want to breathe is out on the water, next to you. But..." He stood as the doorbell rang and Tink's bark intensified to insanity level.

Miles headed toward the chaos. "The water will always be there," he said over his shoulder. "And so will the air."

They would. But would she?

She hated that she even had the thought.

"Wow, HE'S GOOD." Asia skimmed the report that Miles had just printed out, shaking her head.

"Miles or Spencer?" Dane asked, bringing some levity to what had otherwise been a pretty tense half-hour or so.

"Both." She looked up. "This all looks accurate, but nothing terribly new. I placed him at Innovative Manufacturing in that job, which was a coup for him, and for me. It was one of the highest-level executive job recruitments I'd ever done."

"And that's how you met?" Miles asked.

She nodded. "We'd actually only emailed before that,

which is how so much of the business is done. But he was in Columbus for the final interview, and when he got the offer, he emailed me, suggested dinner to celebrate, and..." She lifted a self-conscious shoulder. "We started seeing each other for a few weeks, while he was in town for training. It continued when he came back from London, almost every month."

"Before that, he lived in Oklahoma City," Miles said. "Does that match what he told you?"

"Oh, yes. I mean, obviously, I'd seen his resume and talked with former employers. He had stellar recommendations." She flipped the page. "Is there more about his, um, marriage?"

"Just what you see there. He's married to the daughter of a British aristocrat—a baron and Member of Parliament." Miles glanced at his screen. "I found wedding pictures, if you—"

"I don't need to see them," she said.

"Do you mind if I do?" Dane asked, coming around the desk. "If I see the guy creeping around the townhouse, I want to know what he looks like."

"Of course," Asia replied. "You can look, too, Eliza."

Eliza took a few steps behind Miles and squinted at the screen that showed a wedding announcement from a small British newspaper. The headline was all about Charlotte Simmons, the bride and the daughter of a wealthy, titled aristocrat, but Eliza's attention was on the groom.

Even in two dimensions and grainy from being expanded on the screen, it was easy to see Spencer

Keaton was a good-looking man. He was much taller than the woman at his side, broad and built, sporting what looked to be an expensive tuxedo, dark hair slicked back, a cocky smile tipping his lips.

"Here's another one," Miles said, clicking the screen. "From a fundraising dinner they sponsored at their home."

"Their home?" Eliza blinked and leaned closer. "Where do they live, Buckingham Palace?"

"The Honorable Dalton Simmons is a baron, and head of one of the wealthiest families in the U.K.," Miles said. "Don't know if they still do dowries over there, but the Honorable Miss Charlotte—not officially a 'lady' like her mother—surely has a sizeable trust, and more than one home."

Asia sighed, fluttering the printout onto the desk. "No wonder he was, uh, taken with her."

But Eliza wasn't sure if it was just the money. Not only was the new Mrs. Keaton quite beautiful, this picture was much clearer than the first one. There was nothing cocky about Spencer's smile here, as he was caught in the very act of looking at his wife like she'd hung the moon. Maybe he'd married for love *and* money.

She glanced at Dane, who stared at the image shaking his head. "Were you able to find out when he left London for Florida?" Dane asked Miles. "Or if he purchased a return flight?"

"Not as easy as it sounds," Miles said.

Dane tipped his head as if he didn't agree. "It could be, but also not exactly legal, either," he said.

"True," Miles conceded. "From what I can tell, he does travel to other countries for work. Would he come to Florida for that job, Asia? Is it possible he was here on business and just decided to drop in to say hello, even if his calling card is a bit suspect?"

Asia shook her head. "I don't think they have accounts in Florida, and he's the head of European operations. It's unlikely he's here on business."

Miles studied one of his many monitors again. "Is there any way you've misinterpreted the fan he left? Is it possible you've jumped to a conclusion?"

"It could be a kid's toy," Dane said.

She looked from one to the other, her dark eyes wide. "I mean, I guess anything is possible, but didn't you say you ran a test and couldn't find anything about me for over a year and then—wham!—my name showed up on that database from the housing complex? It's too much of a coincidence."

Miles nodded. "I don't disagree, but I'm not seeing red flags here. I will continue to dig." He rubbed his goatee, thinking. "Are you sure there's no one he knows in Columbus who would have known you had a child? Is it possible he's just here to find out if Zee is his or not?"

"I can't think of anyone, but someone from my old firm could have contacted him out of the blue. Maybe another high-level position came up and they wanted to know if he's happy at IMP, then my name came up. But I didn't tell anyone at that company that I was pregnant."

"Columbus, Ohio isn't a big town," Miles said.

"And executive recruiters surely talk to each other

and your name might have come up," Dane suggested. "That's all it would take for him to find out."

She dropped back on the sofa. "You're right. And if he heard I had a child, he'd want..." Her voice trailed off as she sighed, the unspoken and obvious hanging in the room.

He'd want to meet him, Eliza thought.

"I should tell him," Asia whispered.

Dane came around the desk to sit next to her. "Asia, every person you've told today has lifted a load off your shoulders."

She turned to him, leaning closer, giving Eliza a moment to study their interaction and feel the undeniable chemistry between these two.

"He didn't give me a way to get in touch with him," she said, her voice faltering as if she heard the weak argument.

"But if we stay at the townhouse, he's likely to show up again."

Asia closed her eyes in resignation. "I guess I could do that."

"Just think about it," Dane said, taking her hand. "Let's go back and check on Zee, talk it over with your parents, and make a decision."

His tenderness touched Eliza, giving her a burst of pride in the good man she and Ben had raised.

Asia shifted her gaze from Miles to Eliza. "Thank you both for being so understanding and kind. I appreciate it more than you know."

"We're here for you," she said. "I have one cottage

currently unrented, and I can keep it free for at least a week. If you want to stay in Slipper Snail while you consider all your options, you're welcome to do that."

"Thank you."

"That's so nice, Mom," Dane said. "Thanks."

Eliza walked them out while Miles spent a few more minutes working, giving her time to hug them both again and offer more encouragement. Tinkerbell at her side, she watched them drive off, standing in the driveway for a moment to process it all.

On a sigh, she started to turn just as a white SUV came around the intersection at the edge of Miles's property. Out of habit, she reached for Tink's collar, not that the dog was much of a runner, and kept walking.

"Excuse me? Ma'am?"

She turned, realizing the voice came from the driver of that vehicle, now stopped at the end of the driveway.

"Yes?" She took one step closer and froze, chills marching up her spine as she blinked at the eerily familiar face alone in the SUV. The chiseled jaw, the high cheekbones, the almost but not quite cocky smile that she'd just seen on the screen.

For a moment, she couldn't speak. How was this possible?

"Um, that car that just left?" he said. "That woman I saw you hug?"

He'd been *watching* them? More chills exploded. "Yes?"

"I take it you know her."

She nodded, not trusting her voice.

"Would you give her something for me?" he asked, reaching toward the passenger seat.

Eliza took a step backwards, her mind blank with shock at the sight of Spencer Keaton.

When he turned back, he lifted his brows. "If it's not too much trouble, ma'am. She's an, uh, old friend, and I want to give her something. Would you mind?"

Swallowing hard, she took a few steps closer, vibrating with uncertainty and curiosity. It wasn't her place to say anything or do anything, but...oh, she wanted to. How wrong would it be to just ask, "What are you doing on Sanibel Island?"

But she didn't say a word.

"I don't want to bother her," he said, as if he read the hesitation in her gaze. "I don't have any right to do that, but I owe her something. So much." He gave a soft laugh that somehow made him even more handsome. "Anyway, like I said, I'm an old friend and...here." He held out an envelope. "Would you give this to her? I'm really sorry if it's an inconvenience but—"

"Did you follow her here?" she asked as the weirdness of the situation finally hit her.

"I, uh, did, yeah. I know that seems super strange, but I swear—I swear to God—I just owe her something and I know she probably won't talk to me, so please." He held out the envelope. "Just give this to her and I swear she'll never see me again. I mean, unless...no. Just, please."

She closed the space between them, aware that Tinkerbell matched her step for step, not barking at the man but watching him with a wary gaze.

"It's not for her, exactly," he said as she took the slim, sealed, business-sized envelope from his hand. "It's for the baby."

Eliza gasped and he just nodded, then held up a hand in thanks. Without another word, he drove off—not gassing it or tearing out with attitude, but just rumbled down the street, leaving her in utter and complete astonishment.

She stared down at the envelope, which merely said "Asia" on the front.

Well, this certainly changed everything.

Chapter Six

Claire

W hen Claire returned home after a morning of studying Florida taxation law at the local library, she felt completely ready to take the next section of the practice bar exam. It had to be done on her computer, timed and supervised, so she prayed that the house would be quiet today.

Except...why were there three cars in the driveway?

DJ said he was spending the day at Luigi's, which she hoped meant he was getting closer to a commitment to buy that restaurant. Noah was at work in Shellseeker Beach. And didn't Sophia have her class at the local high school today?

She parked on the street and opened the car door, hearing a splash from the backyard pool, along with the ubiquitous sound of rap coming from the portable speaker Sophia seemed to have glued to her. Then a few female screams, a booming male voice, and a giant splash.

Really, Sophia? She'd invited friends over?

On a grunt, she left her car and bags, slamming the door to channel her frustration. She marched to the front door, which was unlocked, and walked inside. There, she glanced left and right into the living area and dining room, then rounded the corner to the family room and kitchen that looked out to the pool.

At least six teenagers stood around her pool, with a few more in the water, and a mountain of backpacks and sneakers had been strewn over the sofas and chairs inside and out.

She took a few steps closer to the sliding glass doors, which were wide open, scanning the bodies of buff young men and darn-near naked girls—two in the water, two lounging on chaises—one bikini-clad girl dancing to a bass-heavy beat with fast-talking lyrics.

Sophia sat perched on the pool's edge, talking to a boy, which didn't really surprise Claire. Not the boy, but the fact that Sophia rarely got in the water. When she did, it was in the shallow end, except for one time when she scared the life out of Claire by staying under for too long. After that incident, DJ had told her Sophia wasn't a great swimmer, which she thought was odd for a California girl.

But she was a great socializer, and right then—when she was supposed to be in school—she looked to be in her glory.

"This is not happening," Claire murmured to herself. "I am scheduled to take a test in half an hour."

She stood for a second, trying to decide what, well, what a *mother* would do. She'd never been one, and certainly had never put her own mother in a situation like this.

Walk out and announce they all had to leave?

Quietly pull Sophia aside and ask her to take the party somewhere else?

Turn up her white noise track on the headphones and tough it out on taxation?

Before she could pick a course of action, she caught sight of Sophia pushing to a stand, then prancing toward the doors in a bathing suit the size of three Band-Aids.

"I know there's tequila in here somewhere!" she shouted over her shoulder.

"Find it, woman!" a boy called.

"And limes, please!" another girl yelled.

"Shots, baby, shots!"

"I'll do my..." Her voice faded into nothing as she turned and came face to face with Claire, then she froze, closed her eyes, and breathed a curse. "I thought you were gone at the library all day."

"I thought you were in school," Claire shot back.

"I was but..." Sophia swallowed. "But..."

"But you decided not to go to class."

"I was gonna, but I met up with some..." She looked over her shoulder as another boy did a cannonball that soaked the deck. "Dad said he wanted me to have friends," she added, an edge of defensiveness in her voice. "He said they could come over."

"Not a half dozen in the middle of the day. And certainly not to drink *shots*." Claire narrowed her eyes, discomfort stinging at the back of her neck. "I have to take a practice exam for the bar."

She lifted a shoulder. "Take it. I'll tell them to keep it down."

"Sophia." She tried not to grind out the name. "They need to leave."

"Leave? Why?" Her voice rose an octave. "I'm not a prisoner who can't have friends. I told you, my dad said—"

"He's not here, I am. And you can have your friends over, but not now and not with alcohol." She crossed her arms, feeling very mean and bad-mothery, but not caring one bit.

She didn't need a parenting manual to know what was right in this situation with a seventeen-year-old. And drinking wasn't.

"What are you going to do?" Sophia countered. "Send me back to California? I think you'd like that, wouldn't you?"

Claire drew back, surprised by the attitude. Sophia was dramatic, she was loud, and she loved nothing more than to be the center of attention. But she hadn't been rude or disrespectful since she'd arrived.

"I wouldn't like that at all," Claire said calmly. "I would just like today to be quiet so I can take a practice test for the bar exam. Simple and easy. Please ask your friends to pack it up and take your party somewhere else. There's a big beach about ten minutes away. And don't even think about taking anything to drink."

Sophia muttered another curse under her breath, then spun around and marched outside. "Bad news, bros. We gotta split. My dad's, um, friend is here, and apparently she's allergic to fun."

Irritation and disappointment went to war, raising

her hackles, but Claire easily managed not to respond. Instead, she headed back into the house and walked toward her bedroom, where she had a work desk and computer station set up for studying and testing.

It wasn't until she got there that she realized her eyes were stinging with tears. Closing the door behind her, she leaned against the wood and let them out, emotions tangled in her chest.

All her life, as a single, childless woman, she'd fantasized about being a mom. Of course, she dreamed of the baby she'd given up for adoption, and now he lived in this house. And after reuniting with his father, she'd started having fantasies of forever with both of them, and always knew that meant being a stepparent to DJ's girls, but she thought she loved that idea.

This was what she wanted, right? Not...work. The Florida bar exam and the law practice she wanted to open needed to be second after a lifetime of having her career as the one and only thing in her life.

But that didn't mean she had to *like* being sworn at by a sullen teenager, did it?

She heard them all talking—the laughter stopped—through her bedroom window that faced the pool. Her shades were still drawn from the night, and she made no effort to go over there and open them to check things out. After a few moments, she heard the side gate open and close, and more voices in the kitchen and family room, then the slam of the front door.

Finally, some car doors and engines and then...quiet.

She waited a bit, digging for peace and calm, then

went back out to find a completely empty—and incredibly messy—house. Sophia didn't have a car, and DJ had dropped her off at school this morning. That meant she was in a car with someone else driving. Had they been drinking?

She whipped around to look at the chaos on the patio, seeing a few cans of soda, but no...oh, yeah. There was a beer can.

Now what? Sophia would probably be fine, but what if there was an accident? Not only might Claire be liable —the lawyer in her always rose to the top—DJ would be furious. Maybe she'd handled this all wrong. Maybe she should've let them stay here and guaranteed no one drove after drinking. How was she to know?

She needed to call DJ. Or Eliza. Or Noah. Even her own mother, if she weren't on a boat cruising around the Keys with her new husband. She needed advice.

On a frustrated groan, she looked for her handbag, only then realizing she'd left it in the car with her keys and books. Darting to the front door, she opened it and sucked in a noisy breath.

Her car was gone!

Had Sophia just driven it away? Jumped in, saw Claire's handbag and books and just...pressed the ignition and took off? Seriously?

More tears sprang to her eyes as she stood, utterly helpless and furious. And completely stranded unless she wanted to walk somewhere for help.

Why had she wanted a family so badly? Because the one she had wasn't working at all.

"Claire?" DJ came out of the kitchen of the local pizza restaurant looking very much like he worked there. It wasn't just the apron around his waist or the flour dusted on his hands. He wore the expression of a busy cook who'd just been pulled from the lunch rush for a personal problem.

Well, he had. And the last time she checked, he didn't work here, so Claire refused to feel bad for using brains and resources by knocking on a neighbor's door to ask to use a phone...except she didn't know any phone numbers by heart, since they were all stored on her phone.

The kind neighbor offered to give her a ride and, since Luigi's was the closest option, here she was.

"I didn't expect you here today." He brushed his hands and reached for her, looking hard into her eyes. "What's wrong? Is it Sophia?"

"Yes."

"Is she okay?"

"Yes. No. I don't know." Her voice cracked from unshed tears, and he instantly took her hand to guide her into a private dining room off the front entrance that was, thankfully, empty.

"Claire, what happened?"

She took a deep breath and told him the story, leaving out Sophia's horrible attitude, but included the booze, because he needed to know that she might not be safe.

"Can you find her and make sure she's not drinking and driving?" she asked.

"Oh, she wouldn't do that. She's smarter than that, and kids? You know, if one beer is all they're doing, then—"

"She stole my car! Or someone did. That's a third-degree felony with up to five years in prison. And with alcohol in your blood? Even with no aggravating factors, that's a misdemeanor."

He laughed softly, the reaction like a slap in the face. "Step away from the bar exam, Counselor, and calm down."

Was there anything worse than being told to calm down when a person was still vibrating from the problem at hand? Claire closed her eyes and gathered her wits.

"Then I will attempt to think like a parent," she ground out, "since you won't. Your daughter may be in danger. Doesn't that merit just a little stress?"

"Stress is never good, and I think you need to remember that you don't have a lot of experience with teenagers."

Her eyes flashed. "I'm aware of that. I told you I did my best to handle it as well as could be expected, but Sophia was..."

"Mad as hell, I'd imagine," he said on another quick laugh that did nothing but make her stomach clench.

"Yes. Yes, she was. And disrespectful."

He tipped his head and gave her a look. "She's seventeen. They don't know any other—"

"DJ!" she snapped at him. "Are you really going to

take her side in this? What she did was wrong and unacceptable. I need you to call her, to get my car—and purse and phone and books—back to me, and to discipline her. Period. End of story."

He stared at her for a long time, silent, his dark eyes completely unreadable.

"Gimme a second," he finally said, turning and walking out of the private room with an audible sigh that clearly communicated he was not happy.

He was not happy?

She crossed her arms and dropped into an empty chair at the closest table, closing her eyes as the adrenaline of the last hour finally dumped and left her cold and sad and truly worried. Eliza was right about one thing—she needed to have a long and very serious conversation with DJ.

But if this was any indication of how that talk would go? It wasn't one she wanted to have very soon.

After a few minutes, he came back in. The apron was gone, the flour was washed off his hands, and his smile was back in place.

"She's on her way over," he said. "Very sorry she upset you, very contrite, and didn't realize you needed your car. It's all good."

Claire choked. "Good? No, DJ. Nothing is good. She's lying. She knew my stuff was in the car when she took off without asking me, and she is not sorry she upset me. And neither are you, I guess."

"Claire." He pulled out another chair and turned it around, straddling it like he was settling in for a nice, relaxing conversation. "You don't understand teenagers. They aren't like any other species on Earth. And she's been through a lot, moving across the country and breaking up with that guy. Now she's got this new family with you and Noah. Can't blame the kid for having a little harmless fun."

She just stared at him, long enough that she could almost feel her heart cracking, long enough that she could hear all the questions—the real ones—she knew she should be asking him. She'd hoped it would be at home, alone, maybe with a glass of wine or in each other's arms.

But this was the time she got, and she was taking it.

"Do you love me?" she asked.

"Come on, Claire. This is crazy."

"No, I want to know. You've never said it, not in so many words."

He stuck his hand into his salt and pepper hair and pulled it back, a frown tugging his brows together. "You know I don't believe feelings have to be spoken to be real. I love the moments I'm in with you, and I love the way we make each other feel. For me, that's enough. I hope it is for you, because we're in this life together right now, and I want harmony."

Well, that was an answer, and she should be smart enough to hear the truth in the subtext, which was...

"You don't love me," she said matter-of-factly.

He blinked. "Now? You want to have this conversation now?"

"I do."

"Well, I don't. I'm working on a big...new dough with Luigi and we were up to our eyeballs in yeast, so—"

She leaned forward and quieted him with a hand on his arm. "DJ, I would expect a man who loved and valued me to defend me over anyone—anyone at all, including his daughter—in a situation where I am clearly in the right and she is in the wrong. So, I'm giving you a chance to say it. Do you love me?"

He grunted and dropped his head back, looking skyward. "I don't know the meaning of the word, Claire. And if I did, it would just scare me. I'm not ready to make a commitment."

"I'm not asking for one. I'm asking a simple question, DJ. I need you to answer it."

He straightened his head and looked directly at her, pain in his eyes. "I screwed up my marriage so bad. You know I was the one who messed up by being everywhere and anywhere but present in that relationship."

She nodded, listening.

"I don't want to do that again."

"You *are* doing it again."

"But I'm not married to you, and I am present in this relationship, to the extent that I want to be."

"What does that mean?" she demanded, a new bout of confusion taking hold. "I don't understand, DJ. I need an answer. In plain English, not New Age garbage. I need to know what I'm doing here."

He looked hard at her. "You chose to stay, Claire. I didn't make any promises, I didn't beg or plead, I just offered you what I've always offered you. Me—in this moment. That's all, and you accepted it. And when you made that decision, Sophia was already living here."

He wasn't wrong. When she'd been offered the shocking promotion that would have taken her back to New York permanently, she'd happily turned it down.

She'd decided to take the Florida bar, start a practice here, and live "in the moment" that Dante Joseph Fortunato had offered her. She'd finally be a mother to the son she gave up, and, yes, Sophia had come from California and Claire had been ready to accept and eventually love her.

It all seemed so full of potential at the time.

"So what changed?" he asked. "Why do you need words of love now when before all you needed was me? Us. The family, our home, the life we were building."

But they were a fractured family, the home was a rental house, and lately she didn't feel like they were building anything, least of all a *life*.

"Because without love—real love—there's no foundation," she whispered as the realization hit her. "And without a foundation, things...fall apart."

"I'm willing to take that chance," he said. "Are you?"

As she opened her mouth to answer, the door flew open so hard it hit the wall behind it.

"Oh my God, Claire. I'm so sorry!" Sophia, wearing nothing but a tank top and bikini bottoms stood barefoot in the doorway, holding out Claire's shoulder bag strap hooked over one finger. "I just figured you meant for me to take your car. I had no idea your purse was in it."

"It was on the front seat."

"But my friend threw it in the back when she saw it." She held out the purse with a huge and incredibly insincere smile. "Super sorry, Claire. Hope I didn't wreck your test...thing."

"Oh, it's wrecked."

DJ leaned forward. "But you can pay a fine and take the test another time, right?" he asked.

"Or Sophia could pay the fine and learn there are consequences to actions." Claire pinned her gaze on the young woman in front of her.

Sophia scoffed. "Seriously? I'm, like, doing you this huge favor by leaving my friends and bringing you the car and...this cheugy Kate Spade bag." She jiggled the bag with no explanation of what that word meant. "And you want me to pay some fine?"

"I want you to admit that what you did was wrong, recognize that there are consequences for that, and offer up a sincere apology."

Sophia rolled her eyes, dropped the bag on the floor with a thud, and held up her hands in fake resignation. "Sure. Yes to all that. See you guys later. Your car's out front. My friends are waiting for me. I might not be home for dinner."

She pivoted and disappeared, leaving them sitting in the empty room with a cavern of silence and pain between them.

After a moment, DJ stood and walked to the bag, gingerly picking it up. Silently, he set it on the table next to Claire.

"I'm going back to the kitchen. I'm sorry you are

struggling with a teenager, Claire, but you know she's a good kid. And as far as all that other stuff..."

All that other stuff? Had he really said that?

"Well, you know where I stand," he finished.

"No, I don't," she said. "Which is why I asked."

He sighed and reached for her, grazing his knuckles down her cheek. "I believe in you, in us, and in this family. I don't want it to end...now. But no one knows what could happen." His gaze flickered in the general direction of the kitchen. "Anything could change at any time."

"What does that *mean*, DJ?" she demanded. "I've sold my New York apartment, quit my job, am going to hang a lawyer's shingle in Lee County, and am studying my brains out to pass the Florida bar. I did all that because—"

"Because you wanted to," he finished before she could. "And I'm glad you did. But those were your decisions, Claire, not mine." He leaned over, pressed a light kiss on her forehead. "I won't be long. See you when I get home. I'm really in the middle of something big here."

He left and she stared at the door behind him. Well, she had the talk. And just as she'd feared, it had blown up in her face.

Chapter Seven

Dane

The call from his mother with the news that she'd seen Spencer and had a letter from him addressed to Asia had Dane chomping to see what the man had written. Asia, on the other hand, didn't seem remotely interested.

When she finally ran out of excuses—Zee had to nurse, then he had to sleep, Roz was at work and couldn't watch him, she had some scheduled work calls—she finally agreed to go with Dane to Shellseeker Beach.

But she huffed, puffed, and acted like this was a huge mistake.

Dane reached over the console and took her hand. "At least you're going to find out what he wants."

"There'll be a catch."

"But information is power," he insisted. "And you need some of that."

She dropped her head back and closed her eyes. "He always had the power, and he will again. Just think about what he did, Dane. He was lurking around the town-house, saw us, and *followed* us to Miles's house."

He had thought about it, and he hated it. He was quiet for a few seconds, then gave her hand a light squeeze. "I have really tiptoed around this subject, but would you do me a favor and answer my most burning question?"

"What did I see in the guy?"

Dane laughed softly, not at all surprised she read his mind. "Actually, yes. That was the question, word for word." He threw her a look. "I'd love to know."

"I'd love to know, too," she said dryly. "Because I often wonder."

"I'm serious. What was the attraction? Why did you stay with him for so long? And, when you found out you were pregnant, would you have...married him?" He tried not to let his voice rise with disbelief. "I mean, obviously, he was awful."

"Actually, it wasn't obvious at all. He was—is, I suppose—charming and personable and very, very successful. He's great-looking, easy to talk to, and quite generous. He was crazy about me, and...and..."

He braced himself for something like "amazing in the bedroom," doing his best not to react to each enviable character trait the guy had.

"He was a powerful presence, and I was drawn to him," she finished.

"So, you *would* have married him, control issues and all?"

She considered the question, quiet for a long time.

"You aren't sure?" he asked after a beat.

"I'm just thinking that it took many months in therapy with a brilliant woman named Nancy to figure out the real answer, and I'm wondering how much to share."

"Share anything you're comfortable sharing, Asia. I care about you, and I won't judge you harshly. Everyone makes questionable decisions in relationships."

"Have you?" she asked. "You never talk about your exes."

"There aren't a slew of them," he said on a quick laugh. "Three, actually."

"Really?" She turned in the seat, facing him. "I'd love to hear about your past instead of dwelling on my own, even if only for a minute. Then I'll answer your questions, I promise."

He nodded and navigated some traffic, scanning the cars behind and around him, making sure they changed lanes, took side streets, and didn't get followed again.

"Start with your first girlfriend," she said.

"Okay. That would be Emily, a girl in high school, also on the competitive math team."

"Ah, the hot mathlete." Asia laughed.

"Not hot, neither of us, but we had a decent run as a couple. Split up by mutual agreement when I went to Caltech for college. Then, in my junior year, I had another fairly serious girlfriend." His felt his smile grow, making Asia chuckle.

"You liked this one, I can tell."

"I did like her. Her name was Jamie Ferreira. She was shy and sweet and very smart. But she was from Michigan and really close to her family, so she went back there after we graduated. I got the job in Silicon Valley, and we couldn't make long-distance work."

"Was that sad?" she asked.

He lifted a shoulder. "Disappointing, but I wasn't crushed."

"And Girl Number Three?"

"Now that? Crushing."

"Oh! She broke your heart?" Asia guessed.

"Worse. She broke my...program," he said on a laugh.

"What?"

"She was part of my team at Ambrosia, and we worked very closely together on artificial intelligence software for a massive government contract. Just before we bid, she left the company and 'developed' a similar product somewhere else, and they got the millions."

"Oof. Corporate espionage?"

"Sort of. Anyway, she's mired in a lawsuit filed by my company, and the last time I saw her was at a deposition a few years ago."

"And that's it?" she asked. "No more girlfriends?"

"Until this unbelievably gorgeous woman asked to move in with me, and then we wrote two songs together— and sold them, thank you very much—and in the process, I fell so hard I'm surprised it didn't leave a hole in the floor."

"Aww, Dane." She threaded her fingers through his. "You were just minding your own business and I wrecked your life with my messy past."

"So not how I see it," he said, turning onto the beach road that led to Shellseeker, and stealing a look at her. "Is that enough about me to get you to tell me more about you?"

She nodded. "Thanks for sharing all that, though. And to answer your question of a few minutes ago, yes, I probably would have married him and moved to London and had Zee there. I knew he had a bit of a dark streak and needed to call the shots, but it worked for me."

"How?" he asked.

"By following his rules and letting him be the boss."

"Asia." He grunted. "That can't be healthy."

"It's not, hence the therapist. And she made me see that my comfort zone is being controlled."

"I heard you say that, but it doesn't compute. You're so independent it hurts. No one and nothing controls you."

"Not true, but even if it is, that's because of the work I did with Nancy." She plucked at a thread on her jeans, thinking.

"Nancy, the therapist. What was that like?"

Asia sighed. "I loved therapy," she said wistfully. "Nancy had this sweet lavender-scented studio just off the OSU campus and every time I walked in, I felt... lighter. She had silver hair and brown eyes and a soft voice that coaxed my scared and pregnant and deeply broken self back to emotional and mental health."

"Wow, what a testimonial."

"She helped me to see that all my issues started with my mother."

He gave a wry laugh. "Don't they always?"

"Usually, but not always. But in my case, being

controlled by Roselyn Turner was so much a part of how I was hardwired that I automatically sought out a man who did the same thing. I let her—then him—tell me what to say, how to act, how to dress. Taking orders from someone who I think needs me is my comfort zone, and I had to learn to get out of it."

He considered that as they rumbled over the sand and stone parking lot behind Shellseeker Cottages.

"But I will never do it again," she said, determination in her voice.

"I don't intend to ever try to control you, Asia. And you've obviously learned how to step out of that zone with your mother. And Spencer can't control you anymore."

"Really? 'Cause all he did was wave a piece of paper at your mother and here I am, running toward it. And maybe him." She glanced around. "He could be anywhere, watching me."

"I paid attention, Asia. No one followed us, because I didn't take the usual route and no one was behind us."

"Look at you, James Bond."

That made him laugh, but he turned off the car and looked at her. "He's not controlling you," he said. "You're here because you want to find out why he showed up, and what he has to say."

"Trust me, it will be an order to do something. I don't know what it is, or why, or anything, but at the root of what is in that letter will be a measure of control. And, mark my words, as God is my witness, I will not let him have that."

"I one hundred percent agree." He brought their still-joined hands to his lips. "You have my word and full support that no matter what it is, he gets no control over you, ever."

"Or over Zee."

He nodded. "Or over Zee."

She held his gaze, long enough for him to get lost in her dark eyes. "I have your promise?"

"You have my most sincere promise, pinky swear, all sealed with a kiss."

"Thank you." She leaned closer and took that kiss. "And thank you for letting me be your lucky Girl Number Four. I will not move away, steal your ideas, or break your heart. I promise you that."

They kissed again. "Then let's go see what the guy wrote."

"And know this, Dane Whitney," she said before they got out. "He will never get control over me. Never, no matter what it says in that envelope he gave Eliza. He will not."

"I will fully support that."

Chapter Eight

Asia

Asia's hands quaked as she sat alone in the Disney-decorated spare bedroom where she'd taken the sealed envelope to read the contents alone.

She stared at the familiar handwriting and the words that swam in front of her face, reading the whole thing again, top to bottom. As she had when she'd first unfolded the letter, she sucked in a soft breath at the second line, right after "Dear Asia..."

I have learned through a mutual acquaintance that you have a six-month-old son, who I am assuming is my child.

And again, she closed her eyes and let that sink in. Someone had told him, and, really, she wasn't surprised about that. He was obviously asking around about her, and it was only a matter of time until a person who fell into both their worlds—Columbus really *wasn't* that big of a town—told him that Asia had a baby.

But it was the next line that really blew her away.

I have come to offer my financial support and hope that you can find it in your heart—and in your child's best interest—to accept it.

A few things jumped out at her in that sentence.

Financial support? What did that mean, other than strings that would tie them together?

She supposed the use of the phrase "find it in your heart" meant he knew just how much she despised him. And lastly, maybe most important, he called Zane *her* child—which meant he knew he'd have no role in the baby's life.

But even after parsing all those words, she was beyond wary of this offer.

She skimmed the rest again. As she suspected, he'd found her name and address on a database that he was able to purchase through the gray market on the internet, but he made it clear he hadn't started looking for her until after he found out about the baby.

He closed with an apology she'd longed to receive, but still didn't feel was genuine. At least, not to her.

I owe you so much, Asia. I am so deeply sorry for what I did to you. That doesn't even cover my regret and shame. You don't owe me anything, but I owe you and this child and I know that.

Please meet with me so we can make the arrangements as soon as possible. I promise that afterwards, I will leave and you won't have to worry about me anymore. I have a temporary local number, so you can reach me here.

After the number, he signed with a simple S.

"Knock-knock." Dane stood in the doorway. "I don't want to invade your privacy, just see if you're okay."

"I'm...okay." She let out a sigh. "Shocked, confused, and ducking the curveball just thrown my way, but okay."

"Can I..."

"Yes, please." She gestured him closer and patted the bed next to her.

He took the offer, studying her closely. "You don't look too upset. That's good."

"I'm ...confounded." She handed him the letter and huffed out a breath. "Read it and weep. Then help me figure out the catch."

His frown deepened as he took the letter and began to read while Asia leaned back on her hands, her gaze rising to the plastic snowflakes that hung on fishing wire from the ceiling.

Child support. Was it guilt money? A payoff? Some convoluted form of blackmail? Or a very crafty way to stay in her life?

Or was it, as he'd said, "*A genuine offer of funding for the child I helped bring into the world.*"

Maybe it was, but there was no way it was free-and-clear money. He had to want something—her love, her attention, her time or...a role of some sort in Zee's life. Nothing came from Spencer Keaton without a string attached to his oh-so-controlling hands.

"Wow," Dane whispered as he finished. "That's not bad news, right?"

She shot him a look. "I don't trust him to give me anything that doesn't come with stipulations."

He flipped the paper over, but it was blank, then let his hand fall to his knee, still holding it.

"He says he doesn't want anything." At her look, he fluttered the paper. "I mean, he probably has a very guilty conscience."

The first tendril of worry started to worm around her heart, a fear that Dane would make her accept this.

"You don't understand that he is a master manipulator, and I guarantee you this doesn't come without...a *quid pro quo*. He might want to give me money, but he has to want something in return."

"But he says—"

"I know what he says," she fired back, a little sharply. "And I also know what *you* said in the car not a half-hour ago. You promised not to fall into his trap of control, or at least not to let me fall into it."

"Asia." He put the letter on the bed between them and looked into her eyes. "I swear I will keep that promise, but you can't be so blinded by your anger and resentment toward him that you don't accept what might be —*might* be—a legitimate offer of child support."

"But you don't know him, Dane," she said, working to keep her voice steady. "This could also be the first step to a legal battle for shared custody, or his way of trying to get me to allow him to take Zee to London. Or maybe he's buying my silence, because a baby out of wedlock might rock his new wealthy in-laws. Or he wants me back again, part-time, of course."

He just stared at her.

"Which I will not do," she added, seeing instant relief in his eyes. "Don't worry, Dane. I'm not...for sale."

"I know," he said. "And I do realize that I don't know the guy, but isn't it remotely possible this is exactly what he says it is? Sure, it could be driven by guilt and fear, but that doesn't make it less valuable. And best of all, if he's out of your life forever, it's the best gift of all. We can get Claire to draft a legal document that states he gives up all parental rights, and you can be free of him."

Which was what she wanted so much, but somehow doubted it could end that way. "I don't want to meet with him," she said.

"Then I will. I'll talk to him and find out what he's offering."

"No. No." She shook her head, that tendril of worry choking her now. "What was crazy was believing your first promise to me."

"Asia!" He took both her hands. "Don't say that. I'm not trying to convince you to let the guy have one iota of control in your life, or in Zee's. I'm simply saying you should hear him out. I'll go alone or with you, and no Zee. Don't ever let him see your baby, but if he's willing to provide you with some support, you should at least hear him out. If for no other reason than it could provide some security for Zee. He's your first priority."

She just closed her eyes. "No. Maybe. I don't know."

"Think about it."

"I doubt I'll think about anything else," she said.

He lifted the letter again, his gaze moving over it. "He calls it child support for life, and hopes it's enough. He has a good job, right?"

"Seven figures with a bonus, and his wife's loaded." She hissed a breath. "For all we know, she's infertile and wants his baby."

"Stop it," he said. "You're jumping to insane conclusions."

She groaned softly, nearly strangled by the fact that Dane seemed to be taking Spencer's side. She just sat very still for a moment, trying to breathe, trying to ground herself like Nancy taught her.

Dane took her hand. "If we meet with him, no matter what you decide to do, you have my full support, whatever that decision is."

There was something about the way Dane said...*if we meet with him*. It wasn't a done deal, and she wasn't in this alone. That, at least, felt good.

Dane stroked her knuckles with his thumb. "Or I can meet with him alone, tell him to get the hell out of your life, and send his blood money where the sun don't shine."

She snorted softly, the words so utterly out of character for this man. "Whatever you do, Dane, just...don't take his side over mine."

"I never would."

"You just did," she insisted. "You think it would be smart to take that money, no matter how the strings attached to it strangle me."

"Asia, all I'm saying is that you should consider what he has to say, and *if* it is as innocent as child support he legitimately owes you, then think about it—especially if he'll sign something that will make him permanently disappear. That's all I'm saying. Nothing else, I promise. I'm not on anyone's side but yours."

She softened a little, leaning close to him, knowing he really did want the best for her. She certainly couldn't say that much about Spencer Keaton.

"I need to think about it," she finally said.

"Fair enough. There's no timeline. Let him know tomorrow, and take tonight to sleep on it."

She made a face. "I can't tell Roz. She'd force me to take whatever he's offering so fast, my head would spin."

"Asia." He eased her closer. "No one—not me, not Roz, and not this clown Spencer—can force you to do anything. You are your own woman, utterly and completely."

For a moment, he sounded so much like Nancy, the words really did ease her heart.

"My mother just told me one of the cottages is empty and offered it to you. Would you like to stay in something called Slipper Snail?"

"Yes," she said without a moment of doubt. "I'd feel safer, and I don't want him anywhere near my parents' house."

"And Zee?"

"He stays with me and..." She put a hand on his arm. "And you, too. Please?"

"Don't ask twice. I'll get the key from my mother and you can get settled in there now. I'll bring what you need, and Roz can bring the baby."

"I'll decide whether or not to see him really soon, I promise."

"Okay. Every single decision is yours, and I'm right next to you all the way."

It was exactly what she needed to hear.

Chapter Nine

Noah

At least it was quiet. Weirdly so, if Noah was going to be honest.

The small house with the makeshift family sounded downright desolate after Noah came home from closing up the rental cabana for Deeley. He'd grabbed his favorite ribeye cheesesteak at Jerry's on the way home, since DJ had texted him that he'd be working late at Luigi's.

Except...the man didn't *work* at the restaurant—he was supposed to be considering buying it. There'd been a strange vibe in his father's text, too, Noah mused as he read it again. But maybe he was imagining that, and DJ was merely up to his eyeballs in making dough with the old Italian guy who'd become a good friend.

But he could swear he was...hiding something. Was that possible?

Noah had considered offering to go in and help, but backed off. It was one thing to learn the art of making pizza in their small ovens at home, or at the tea hut when he and DJ ran a pop-up event. But it was downright uncomfortable to go into Luigi's kitchen like some kind of apprentice when the staff was running around doing real work.

Plus, he needed the time to write his book.

Sophia was nowhere to be found, which was a gift from God Noah didn't question. He knew his mother was in her room, studying for the bar, because he'd texted her to see if she wanted her favorite mahi mahi tacos from Jerry's. But she turned down the food and said she'd be knee-deep in...something legal.

So no family dinner tonight, he thought as he pulled the sandwich out of the bag and got a soda from the fridge. No family at all, and that didn't feel quite right. And when he pulled the tab on the can and it hissed noisily, it felt like an echo in the silent house.

"Malcontent," he murmured before taking a bite of cheesesteak on a freshly made hoagie roll.

If it was noisy, he wasn't happy. If it was quiet, he was lonely. He needed to just settle down and be content with the amazing life he'd somehow carved out for himself.

And use this time to plot the book that was kicking his butt and hurting his head as he rammed into something he imagined was "writer's block."

Pulling out his phone, he tapped the Notes app and reviewed what he'd written the last time he attempted to work on the quasi-autobiographical story of a man who loses both parents in 9/11 and ends up in foster homes.

Okay, not so *quasi*. But reality and fiction weren't coming together as nicely as he'd hoped.

"Hey, you."

He looked up at Claire, whose voice seemed strained and subdued.

"Hi, Mom." He still liked the sound of that on his lips, since he was, after all, the man who'd lost both parents in 9/11 and ended up in foster homes. Until this woman, his biological mother, re-entered his life. He just loved calling her "Mom."

"Ribeye cheesesteak?" she guessed, taking a whiff.

"Yeah. I really could have gotten you those tacos—"

She waved off the offer with a smile. "Not hungry at all, honey. Thanks. How was Jerry's?" she asked, grabbing a glass from one of the cabinets and taking it to the fridge.

"Kind of empty, honestly."

"Mmm." She pushed the ice maker and filled the glass, then added water. "You know, I think I like Jerry's better than Bailey's for the to-go food, though they're both darling grocery stores."

"Darling?" He smiled around the next bite.

"Can't think of a better word," she said on a laugh, joining him at the kitchen counter.

"Has the bar exam stuff fried your brain tonight?"

"Kind of." She rolled her eyes. "Civil law is so boring. And I missed my taxation practice test, so I'm still studying for that."

"You missed a practice test?" he asked after swallowing, wiping some sauce from his mouth with a napkin. "Not like you, Claire Sutherland."

He expected her easy laugh, but didn't even get a smile. "Yeah, well. You know."

No, he didn't know. "You okay?" he asked, lowering the sandwich before taking another bite, seeing the strain in her eyes and shadows under them. "You look like you had a tough day."

"Mmm." She covered with a sip of water, but not well enough.

"Mom? What's wrong?"

She put the glass down, running her fingers along the condensation, silent. Finally, she looked up, her dark eyes brimming with emotion—and tears.

"Everything's wrong," she said on a near-sob.

He put the sandwich down and reached for her. "What's going on?"

She sighed and accepted the hug, drawing back as she shook her head. "I don't know if I should talk about it."

"I do. Talk. Now. Everything. Did you have a fight with Dad? Or Sophia? She's always at the center of drama."

Claire almost smiled, but then sighed and closed her eyes. He recognized the wind-up for whatever was on her mind, so instead of talking, he just waited patiently for her to share.

"You hardly ever call DJ 'Dad.' Have you noticed?"

Not what he was expecting, but okay. "I do, occasionally. I mean, we're always working together and lots of times people and customers are around, so 'Dad' seems weird." He frowned, not sure where she was going with this. "Why?"

"I don't know. I just..." She released another heartfelt sigh. "Yeah, I guess I did have a fight with him. And

Sophia, but not at the same time. It was a crap day, Noah."

"Oh, man." He put a hand on her shoulder. "Want to tell me about it?"

"Yeah, but...should I? You see, I don't know the ins and outs of being a family. I was an only child and my parents were anything but traditional."

He snorted, thinking of her crazy French mother and the man he'd never met, the oversized-in-death Dutch Vanderveen, the pilot and bigamist.

"So, I don't know how to handle some of these things," she continued. "Like disciplining a kid who isn't mine, or expecting DJ to see things my way, or...how much I should tell you."

"Tell me everything, and remember my background. I'm no family expert, but I've seen some on TV."

She smiled at that. "Sophia decided to cut her class at the high school and have a party here, with boys and alcohol."

He lifted a brow. "*Oookay*, not cool but not, you know, too far off the mark for a senior in high school. At least she's making friends, which is surprising, since she just started taking a class or two there."

"I know, you're right. It wasn't just that she had kids here, although they may have driven after drinking. And that scares me, plus it presses all my lawyer hot buttons."

"Is that what you fought about?"

"Not exactly. But we had some harsh words because I had a practice test scheduled, and you can't re-do those easily. She was really nasty, and then"—she angled her head—"she took off in my car with my keys, purse, and books on the front seat, and left me here, stranded."

"Ouch." He made a face. "What did you do?"

"I got myself to Luigi's and..." She swallowed hard. "Then I think I had a big fight with DJ, although with him, who knows? It was really unpleasant and made me question everything."

"Oh, Mom." He reached for her again. "Like I said, no expert on families, but I think you and DJ having a disagreement over something like that is pretty normal. Sophia is a flashpoint and is going to cause friction wherever she is, and DJ's loyalties are torn. Don't get too bent out of shape about it."

She nodded glumly. "I know, but something about the conversation felt...serious. I'm not entirely sure where I stand with him." As soon as she spoke, she gave him an uncertain look. "That's probably too much information for our son to have, huh?"

"Not too much, but I don't need the details," he said. "We're all trying to do our best and really enjoy the moment that we're in. I know, I know." He held up his hand, laughing. "I sound exactly like him and one of our Paulo Coelho books we like to read, but I mean it."

"It's hard to enjoy the moment when I feel like Sophia has fractured things."

"Yeah, she makes trouble. And noise."

"So much noise," Claire said on a laugh.

"But she is who she is, and, believe it or not, I think she's learning a lot from being around you."

"Me?" she scoffed. "She mocks me. And my stuff.

She called my bag...chewsomething? Chew-gie? What does that even mean?"

He laughed. "Cheugy—spelled c-h-e-u-g-y, I think. It's a Gen Z and younger expression for something that's...I don't know." He wasn't sure how sensitive she might be about her handbag.

"Worth a lot?"

"Uh, not exactly. More like not, you know, cool."

"Well, I never pretended to be cool."

"I wouldn't take it to heart," Noah said. "Sophia is seventeen and you're..."

"*Not* seventeen," she finished with a chuckle. "Hence the uncool bag. Which I happen to think is lovely, especially when it's not being driven away in a stolen car as part of a felony, misdemeanor, and possible DUI, thank you very much."

"Man, you are a lawyer."

"Which is probably...cheugy to the max."

He laughed, happy to hear her make jokes again. "And as far as DJ?" he added. "The man is crazy about you, so I bet he comes home, makes up, and...that's all I want to think about."

She gave a soft chuckle. "Oh, Noah, you're such a good kid. Why are you sitting here eating alone and not having family time of your own with Katie and Harper?"

"Good question," he said, returning to the abandoned sandwich. "The answer is because I want to write my book, but..." He shook his head. "I think I have a classic case of writer's block, which stinks."

"What's blocking you?"

He opened his mouth to answer, had no idea, so he took a bite instead but thought hard as he ate it.

"I'm excited about writing," he finally said, wiping his mouth again. "I love the act of creating a world with words and inventing people from scratch to make them do what I want, but..." He dug a little deeper, grateful that his mother was a fantastic listener who just waited patiently for him to find the answer. "It's too close and autobiographical," he finally said, surprising himself with the answer. "Every time I change what happened for the sake of the story, it feels like I'm lying."

"Hard to make up people from scratch when they already exist," she said.

"Yes!" He pointed at her. "That's just it. I'm straddling this line between fiction and biography that doesn't feel right. And—this is really stupid—I keep thinking what people who know me are going to say when they read it. I am a storyteller, but is this the story I want to tell?"

"I bet lots of writers feel that way when they first start."

"Maybe, but what is monumentally stupid is thinking it could get published at all."

She eyed him for a moment, thinking. "I have a suggestion. Why don't you just sit down and write something totally different tonight, just to exercise your storytelling muscles with no expectations about what you're writing or who's going to read it."

"That's smart."

She tapped her temple. "Amazing there's anything

left up there after civil law and taxation sucked up all the gray matter."

"Still," he said, thinking. "I might try that freestyle technique. It's a good idea." He inched the plate toward her, offering the other half of his sandwich. "You sure you don't want something for dinner?"

She shook her head. "You eat it, honey. I'll get some cheese and crackers and go back to the books." Pushing up, she picked up her glass and studied him. "Thanks for the pep talk, my sweet son."

"Anytime, except you gave me advice and I didn't give you anything, not even a sandwich."

"It's fine. Enjoy the rest and happy writing."

"Thanks."

As she started to walk out of the kitchen, a thought occurred to him. "Mom?"

"Hmm?"

"I do have a little bit of advice, not just for you, but for all of us."

"What's that?" she asked, interest sparking in her eyes.

"Why don't we do something as a family—the four of us, you know? And I don't mean make pizza or go to the beach, because that's all we ever do. But something touristy or fun? Maybe even a little vacation or...something. The stuff that none of us got to do together in all the years that have passed."

She considered that, nodding. "I love that idea, Noah. Let's both think about possibilities and bring it up with DJ and Sophia."

He lifted his soda in a toast. "We got this covered. Trust me."

"We do," she agreed. "Now, go write and don't think. Just...create."

"I think I will." For the first time in a long time, he couldn't wait to hole up in his room, open his laptop, and do something new and exciting on the page.

Chapter Ten

Eliza

When Claire cancelled their walk the next morning, Eliza was more disappointed than usual. Yes, her sister had backed off a few times due to studying, but with so much going on right now, Eliza had really been looking forward to a heart to heart during their morning walk.

So, when she strolled down to the tea hut instead of the beach, Eliza was doubly happy to see her daughter at one of the tables, sipping iced tea with Teddy while Bash sat in the sand filling buckets with sand and dumping them...on Olivia's feet. And lap.

Laughing at the child who already felt like a "grand," she called out, "Livvie! What a lovely surprise. You're never here this early."

"'Liza!" Bash shot up from the sand, running to her, hands outstretched.

"There's my little man!" She scooped him up and swung him around with a soft grunt, because the toddler was growing, and fast.

"Tomorrow's my birthday!" he announced as she lowered him to the ground.

"And don't I know it, Mr. Three Years Old Tomorrow." Taking his hand, she walked the rest of the way to the sand to join Olivia and Teddy. "What's happening for the big birthday?"

"We'll be having a party," Teddy said with a satisfied smile. "I mean, have you met me?"

"You do like a party, Teddy, but tomorrow?" Eliza pulled out the third chair. "Mid-week crazies around here. Four check-ins, and..." Before sitting, she let work go and planted a kiss on her daughter's sun-warmed hair. "I'm so happy you're here."

"No party tomorrow," Teddy assured her. "We're just planning something for the near future."

"But tomorrow," Olivia said, "Deeley and I are going to take him to Ding Darling for the day. Nothing like a wildlife sanctuary for a three-year-old."

"He'll love it," Eliza said. "Teddy, do you remember when we did the field trip there with Harper's Vacation Bible School?"

"Oh, we had a wonderful time. No one should be on Sanibel Island and not see that glorious place," Teddy said, then turned to Eliza with a frown. "I thought you were waiting for Claire to take your morning walk."

"She bagged today," Eliza said, and then remembered something else that was in her sister's text. "Although she did ask me if I could recommend something she and DJ could do with Noah and Sophia, like a family outing. Is Ding Darling too obvious?"

"Oh, they definitely should go," Teddy said. "It might be a tad slow for Sophia, but even a jaded teenager will get swept away by the beauty of that preserve."

Olivia smiled at her. "Spoken like a true Sanibel native, Teddy."

"That I am, my dear, and proud of it."

"I'll tell Claire when I see her," Eliza said, then scowled. "*If* I see her. The bar exam prep has her so busy. It's not like her to text me, you know? I was surprised she didn't call. And I really wanted to hang with her today."

"Hang with me." Olivia leaned toward her. "There's much to gossip about. I talked to Asia last night and she filled me in. Teddy and I were just discussing this mysterious child support offer from the ex. What do you think?"

"I don't know what to make of it," Eliza admitted. "I guess it's good that he knows about Zane. I would imagine she's been carrying a terrible burden of guilt that she can let go of now."

"And so has he," Olivia said. "I'm sure his guilt for being the world's worst human is what's driving the offer."

"Agreed." Eliza nodded. "Which is why I'm with Dane, frankly. She should meet with the guy and hear him out."

"Eh, not sure about that." Olivia raised a skeptical brow. "Last night, I swung by Slipper Snail while Dane was at Little Blues, so she and I had a good, long talk. 'Specially long, 'cause my angel boy napped for an hour." She reached down to flutter Bash's hair, getting a sweet smile that touched Eliza with how strong Olivia's bond had become with this boy.

"What did she say?" Teddy asked.

"What *didn't* she say? It was like a dam broke after all these months of being friends and her not telling me about the guy, so I got an earful about Spencer Keaton. She doesn't trust him."

"For good reason," Eliza said. "He cheated on her in the most unimaginable way."

"That doesn't make him a fully bad man," Teddy said.

They both shot her looks of incredulity, and the older woman lifted a shoulder. "You aren't forgetting Dutch, are you?"

"My grandfather, the serial cheater?" Olivia choked a laugh. "How could we?"

Eliza winced at her father's sad and ugly legacy.

"He was unfaithful to Camille by marrying Birdie, but remember, he had an altruistic reason that was all about his guilt," Teddy said. "And guilt, I can tell you, can bring a man to his knees. Having lived with a man who was mired in it, I'm not at all surprised that Asia's ex would make this offer. It might be the only way he can sleep at night."

They all nodded, mulling that over for a minute, then Teddy changed the subject with some pictures on her phone from Camille, sunbathing on the deck of Buck Underwood's boat.

"She looks amazing and young and so happy," Olivia said.

"You'd never know she had open-heart surgery a few months ago," Eliza added.

"I'd say her heart is healed," Teddy mused, examining the picture. "That's the face of a woman in love." She slid the phone into the middle of the table with a smug expression. "That is all the proof you need that a woman can survive, thrive, and find love again."

Eliza studied the picture, something shifting in her heart, powerful enough to let her release a soft whimper.

"Mom?" Olivia asked instantly. "What's wrong?"

"Oh, nothing."

Teddy reached a hand over and put it on Eliza's arm, pressing down. "Not nothing," she said. "I can feel you humming with..." Teddy's brows drew together. "A deep blue aura of doubt."

Eliza smiled. "No secrets when your closest friend is an empath."

"No secrets when you're sitting next to your daughter, either," Olivia said. "Is it Miles, Mom? Are you still struggling with *your* second chance?"

"No. Yes. Maybe. Sometimes."

They all laughed at that, including Eliza.

"Like I said, deep blue doubt," Teddy said.

"I don't think I have doubts." Eliza looked from one to the other, extremely happy to have these two as a sounding board this morning. "But I woke up feeling...out of sorts."

"Because you should wake up feeling...a man." Olivia poked Eliza's arm playfully. "Next to you. Named Miles, who's so crazy about you it kind of hurts to watch."

"I can't argue any of that," Eliza said.

"Then what are you doubting?" Teddy asked. "Your year of mourning is up, your son has accepted Miles as the man in your life, and your daughter is sitting here giving you permission to wake up next to him."

"You sound just like Claire," Eliza said, tsking and tipping her head toward the sand. "And please don't let Bash hear that scandalous talk about his Grandma 'Liza." But he was a good six feet away and oblivious to the women's conversation.

"What's really stopping you, Mom?" Olivia asked, quite serious. "Do you even know?"

"No, I don't, except I guess I'm waiting for...a lightning bolt. A moment of clarity. That ah-ha instant when I know beyond a shadow of a doubt that I am well and truly in love."

"Not sure it works that way," Olivia said. "What do you think, Teddy?"

She shrugged, wiping back a stray silver curl that had escaped her clip. "I don't know about that kind of certainty. I don't think you ever have that, not completely, with love. But what do I know? I'm seventy-three and never married. I'm clearly not the best person to ask."

"But you're the wisest person I know," Eliza said.

"Oh." Teddy gripped her hand, not to feel her aura, but to express her love, and Eliza felt it right down to her toes. "Thank you, sweetie. I am honored to be the sage on the sand here at Shellseeker Beach, but I'm afraid I can't give you a cut-and-dried answer. I do think your heart is open to him, and you know Miles is an extraordinary man."

Eliza nodded. "He's going to propose, and I...I don't know what I'll say."

"How about yes?" Olivia shot her a look. "Mom, you'd be crazy not to marry Miles."

"But do I have to? I was married once, and it still feels like that should be something you only do one time in your life."

"Spoken like a woman whose father married three times, twice simultaneously," Olivia cracked. "I guess you come by that fear of walking down the aisle kind of naturally."

"That could be it," Teddy agreed. "In fact, if you hadn't discovered all you did about your father after coming here, I'm not sure you'd have this hang-up about a second marriage at all."

Eliza nodded slowly, mulling all that. "Maybe."

"Don't let Dutch win," Teddy whispered. "He has no right to do that to you, and from the grave, no less."

"Is he in a grave?" Olivia asked, frowning.

"He's in a box in my bedroom," Teddy said.

Eliza drew back, not sure she'd known that. "Really? Is that what you want?"

Teddy sighed. "I don't think it's about what *I* want," she said. "I personally think a final resting place should be where the person who died wants it to be."

"Ben refused to tell me where he wanted to be," Eliza replied, glancing toward the water. "So I put him where I wanted him, right out there in the sunshine and blue water." She turned back to Teddy. "And I have to tell you, it was liberating. Maybe you should do the same thing."

"I can't," Teddy said. "Dutch wanted his ashes to be

in the sky, which should surprise no one who knew that pilot."

Eliza felt a frown tug and she glanced at Olivia, who looked as confused. "How does one put ashes...in the sky?"

"Right?" Teddy snorted. "I suppose I could go up in some little airplane that is safe to open a door, but...is there such a thing?"

"I can try and find out," Eliza offered. "Miles might know."

"Is that what Dutch expected you to do?" Olivia asked. "Find a plane and dump him out? Or buy a seat on a rocket to space? That's a dilemma."

"I honestly don't know what he expected me to do," Teddy admitted. "He just told me once that I should bury him in the sky, where he belongs." She waved a hand. "Don't worry about it, ladies. He's fine for the moment in my room. Let's get back to you, Eliza, and what's stopping you from looking as happy as Camille and"—she pointed to Olivia—"this joyous newlywed right here."

Olivia gave a big grin and fluttered the diamond ring on her left hand, making them laugh.

"I don't know, but I'll figure it out," Eliza promised them. "I can say with some certainty that my doubts don't have anything to do with Dutch. I think if anyone is to blame, it's Ben Whitney."

"Dad?" Olivia sat up straight. "Did he ask you not to marry again?"

"No, he didn't." But he never gave her a blessing,

either. "Ben did nothing but be the most perfect man, the best father, a great lover, and the only husband I ever wanted. I know I have officially passed my 'grieving' period and I am ready to move on emotionally, but some days, some mornings, I wake up and..." She hated that her eyes grew misty. "I don't know if I can ever love anyone like that again, or be that connected to another person. I already had 'The One,' you know?"

"Oh, Mom." Olivia pressed her fingers to her mouth. "I'm sorry it still hurts."

"It doesn't hurt like, well, like it did. But the very thought of—"

"Hey, ladies."

They all turned at the sound of Dane's voice and the sight of him coming down the path from the cottages.

"More later," Eliza whispered under her breath. "I don't want to talk about this around him."

Olivia and Teddy agreed with silent nods, then they all waved Dane over.

"Hey, bro," Olivia called. "Grab a chair and a tea and tell us what's new."

"Love to. I'll skip the tea, though. Asia and I already had coffee, Zee is fed and happy, and..." He plopped into a chair and looked from one to the other. "She called Spencer Keaton."

The three women all reacted with surprise while Dane settled at the table and got a sandy high-five from Bash.

"Well, what did he say?" Olivia demanded. "Tell all, please."

"Not too much to tell yet. We're meeting him in a little bit."

"Is he coming here?" Teddy asked. "I need to meet him."

"Yes, she does," Olivia agreed. "Let Teddy suss out his aura and find out if this is a legit offer."

"Asia doesn't want him to meet Zane, and wants to be on neutral territory, which I totally get. We're going to have a coffee with him, and were hoping we could scare up a babysitter in this group, because she doesn't want to tell her mother yet."

"He's not insisting on at least meeting the baby?" Eliza asked. "I'm surprised at that."

"He's not," Dane said.

"Well, what did he say?" Olivia pushed. "What was he like? What did they talk about? Did you hear any of it?"

"I heard all of it, because she had him on speaker."

"What changed her mind? When did she call him?" Olivia tapped the table, impatience in every question.

"I changed her mind," he said. "We talked late into the night after you left, Liv, and more this morning. She's weighed the pros and cons—"

"Dane Whitney-style," Olivia teased.

"You got that right. And there's not really a con other than the emotional impact of seeing him. I'm going to be with her every minute. The fact is, the guy's offering child support and, maybe more important, he's agreed to sign away any and all rights to Zane. In fact, he says it is not necessary to even see him."

"Why would he do that?" Eliza asked, shaking her head. "Why wouldn't he at least want to see his own child?"

Dane shrugged. "I don't know what makes this dude tick, Mom. But to answer all your questions, Liv, she called him a little while ago and he opened with what sounded like a very abject apology and—"

"What did Asia say?" Olivia asked, making Dane sigh with frustration that he couldn't finish a sentence.

"Not much. She's furious at him, and hurt. She didn't call him to chat and get the latest on his happy marriage in London, if that's what you mean. It was brief, businesslike, and we're meeting him at a local restaurant."

"Can you take a lawyer?" Eliza asked. "You might want Claire with you."

"No, I think that would just send the wrong message."

Olivia snorted. "She cares what message she sends that loser?"

"All Asia wants is to hear the details of his offer and keep the whole thing as quick and painless as possible," Dane told her. "Honestly, it sounded like that was what he wanted, too."

"So why is he doing this?" Teddy mused. "If it was guilt, he'd be more...emotional, don't you think?"

"You want to know what I think?" Dane asked. "After hearing the guy, I think he wants to cover his bases so something doesn't come back to haunt him in the future. He sounded all business to me, like this was more of a transaction than a big heartfelt deal."

"And how did that make Asia feel?" Teddy asked.

"I think better, to be honest, but..." He looked past them to the path, pointing. "You can ask her now. She's got Zee. Who's our sitter?"

All three hands went up and he laughed, standing. "I knew I could count on you guys."

"So?" Olivia asked when he went to greet Asia and was out of earshot. "What do we think of this new development?"

"I guess it's good," Eliza said, although she wasn't certain.

"I'd like to meet him," Teddy said. "Then I'd tell you what I think. And you, Liv?"

She made a face. "I'm a skeptical person who has been burned by trust in the past. I'd be careful what I signed."

"Thank you for babysitting," Asia called when she came closer, shutting down their chatter. "We won't be long."

They talked some more about the situation, but it was clear Asia was anxious to get her uncomfortable errand over with, so Teddy took wee Zee up to the house. Olivia chased after Bash, who wanted to go to the water, and Eliza stayed at the table with Dane.

"Can I tell Miles?" she asked when they were alone.

"Sure, but why? You said he did as deep a dive as he could into the guy and found nothing of any concern."

"I'm curious what he thinks of this new development."

"Sure, you can tell him. I'll let you know what the

offer is." Dane let out a sigh and stood to go up to the house, obviously ready to go, too. "This might be a gift. And not just the support, as I said. Asia wants him to disappear from her life for eternity and if he agrees to that, she's going to be happier. Honestly, Mom, that's all I want for her. Peace and security."

Eliza reached for his hand. "You're being wonderful in this situation," she said. "Your father would be proud."

He gave her a sad smile and nodded his thanks, then took off to meet Asia. After a moment of watching him and letting emotions wash over her, she lifted her phone to call Miles.

"Hey, gorgeous." He always answered on the first ring when Eliza called, and there was always a smile in his voice. She loved that. She loved everything about him, in fact.

But did she love *him*?

"E?" he asked when she didn't say anything. "You still there?"

"Oh, yes, I was just...thinking. Sorry. There's a new twist in the Spencer Keaton saga."

"Really?"

"She and Dane are meeting him right now. He knows about the baby and has come to offer child support."

Miles was silent for a few seconds as that sunk in, then asked, "And he did this by leaving the silent message of a fan at her door?"

Eliza stood and inhaled the fresh salt air, thinking about that. "That is strange, yeah. I don't suppose you found anything else of interest on this guy?"

"Nothing new, but I'll keep looking. I got another new case today, so I'm pretty busy, but I'll squeeze it in. But what I really want to squeeze in is you."

She laughed. "Sounds like I better get in line."

"I have a dinner meeting with a client, but I'm free after eight or so. How about a moonlight cruise?"

"Oh, that sounds divine. Text me when you're on your way home tonight and I'll be there."

She was still smiling when she went up to check on the baby. True, she might not want to marry Miles Anderson—or anyone, for that matter—but she sure was happy to have him in her life.

Could she, as the expression went, have her cake and eat it, too? Or would it have to be wedding cake? Because Eliza knew herself well enough to know that was just not happening.

Chapter Eleven

Dane

Asia chose a well-loved restaurant because she said it seemed open and safe, but they hadn't counted on having to wait for a table when they arrived early for the rendezvous at the Lighthouse Café.

Spencer still hadn't arrived when they were taken to a booth for four against a wall that, like the entire place, was filled with framed images of seascapes and lighthouses. Dane slid next to her, taking her hand.

"I came here once with my mother," Asia said, glancing around like they were just typical tourists enjoying one of the local favorites. "The French toast is amazing, and the waitress said the café had been written up in *Bon Appetite* magazine."

"Aje, you don't have to make small talk," he said. "I can practically taste your nerves."

She nodded, then sighed, sounding sad. "It's a shame, you know?"

"This whole thing with Spencer?" he guessed.

"The fact that a few days ago we were high on life and a contract to write songs. We haven't even thought about it since he showed up."

"Think of it as material for our next song," he said.

"Nothing like a good ballad about a bad ex." He winked. "We could call it 'Blast From The Past.'"

She rolled her eyes. "You love a good cliché, Dane. I can do better than that." Leaning in, she whispered, "Who needs an ex when you have a Y...like why did I think you were a good idea?"

He threw his head back and laughed. "You're so good at that, Asia."

She laughed, too, then glanced at the door as it opened, and the chuckle caught in her throat.

"He's here," she managed.

Dane sneaked a quick look, knowing instantly that the man who was at least six-two and held the captive gaze of the hostess had to be Spencer Keaton. He wore a button-down shirt and khakis with a leather messenger bag hooked over a shoulder, which stood out as wildly overdressed for Sanibel Island.

Dane squeezed her hand, his attention back on Asia. "We got this, Aje. You and me. You're not alone."

She mouthed a thank-you and looked toward the door again. "As soon as he's done flirting with the poor hostess."

"He looks, uh, formidable," Dane said with an easy laugh.

"I told you, he is. Look at the way he walks. All that Mediterranean swagger from a Greek mother, and hours upon hours in the gym."

Dane barely hid his eyeroll. "I just do hours upon hours at the keyboard—music and computer."

"Just brace for charm," she warned under her

breath. "I'm sure that's how he got the British aristocrat to marry him while I was back in Ohio taking pregnancy tests."

He arrived at the table and looked down at them. Dane's first thought was, *dang, Zee got this guy's eyes*, no matter how much he liked to think the baby favored Asia's side of the gene pool.

"Asia," Spencer said softly, tossing the bag into the booth as Dane stood in greeting.

Asia didn't move, except to nod at him.

Spencer's eyes flickered and shifted to Dane. He extended his hand and said, "Spencer Keaton."

"Dane Whitney."

The two men shook hands with the seriousness of a chess match opening. Spencer slid onto the leather seat across from them, then there was a beat of awkward silence.

"Thank you," Spencer finally said, looking directly at Asia. "I appreciate you doing this."

She was quiet for a moment, probably not prepared for that opening salvo, maybe expecting him to be nervous and make some small talk. But he was all business, in demeanor and dress.

"I asked Dane to come," she said softly, as if his presence needed explanation.

"I know, you said that on the phone," he replied, and somehow, the comment gave him the upper hand. Like nothing surprised him, which Dane didn't like.

Have some humility, dude. You totaled the woman's life.

He glanced at Dane with a hint of a smile. "Happy to have you here, too. This isn't easy."

Asia snorted as if to say, "Understatement alert," but that just made Spencer sigh.

"Asia, we don't have to be enemies," he said. "I come in peace. Literally, across the ocean, bearing..." He patted his bag. "Something I think you'll love even more than you, uh..." He chuckled softly. "Hate me."

She glared at him. "Is it a joke to you, what you did?"

"No, Asia, it's not. I'm trying to make you comfortable."

She drew back, giving him a *get real* look. "Nothing about you is ever going to make me comfortable again."

"I get that," he said with a whisper of subtle condescension. "And that's why I'm here. Would you like to know my plans?"

"I would have liked to have known your plans before you got married," she said, keeping her voice low but her anger came through. "That would have been nice, don't you think?"

He looked down at his placemat, silent while the waitress put a glass of water in front of him.

"Are y'all ready to—"

"We'll need a few minutes," Dane said with a tight smile. "I'll, uh, let you know."

She got the message and disappeared again, another few seconds of aching silence in her wake.

Spencer inched slightly closer, holding Asia's gaze. "Let me just say my piece, Asia, and then we can move on."

She nodded and took a sip of her water as he put his elbows on the table and took a breath.

"I want to help you take care of the child."

"The child?" she scoffed under her breath.

"I thought you would prefer if I didn't...talk about him."

"What I'd prefer is that you didn't *know* about him," Asia said.

Under the table, Dane put a hand on her leg, giving her thigh a calming squeeze of support.

"I'm glad I do," Spencer replied. "I am so grateful to be in a position to meet my obligations as his biological father. I'd rather do that now, when I can really help you, rather than years from now when...it's so late in his life."

Dane studied him, wondering if he'd missed some subtext. He wasn't the greatest reader of people, but if he had to say? This dude honestly looked nothing but sincere and warm.

Was that the charm Asia had warned him about?

"Well, it is what it is," Asia said, swallowing as if the man's kindness wasn't making her feel any better. "Say what you came to say."

"Fine." He pressed his hands together, the tips of his index fingers settling into the triangle of whiskers under his lips. "I would like to put one million dollars in your name in an account that will be safe and grow, and that you can access when your son turns five years old."

Asia's head jerked up and a gasp slipped through her lips. "A million..."

"Please don't be surprised, Asia. I am a man of my word and responsibilities."

She stared, visibly processing this. "What's the catch?"

He lifted one sizeable shoulder. "There isn't one. To help you, I had my accountant arrange to have the money bear the maximum amount of interest with the least amount of tax hit. You can disperse or access it as you like, or leave it there to continue to grow. The account will be in your name and..." He flipped his hands. "That's it."

She stared at him, looking like she might not have heard anything past...well, a million dollars. But Dane did. He heard it all...what was said and what *wasn't* said.

"May I ask a question?" He leaned in.

"Of course," Spencer said graciously.

"What are your intentions regarding custody?"

"I have none," Spencer said without a nanosecond of hesitation. "I have a document right here in my bag that states I relinquish any and all custodial attachments to the child, and an affidavit stating I will not make any effort to contact him." He shifted his gaze to Asia. "I know that you've told people...a different story," he said softly. "I can assure you that I have no intention of contradicting that."

"Kinda too late," she said, dropping back in her chair. "You dropped that fan, I got spooked, and... Why did you do that, anyway? Why not just call me or...or have your accountant call me?"

"It was clumsy," he said softly with a sigh that sounded genuine.

"It was creepy," Dane shot back.

Spencer closed his eyes. "I realized that after the fact," he said. "I came to your apartment, no one was home, and I didn't want to leave a note, but I wanted you to know I was here. I guess I wanted to prepare you, and..." He shook his head. "Clumsy," he repeated.

Except he had to buy the fan before he got there, Dane thought. So it was far more deliberate than he was letting on.

Asia shifted in her seat like she was thinking the same thing. "And then you followed us? And approached Dane's mother in the street?"

"Is that who that was?" he asked. "I'm sorry if I intruded on family time. I simply wanted to get the message to you, and I knew if I tried in person, it would not go well. I needed an intermediary. Honestly, that was my only intention." He waited a beat, then asked, "Would you like to look at the paperwork?"

"Can you just leave it for me?" Asia asked. "I'd like to take anything and everything to an attorney."

"Of course." He flipped open the messenger bag and pulled out a thin manila envelope that he placed in front of her. "But I need signatures quickly, as I have to get back."

"To your wife," she said, the words slipping out like she had no control over them.

Once again, he closed his eyes. "Asia, please."

She straightened as if a lightning bolt of fury shot up

her spine. Before it reached her brain and spilled out more nasty words, Dane put his hand on her back, adding what he hoped was the right amount of pressure to quell the anger.

"Let's take a look at it, Aje," he said gently. "We'll get Claire's help, and you can make a decision."

She nodded, looking up at Spencer. "Fine."

He slid into a charming smile. "Good girl," he whispered.

This time, Dane sat straighter. "She's not a little girl who needs your approval," he said under his breath.

He tipped is head in acknowledgement, chastised and wise enough not to argue.

"You have my number, Asia," Spencer said. "I can be here a few more days, max, if you need to talk or if you have questions. I don't know what they'd be, however. It's a million dollars, free and clear, for your child's future. And there's nothing for you to do but sign the contract and termination of my parental rights, and I'll transfer the money into your name. All ties to me are severed and my responsibilities are met. It couldn't be easier or more in your favor, to be perfectly honest."

"Okay," she said softly and barely had the word out before he stood, holding out both hands to stop them from getting up, too.

"Let's make this happen, Asia," he said with a quick smile, then he nodded to Dane. "Pleasure to meet you, Dane."

With that, he scooped up the bag and hooked it on his shoulder, heading out with the same confidence he had when he arrived, leaving them both silent and staring at the envelope between them.

LATER, as they sat in the cottage at Shellseeker Beach and reviewed the paperwork, they talked for a long time about Spencer Keaton's motivation for giving her a million dollars "free and clear."

Dane had to agree with Asia that it seemed a little too good to be true, but the guy—*if* he was being honest—hadn't presented one downside to accepting the offer. Except, of course, his history of breaking Asia's trust, and Dane couldn't discount that as he tried to help her decide what to do.

"My gut says run and run fast," she whispered after they'd sat quietly thinking it all through. "He cannot be believed."

"I get that," Dane said calmly. "And you don't have to take the money if you feel like there could be strings that might strangle you. Tell him you want no ties to him and turn it down, but please consider that termination of parental rights. That's the real prize in his package."

She nodded, agony still on her face. "But a million dollars could change Zee's life, Dane. Kids are expensive, and this money will grow and easily pay for everything he needs, including college. Is it ridiculous to turn that down?"

"Not if you're terrified of the strings attached. But if he truly isn't asking for anything except the one thing you want—for him to relinquish any parental rights? Then it is worth considering."

She nodded. "Maybe he just feels like crap for what he did and this is his way of having a snowball's chance of not going to hell."

"Oh, he's going to hell," Dane said with a snort. "But maybe his wife put him up to this. He does have an aristocratic reputation to maintain now. To be fair, he didn't say anything to make you feel bad about your decision not to tell him he was a father. He didn't berate you for keeping him out of the loop. On the contrary, I think he was relieved."

She made a face. "He did say 'good girl,' but..." She rested her head on his shoulder. "My hero called him out on that."

He chuckled, not at all used to being thought of as heroic.

"Did you know that Nancy helped me realize that phrase is a trigger for me and my control issues?" she asked.

He reached for her hand. "I didn't know, but it irritated me. You're not a girl, and certainly not his."

"Thank you." Threading her fingers through his, she stayed quiet for a long time, deep in thought. Then she asked, "Is it possible for a man to really hand over a million dollars without a catch?"

"I guess it truly depends on his motivation," Dane said. "The paperwork is clear that you would never have contact with each other after it's signed, so you can't come after him for more—not that you would. And he is then free to put this chapter of his life behind him."

She flinched at the words. "Was that all I was to him? A chapter? And Zee? No interest at all? He didn't even want to see a picture. Never asked me how he was or what kind of pregnancy I had or..." She swallowed. "I'm sorry, Dane. It's not like I wanted to have a conversation with him, but it still hurts."

"I know it does," he said, giving her hand a sympathetic squeeze. "And, frankly, his apology was robotic, if you ask me."

"Saying a lot from a man who programmed robots," she replied with a smile. "But you know, I didn't expect him to grovel, because that's not his style. I guess I just want to know why he's really doing this. I simply don't believe it's as innocent as...closing my chapter, as much as that idea hurts."

"I didn't mean to reduce that time in your life to a chapter, or the pain he caused you," he said. "I know what betrayal feels like. Remember my ex, the corporate spy?"

"You didn't—"

"But my perception of the man isn't clouded by a deep personal wound," he continued. "He knows he caused that wound and, yes, he does have a different life that he probably wants to live without looking over his shoulder. Who knows what the deal is with his wife? Maybe she did put him up to it. Maybe her rich father is the one pulling the strings."

Her eyes widened. "Do you think?"

"Who knows? Well, Miles might," he added quickly. "Before you sign anything, we really should find out more about this family Spencer married into."

"Good idea," she agreed. "Because if I discover she was behind this, and she is pressuring him into terminating parental rights and buying me off with a million? Then I'd feel better."

"Really?" He drew back, not expecting that. "I'd think you'd hate a stranger dictating your future like that."

"No, I don't see it that way. I'm scared of him pulling strings and manipulating me. If he's the one under control—either his wife's or her father's—then I feel less threatened. Does that make sense?"

He tipped his head, trying to put himself in her mindset. "Kind of. But let's get Miles to find out more about this baron and his daughter. He concentrated on Spencer and didn't look too deeply into the family."

"Good, that's a plan."

"And we can have Claire review that..." He gestured toward the documents. "Although the termination agreement looks pretty straightforward. Then you'll make your decision, and I will support you with everything I have."

"Thank you." She looked up at him and kissed him lightly, then laughed. "And you'll never call me your 'good girl.'"

"Never," he promised. "You are a queen, Asia Turner —strong, brilliant, and beautiful."

"Oh." She let out the single syllable as a whimper,

sliding her arms around his neck to pull him closer. "How did I get so lucky?"

"Well, I don't know if you're lucky. I certainly don't have that guy's, uh, jawline."

She laughed into his shoulder. "He doesn't have your IQ, good heart, and incredibly kind personality."

"Take that, alpha dog," he joked, giving her another kiss. "Let's go get Zee now. I miss that little bugger. Can we tell Roz everything?"

"Yeah, we should."

"Only if you're ready, Aje. All of this, every single move, is your call."

"And that, Dane Whitney," she said, putting her hand over his heart, "is why I like this man so much more than any I've ever met."

And that felt like she'd handed *him* a million bucks.

Chapter Twelve

Claire

Claire had hoped that she'd have some quiet morning time with DJ to talk and maybe plan a family outing as Noah had suggested, but DJ was sound asleep. She assumed Sophia was asleep in her room, too, although she hadn't heard either of them come in last night.

Whenever DJ had gotten home, it had been so late, he'd crashed on the pull-out sofa in the den. That was considerate, if disappointing, but did allow Claire the ability to sleep, and then to work at her desk in the bedroom while she waited for him to get up.

During that time, she easily finished—and aced—the civil law practice test. She also rescheduled taxation, studied procedure for an hour, and resented the fact that she could have gone to Shellseeker Beach to walk with Eliza after all.

She tamped that regret down by diving into torts, her least favorite section on the test that loomed ahead of her.

But the words swam on the page and after five minutes, she pushed up, went into the kitchen for tea, and did a double take at the sight of DJ and Sophia, side by side on some chaises by the pool, drinking coffee and talking.

They were up? DJ had gotten up and hadn't come into their room?

Disappointment kicked her in the gut as she stared at the father and daughter, their heads turned to each other, one making the other laugh.

Why wouldn't he say good morning to her? Explain why he was out so late, and smooth things over from their last conversation?

Swallowing her sadness and the raw sense of rejection, she planted a smile on her face and headed toward the sliding glass doors, pushing them open.

"Look who's out here in the sunshine!" she called, hoping they didn't hear how false the brightness was in her voice.

"Hey, Claire." DJ lifted his coffee cup. "How goes the bar exam wars?"

"Well, I'm not dead yet, so the torts didn't kill me."

She waited a beat for Sophia's greeting, but she just sipped her coffee while Claire walked the perimeter of the pool to join them. She dragged a chair from the table a little closer, the feet scraping the pavers noisily, filling the awkward silence.

"Morning, Sophia," Claire said as she sat. "You were out late."

"She was with me," DJ interjected.

"Oh?" Claire drew back, as surprised by his vehemence as the statement itself. "I thought you were at Luigi's."

"I was, we were." He threw a sly smile to Sophia. "Ended up being a fun party, don't you think, Soph?"

A party?

"It was cool, Dad." She leaned forward and put her cup on the ground, then dropped back to lift her face to the sun. "You never hung with my peeps in California before, so it was great."

"You...hung with her peeps?" Claire asked, giving a soft laugh to the terminology to cover the hurt that hit her. "At Luigi's?"

"You don't have to sound so surprised," DJ said, defensiveness in his tone. "Sophia and her gang came in late for pizza and we were just about closed. So I made them all a few pies and we ended up chilling for a few hours."

Chilling. "Well, that's nice." Claire swallowed, trying to imagine DJ and those kids. She actually could, since he could fit in with anyone. But it hurt that she hadn't been included. "You should have called. Noah and I would have joined you."

Sophia flashed a look that said the very idea was preposterous, but she covered quickly by reaching for her coffee.

"It was really late," DJ said. "The whole restaurant staff was gone."

"Even Luigi?" she asked, wondering how DJ had wormed his way into the business so effectively that he could stay open after-hours, make pizza for private parties, and, she assumed, lock up.

"He was gone by seven," DJ said. "I ran the place last night."

He did what? Claire angled her head, the lawyer in her already lining up a bunch of questions to get him to the point of complete honesty. But before she started a cross-examination, she stopped herself and remembered that DJ wasn't a witness. He was her...partner. Or something like that.

She tried a completely different tack, tucking her feet under her as if she were settling in for a sweet family chat, not a deposition.

"That sounds fun," she said. "So I guess when you buy the business, the transition with the staff will be seamless."

He stared at her for a second, then glanced at Sophia, who looked down again, as if she knew something and didn't want to let it out.

Then Sophia popped up to a stand. "I need a shower, like, desperately. Then I'm meeting Levi at the beach."

"Levi?" Claire looked up. "Who's that? Was he here yesterday?"

"He's a guy I'm talking to and, yeah, he was here, but you spazzed out or I'd have introduced you."

"Nice boy," DJ added. "I liked chatting with him last night."

"Chatting." Sophia snorted. "You're such a dweeb, Dad."

"Why?" Claire asked. "Is chatting...cheugy?"

Sophia almost choked. "Something like that." She shot inside, leaving them alone and quiet for a beat.

"So," Claire finally said to break the uncomfortable silence. "Sounds like that was fun."

"Fun and necessary," he said, a weird sternness in his voice. "After what happened here and how things went down between you two, I thought I—"

"How things *went down*?" Her voice rose but this time, she didn't adjust to sound bright and warm or less than shattered, which she kind of was. "She was wretched to me—rude and disrespectful."

"She's a—"

"Teenager, I know. But I still expect you to support me on this, not celebrate with a private party for her friends after-hours at the pizza restaurant you don't own yet but act like you do."

He stared at her for a moment, then closed his eyes. "No...yet," he finally said.

The words made no sense. "Excuse me?"

"You said, 'The pizza restaurant you don't own *yet*,'" he explained. "I'm never going to own it. So, no 'yet' in that sentence."

And that made even less sense. "You're...not?"

"Nope."

"Did Luigi change his mind about selling?"

"No, and Luigi doesn't know yet. I only made the final decision last night."

Without consulting her. She shoved away another bucketload of disappointment and waited for more. But he didn't elaborate.

"So, what changed your mind?" she finally asked.

"I never made up my mind, Claire. I was merely

toying with the idea and waiting for the answer to be clear in my head, which it was last night."

"At an impromptu party with Sophia and her... peeps." She tried to keep the sarcasm out of her tone, but might have failed.

Either way, he just shrugged. "Answers come when they come," he said, in the most DJ way possible.

"Can you tell me...more?"

"Not much to tell. I realized when I closed up that I hadn't done a new inventory, and the staff schedule changed because Carlos quit, and I forgot to take the cash to the bank. Oh, by the way, that money's in the den, so I need to go now to the bank. Want to come?"

"DJ." She leaned forward, baffled and worried. "I know you've been on the fence about the price and the commitment, but what was it about those responsibilities that gave you the answer?"

"The fact that they were just that—*responsibilities*." He said the word as if it were repugnant to him. "Claire, I do not want to own another business. I do not want the mountain of...of crap that comes with it, nor do I want to be dragged away from what I want to be doing so I can do...scheduling. God, please, no."

She'd had this same conversation with Noah in the past. He'd often said the obligations and tasks of owning a business somehow didn't suit DJ's freestyle, moment-by-moment personality. He had a point, but Claire thought that was just Noah bracing for disappointment if the restaurant purchase fell through.

Then her heart dropped when she realized how this

news would affect Noah, who'd talked a lot about
working side-by-side with his father when DJ bought
Luigi's restaurant.

"But I thought pizza is your passion," she said,
already knowing that argument wouldn't work.

"It is and will always be," he agreed. "But I don't
want the stress or agony of owning a restaurant. I don't
want that anchor around my neck. I love freedom too
much. The chance to, you know, travel and meet people."

Now he wanted to travel? The words hit hard, but
she managed not to react as they played again in her
head. Was *she* an anchor around his neck? Was Noah?

"The whole idea was more than I wanted to take on,"
he said, shifting on the chaise like the admission made
him uncomfortable. "It sounded good on paper, you
know? A pizza joint on Sanibel Island. Good money—not
that I care about that—but a chance to make my pies and
share them with people who come to this island from all
over the world. All the best guys in the business have
their own restaurants, and I thought it made sense."

Right now? Nothing really made sense. "That's what
you said, and why you wanted to buy Luigi's. For something permanent here...with me and with...our family."

He nodded, then shrugged. "I despise that word."

"Me? Or family?" she shot back, her heart cracking.

"Claire! You know I meant the word 'permanent.' Do
you not remember my history? My darkest days? My sole
motivation?"

Yes, she knew it all. She knew that his big job as an
architect had so consumed him that his wife left him, and

he felt abandoned. And he'd had a huge change of heart, sold his successful business, moved to a seaside town in California, and become a shockingly skilled *pizzaiole*. In the process, he embraced a "live in the now" philosophy. Was that history his...motivation?

She was completely confused.

"DJ, what exactly are you saying?" she asked.

He sighed again and looked at her. "Just that I don't do permanent, Claire. I don't like the idea of being tied down."

"And where does that leave me?" she asked on a shaky whisper.

He reached his hand toward her. "Right next to me, I hope."

"But that could change at any second," she added, taking his hand.

"Life could change at any moment," he said with a sad smile. "Remember, I'm the man who was one millimeter away from being hit by a bolt of lightning. Life is too precious to waste doing schedules." He let go of her hand and stood up. "Now, would you like to come with me to the bank? I'm going to deposit yesterday's cash and that will be the last thing I'll do in an official capacity for Luigi."

She searched his face. "What about Noah?"

"What about him?"

"He was...counting on working with you at the restaurant."

He flicked his hand as if that meant nothing. "That kid is all over the place. Working at the beach rental, the tea hut, and writing a novel. The last thing he needs is a restaurant job. He'll be cool. I'll talk to him."

Cool? He'd be devastated. Should she talk to him first and break the news?

"So, you want to come with? If not, I'll just drop Sophia off on her date and hit the bank alone."

"And then what will you do?"

"Whatever the heck I want," he said with a grin. "That's the life I lead and I sure have no plans to quit it. You can always ditch the books and come with me. Who knows where the Gulf breezes could take us, Claire."

She swallowed and managed a smile. "I have to study and work on the bar exam. But...can you leave tomorrow open? Or a day later this week? All day?"

"For what?"

She opened her mouth to tell him she was trying to figure out a fun family outing, but something stopped her. Probably the fact that DJ was allergic to plans and things would go much better if their outing, whatever it was, happened "spontaneously."

"It's a surprise," she said with a playful tip of her head.

"Oh, I like those."

"I know you do, so expect one. And tell Sophia, because I'd like her there, too."

He beamed down at her. "Sounds good, Claire." He leaned over and planted a kiss on her forehead, then headed into the house.

For a long time, she sat and stared at the pool, watching the glittering sun on the turquoise water while she heard the sounds of DJ and Sophia leaving the house with a quick "G'bye!" called from inside.

Then she got up and headed to Shellseeker Beach, because she really needed her sister. And maybe she'd see her son and she could break the news about the restaurant.

"Oh, DJ," she whispered to herself. "There's a fine line between living in the moment and being a selfish ass."

She had a feeling he might be crossing it, but she wasn't ready to give up yet.

Not an hour later, Claire was right where she wanted to be, with the people she wanted around her. Tucked under a sun umbrella at a table in the Shellseeker Cottages garden, she sipped a cold hibiscus tea with Eliza on one side and Teddy on the other.

"You're upset," Teddy noted as she settled across from Claire.

"And you didn't even touch me to catch my aura. My goodness, Teddy, you're good."

"Doesn't take an empath to see the pain in your eyes, Claire," Eliza said. "Does this have anything to do with you not showing for this morning's walk with me?"

"*Everything* to do with it," Claire admitted on a sigh. "Shall I dump?"

"We'd be devastated if you didn't," Teddy said with a laugh.

It didn't take much prodding for Claire to fill them in. With Eliza and Teddy riveted and concerned, it was so easy to share, and know that whether or not they had advice for her, she already felt better. That was the magic of this sisterhood, and she treasured it more than she knew how to express.

"I've more or less upended my whole life for this little family," Claire concluded. "And now I'm wondering if that was the right thing to do."

"It was the right thing for Noah," Teddy said.

"Absolutely," she agreed without hesitation. "I promised him months ago I would be where he was, as long as he wanted me. We lost twenty-six years after I gave him up for adoption, so I have no regrets where he's concerned. But...DJ."

"DJ didn't make any promises when you decided to quit your job at the law firm in New York and move here permanently," Eliza reminded her.

"No, no." Claire shook her head. "He's never done that, and he's always been unapologetically who he is—a man who lives for the here and now, and is not ready, willing or able to make a commitment."

"Did you upend your life for Noah or DJ?" Teddy asked her.

"I upended it for...Claire." She smiled at them. "I'm happier on Sanibel Island than I've ever been anywhere in my life."

"Then this problem is more about your relationship with DJ than how and where you're living," Teddy suggested. "It sounds like that romance is not on solid ground right now."

"Shaky as can be."

"Did this start with Sophia's arrival, though, Claire?" Eliza asked. "Even before she showed up, I remember a lot of morning walks when you shared your concerns about DJ's personal philosophy being a little hard to embrace yourself."

Claire conceded that with a tip of her head. "That's true, and I've always known he wasn't going to run out and buy a ring." She gave a sad look. "I guess I thought if he bought Luigi's..."

They didn't say anything, but they didn't have to.

She sighed. "I know, but I so liked the idea of being a family, and of Noah having his biological parents together. Maybe I'm more in love with the idea of family than with that particular man." Just saying it out loud made her heart sink. "It's going to gut Noah if we break up."

"You don't have to break up," Eliza said quickly. "But you do have to set your expectations properly. And keep talking to him, making him address the issue."

She stirred the cold tea with the paper straw, thinking about this morning's conversation.

"DJ isn't very good at talking. He dodges and makes sweeping statements, but he doesn't really enjoy deep and hard introspection. Truth is, we could talk for hours and I might still not know quite where I stand with him." She leaned into Eliza with a sad smile. "You should count your blessings with a man like Miles who knows what he wants and what he wants is you. I swear he's going to propose any minute."

Eliza's eyes widened. "I hope that's not tonight. We're going out on his boat later. I don't know what I'll say, because I'm just not sure."

"Neither of you are sure," Teddy observed, looking from one to the other. "You"—she put her hand on Eliza's arm—"have a man who wants to commit everything to you, and you're not sure you want it. And you"—she turned to Claire—"want to commit everything to a man who isn't sure he wants it."

"Pretty much sums it up," Claire said glumly.

"You can't force-fit love or family just because you want it to work," Teddy said. "Wanting it isn't the same as...feeling it. Wanting it to work isn't enough."

"But you so deserve love and a family, Claire," Eliza whispered with vehemence in her voice. "No one deserves it more. I just don't want you to settle for a man who isn't willing to give you his heart and soul."

Claire let out a soft grunt. "I don't want to, either."

Teddy patted both of their hands. "Listen to me, girls. Love is both a feeling and a decision. Sometimes it's an action you take, sometimes it's an emotion you experience. Both of you are walking that fine line right now. And neither of you should compromise on what you want and deserve."

"I won't," Claire promised. "I'm not ready to give up yet, but I will when the time is right. Noah thinks we just need more fun family time, something that's not making pizza or being at the beach."

"Oh, I was going to suggest a day at Ding Darling for you all," Eliza said. "It might be fun."

Claire nodded, thinking about the gorgeous wildlife refuge that took up so much of Sanibel. "We've been wanting to go, so, yes. I'll make a day of it for them. The weather's perfect and I think DJ would love that."

"Bring Katie and Harper, too," Teddy suggested. "They'll likely be family, too, soon. And Harper loves the place. She's been a few times and would be a good tour guide."

"A multigenerational trip to the refuge isn't going to fix everything," Claire said. "But I think we all need to feel like a family again, and take it from there. Thank you both so much for the advice, no matter how much I don't love it."

"Yo, ladies!" They all turned as Noah jogged toward them. "All good at the tea hut? I have a break at the beach cabana and thought I'd check."

He stood over the table, his dark hair damp, his broad chest rising and falling with the breath he needed from making the run up from the beach, his warm gaze on Claire.

"You okay, Mom?" he added.

For a moment, she just looked up at him, her whole being filled with an indescribable love. He so *got* her. How was that possible?

"I am now," she assured him, reaching for his hand, hating that she had news that would make him sad. But she refused to erase that smile by delivering it now. "What would you say to a big family outing at Ding

Darling one of these days? Including Katie and Harper, of course."

"I love that idea," he said, leaning over to plant a kiss on her head. "That'll be just what the doctor ordered."

She wasn't sure about that. She wasn't sure about DJ or, really, anything. But she was sure about one thing: she loved Noah Hutchins. Sometimes, he was all the family she needed.

Chapter Thirteen

Eliza

L*ove is both a feeling and a decision.*

Teddy's words echoed in Eliza's head for the rest of the day. She was still thinking about the idea that evening when Miles texted her and told her he was back from his client dinner and asked if she still wanted to take a moonlight boat ride.

She always wanted to see him, always felt lighter on the way over, and always melted into his embrace the minute they were together. Was that love? Was that a feeling or a decision? She went round and round long enough that she was half dizzy thinking about it by the time Tinkerbell bounded toward her car to greet her.

Miles's text said he'd be on the dock getting the boat ready, so she let the sweet pupper lead her there. Vineyard lights twinkled on the dock and *Miles Away*, his beloved fishing cruiser, bobbed in the water, lighting up the canal behind it.

"Ahoy, Captain," she called as she and Tink walked down the wooden dock.

Miles turned from the helm, his smile as bright as the lights around him. "There's my redheaded beauty," he said, his voice husky with admiration.

"Permission to come aboard with dog, sir?" she teased as she reached the end of the dock.

He was at her side with a hand extended in a few short strides. "Permission granted. Treats for all." He gave her a quick kiss, then guided her toward the table he'd set up near the leather banquette, where a bottle of cabernet was uncorked, with two full glasses waiting.

"One for you..." He picked up the glass and handed it to her, then reached into his pocket for a cookie. "And one for Tinkerbell, the second prettiest girl on the boat."

Tink wagged her tail in gratitude, then trotted toward the helm to enjoy her snack, while Miles took the other glass and lifted it.

"I guess we drink to the million-dollar offer," he said.

She gave a dry laugh. "That was a shocker, huh? What do you think?"

He lifted a shoulder. "Sometimes when something is too good to be true..."

"Really? You don't think she should accept what sounds like an extremely generous offer, and no pesky custody battle?" Eliza asked, thinking of the conversation she'd had with Dane that afternoon. "Dane thinks it could be legitimate and quite beneficial for her."

Miles nodded. "They swung by here today and we talked at length. I'm going to root around a bit more, maybe find out what the Simmons family is all about. I do agree with Dane that if this completely severs Asia's ties with him forever, then it could be a very good thing."

"He told me that, too," Eliza said. "I didn't talk to Asia, she stayed for a while with Roz, but I did chat with

Dane, and he only wants what's best for her, and for Zee."

"I agree, he's being analytical, which is good because Asia is driven by emotion on this."

Eliza nodded, knowing that was true. "Well, Dane doesn't do gut feelings too well. He's logical, first and foremost. Although, when it comes to Asia?" She gave a knowing smile. "Sometimes he can be a little...illogical."

Miles laughed as he gestured to the bench for her to sit. "A good woman will do that to you. Trust me, I know." He gave her a playful glare. "Like the one I'm looking at. Can we drink to that, too?"

"Absolutely." She smiled at that and touched his glass with hers. As she leaned back onto the leather banquette, though, her mind was still on the situation Asia and Dane faced. "Have you found anything at all that would make you think this offer isn't legitimate?"

"Not really. But without going to London to talk to people and maybe get a sense of what's going on in this guy's life, I might not find too much. I do have a contact there, former Scotland Yard who is in the investigation business, but he's pricey. If Asia really wants me to pursue that, he could dig around. In the meantime, I'm continuing with online stuff, but didn't make any progress today. I had another client project all day, but I'll make it a priority in the next few days."

Miles pushed up and tipped his head toward the helm. "Want to cruise around the Gulf or hang out at the dock? Your choice, my dear."

She nestled into the seat, grabbing a throw blanket

nearby. "I think I want to cruise for a bit. It's a gorgeous night."

"Then we will cruise."

A few minutes later, they were rumbling through the no-wake section of the canal, past a few more houses and boats. They waved to some neighbors sitting on their dock, and slid through the narrow strait that opened into the bay.

Even in the moonlight, Eliza knew the familiar route that took them to the channel that led to open water. She knew the landmarks in the canals, like the marina and the festive blue roof of Grandma Dot's Restaurant, lit and noisy with the last of the dinner crowd.

She recognized some of the homes and familiar land-scapes, a row of palm trees here, a cluster of mangroves there.

And when they turned right into the bay, she knew the route he'd take around the easternmost edge of Sani-bel, at Point Ybel, where the distinct brown lighthouse stood with a soft yellow gleam as a beacon to welcome or warn boaters.

The familiarity of it all warmed her like the wine, and surprised her when it brought some tears to her eyes.

"It's become home to me," she murmured, just loud enough for Miles to shift his gaze from the water to her.

"I'm sorry, that got caught in the wind. What did you say?"

She stood and joined him, wrapping an arm around his waist. "Sanibel Island is my home."

He inched back and looked at her, a smile threatening. "Is this a big revelation?"

"I guess so," she said on a laugh. "I lived my life in New York, then Los Angeles, and never even considered Florida. But here I am, not even a year since I got off that ferry in Fort Myers, reluctantly responding to a message from some stranger named Teddy Blessing. It's home now."

"And a great one," he said, putting his arm on her shoulders to draw her even closer. "How can I ever thank Teddy?"

She smiled up at him, but still shook her head. "It just hit me so hard, you know? Right now. Like—bang!—I knew it. I'm home, this is where I belong, these are my people, this is my water, that stubby little lighthouse is all mine."

"Hey now, don't disparage the ultimate Sanibel Island landmark."

"I can't disparage any of it," she said with wonder in her voice. "I love this place." She looked up at him, knowing the next thing she should say. The next natural sentence: "And I love you, Miles."

But something stopped her. She had such clarity about her home...but not her heart.

"Do you think," she said instead, "that I just truly am in love with Sanibel, or is it a perfect place to call home and I've made a decision to love it?"

He gave her a look, easing away to put both hands on the helm and guide the boat.

"Does it matter?" he finally asked. "I mean, you love the place, and now you call this island home. Why question that?"

"I don't know, I'm just...thinking. I mean, moving myself here and making a life on the opposite coast with a bunch of strangers, that was a big deal. Major. Never thought I'd do that, but..."

"A bunch of strangers?" he scoffed. "Ouch."

"Well, you were a stranger at one point, but obviously, that changed."

He nodded. "I get that. And I don't know the answer to your question, but I sure am glad that whatever got you here has kept you here and we—the official *bunch of strangers*—are so insanely happy that you are."

He leaned down and planted a kiss on her lips, both of them laughing as they kissed.

"How about we anchor between the bay and Gulf, right in line with that lighthouse you mocked so mercilessly?"

"I didn't mock it! I love it. Just like I love...Sanibel Island."

She could have sworn a flash of disappointment in his eyes, but she looked away and studied the dark water ahead of them.

"So, how's Janie doing?" she asked, feeling like the sudden change of subject was a little bit awkward, but Miles was far too classy to call her on it.

"She's okay. Puking her guts up way more than Olivia does. Pregnancy is hard, she tells me."

"It can be," she agreed.

"But she tried for a long time, so I know they're happy. She's bugging me to come up and see her."

"You should go," Eliza said. "Seeing your pregnant daughter is a joy no parent should miss."

He idled the engine and brought the boat to a stop, quiet as he went for the anchor that he stored in the stern.

"You don't want to go?" she asked when he didn't answer.

"I do, I just..." He threaded the thick line and lifted the heavy metal hook at the end, his finger lightly grazing the sharp and pointed edges. "Sometimes things you say hit me as hard as this thing," he joked, tossing it into the water with a splash.

"What does that mean?"

"It means...sometimes you confound me, E."

"By saying you should go see your daughter? I didn't mean forever, just a visit."

He didn't answer, just guided the line slowly into the water until it was taut and holding the big boat steady. "Forget it."

That she confounded him? "I'm not about to."

He turned to her, his head tilted, an unreadable expression on his face.

"What?" she asked with a soft laugh when his silence lasted too long. "What did I say that confounded you?"

But something told her it was more about what she didn't say that bothered him. She knew Miles well enough to realize that he was giving her the chance to say...*it*...first. But he was dying to.

"What was all that about a decision or a feeling or...

whatever?" he asked. "Why do I get this weird feeling that was not just about Sanibel Island?"

Because he was sensitive and wise and could read her like he read his ocean charts and all those computer terminals in his office.

Should she hide all these thoughts from him? If they were together, then they were *together*. Thick and thin, real and honest.

"It was just something Teddy said to me today," she responded, patting the bench next to her in invitation. "Do you want me to tell you? It has to do with us."

"Us?" He joined her and picked up the wine glass. "Should I be worried?"

"Why do you worry, Miles?"

He slid her a look. "Because I'm crazy about you. I think about you morning, noon, and night. I never expected this...this..." He gestured from him to her and back again. "This to come into my life as I was staring down the barrel of sixty. And now that it has, I'm scared to death to lose it. That's why I worry." He lifted his glass to hers. "Cheers to that, huh?"

"You don't sound very cheerful," she said, but tapped his glass anyway.

"Not knowing where you stand with a woman isn't cheery."

"You know where you stand, Miles," she insisted, then playfully elbowed him. "I turned Jimmy Thanos down cold."

He gave a wry smile. "Which is the only reason why

your ex, who also happens to live on Sanibel Island, is still breathing."

"Tough talker," she teased. "He's also Dane's boss, so..."

That smile wavered. "Is that why you didn't go out with him?"

"Miles!" She choked his name. "I didn't go out with him because *we're* together. You and me. A couple."

He regarded her for a long moment, his green eyes pensive and wise, but he didn't say anything.

"Aren't we?" she asked on a whisper when the silence between them lasted too long.

"Yes, we are, but you know I'm not going to be satisfied with that status quo forever."

She looked down at her wine glass. "I know."

After a beat, he touched her chin and tipped her face up to look at him. "And I know that if I make declarations and ask you for more—for permanence and a possible change of name and address—I'd get turned down."

"Miles, I told you. I simply do not see myself marrying anyone. I had—"

"A blissful, perfect, ideal marriage, I know." He looked into her eyes. "I'm not trying to compete with Ben, Eliza."

"Our marriage wasn't always blissful, perfect, or ideal," she said. "But it was..." How could she put her feelings into one word? What would it be?

"Your only walk down the aisle," he supplied.

Well, yes. At least he understood that. She sighed in

response and took a sip of wine she didn't want, but really didn't have the right words for him. If she told him Ben was "The One—the *only* one" for her, he would be devastated.

"But you will love again, right?" he pressed.

"I think I will," she answered immediately.

He searched her face, inching a millimeter closer. "Will? Or do?"

Her eyes shuttered.

"Never mind." He stood quickly. "I have no right to push you into anything—whether you decide you want it or really feel it." He tugged at the anchor, pulling at the line. "And it's late."

"Miles." She stood and walked over to him, easing the rope out of his hands and letting the anchor slide back into the water. Looking up at him, she put both hands on his cheeks and forced him to look into her eyes. "I'm waiting for that same moment of clarity I had when we motored out here and I saw Sanibel as home."

"You're waiting to look at this unattractive old lighthouse with gray hair and a sore back and see him as something you can love?" he said with a joke in his voice, but she knew he wasn't kidding.

"First of all, unattractive? Stop. Gray and old? You're a silver fox, barely a few years my senior. But most important, I *do* see you as a man I could love. I have known that from the beginning."

He put his hands over hers, pressing her palms into his cheeks. "Well, here's a news flash, E. I love you."

She swallowed and let the words hit her heart as he continued.

"I love everything about you, but the fact is, being 'a couple' just isn't going to be enough for me in the long haul. I thought I could wait indefinitely for you, but the more I'm with you, the more I want...everything. Every day, every night, every bit of you. I'll wait, but not forever."

For a long moment, she held his face, the rocking of the boat under her nearly making her as dizzy as the intensity in his green gaze and the honest ache in his voice. But at that moment, the only sound was the soft lap of waves against the hull, a distant bell, and the splash of a fish somewhere out there in the Gulf of Mexico.

Taking a breath, she closed her eyes and waited for the same sensation of certainty she'd had earlier. The indescribable but extremely real knowledge that she was where she belonged.

Please, please, she begged her heart. *Tell him, tell him. Say the words: I love you, too, Miles. There is a forever future for us. I could change my name and address and...*

No. Her body and soul simply would not cooperate.

When she opened her eyes, she could see by the look in his that she'd waited too long. He let go of her hands and gave a tight smile.

"Let's get the anchor up, E. It's chilly and we should be getting in. I have a ton of work to do tomorrow."

She just nodded and turned toward the table, ready to put the drinks away and stow the cooler for the ride back in.

It was what she always did out here on his boat; it had become their routine.

But tonight, she had the terrible feeling something had changed.

Chapter Fourteen

Asia

Dane had to work the next afternoon, so Asia went to Claire's house with baby Zee in a carrier on one arm and a long legal document under the other. The ranch house looked quiet and deserted, which surprised her, because she expected DJ to be here, and maybe Sophia.

But Claire seemed to be alone when she answered the door and invited Asia in, making a fuss over Zee, who'd just woken up from a nap.

"Hello, handsome," Claire cooed into his bundle of blankets as they walked in. "You are getting bigger every day."

"On solid foods now," Asia said proudly. "Although they are cooked and mashed to a pulp, but..." She tapped her breasts with the envelope she held. "I get a bit of a break."

Claire smiled and gestured for them to come in through the entry, then around the corner that opened up to a family gathering area and kitchen. "We'll be more comfortable at the table. Can I get you something to drink?"

"I'm good, Claire, thank you." The moment she set

the carrier on the table, though, Zee started to fuss. "But my boy might need a little something soon. He always wakes up starved."

"Would you like some privacy to nurse or..."

"I have a backup bottle in my bag which, of course, is in the car. Keep an eye on him for a second?"

"That would be my pleasure!" Claire came closer to the carrier. "Can I hold you, fussy man?"

"He might not like it, but feel free to try." Asia sailed out back to the car, grabbing her bag, which she had wisely packed with a spare bottle of pumped milk in a cooler section.

When she came back in, she half expected to hear the baby wailing in hunger, but all she heard was Claire speaking in a high-pitched, soft voice, tender and sweet.

She stepped around the corner slowly, catching sight of the other woman easily holding Zee against her chest, rubbing his back and humming in his ear. She swayed and bounced with the moves of a professional, doing everything right to calm the baby.

"Wow, you are good," Asia joked.

"Not bad for a rookie, huh?" She turned so Asia could see Zee's eyes looked heavy, whispering, "He might go back to sleep."

"Not when you put him down."

"Then I won't. Right, baby Zee?" she asked softly. "I'll just hold you and hold you forever."

Zee shuddered with a sleepy sigh, dropping his head against her shoulder.

"Oh." Claire let out a whimper. "Someone get me a grandbaby, stat."

Asia laughed at that. "Noah and Katie?" she asked on a tease.

"God, I hope so." Still holding the baby, Claire came to the table and sat down slowly, one hand splayed on his tiny back. "I probably have to put him down to do legal work, but I don't want to."

"Hold him for a moment, Claire. Let me open all this up and spread it out and then you can get all lawyerly. Right now, you just practice being a grandmother."

Claire smiled, dropping a kiss on Zee's curls. "He even smells divine."

"You can babysit anytime."

"Right, like anyone can get near this child when Roz is in the same zip code."

"True," Asia agreed, sliding the documents across the table. "And please let me say again how much I appreciate you doing this for me."

"You're more than welcome. But remember, I'm a corporate attorney, not a specialist in family law. But I can certainly spot red flags in a contract, which it sounds like you want me to do."

Asia sighed and skimmed the legal-sized papers she'd spread out. "I guess my biggest fear is that the red flags are all over the man who gave me these, but not on the papers themselves."

Claire eyed her, lifting a brow. "Don't discount the power of your instinct, Asia."

"I'm not, which is why I'm so hesitant about this,

even though the offer is a wonderful opportunity for Zee, and completely deserved."

"It's certainly the right thing for the biological father to do," Claire said.

"But when that much money is involved, and an agreement to relinquish all ties to his own child? I'm a little nervous and skeptical."

"Which is very smart." Claire's gaze shifted to the documents, then she frowned and looked up, holding Zee out. "I guess I can't multitask as much as I'd like to."

"I'll put him down, Claire. He's sound asleep. You have a magical touch."

As Asia got the baby settled in the carrier, Claire started reading silently, grabbing a pen to make a few notes on a legal pad she had on the table.

"One lump sum in an investment account, but..." She looked up, a frown pulling. "Why an offshore account? It specifies a Cayman Islands bank, which can be a red flag in and of itself."

"He said that protected me from high taxes."

"It does, to some extent, though when you take the money, you'll pay a tax. You can't not declare it."

"Then I imagine it's for privacy," Asia said, making a face. "For him, not me. Maybe he doesn't want his wife to know he's paying off his ex to stay quiet about a baby he fathered. We're really not sure where she stands in all this."

"But he didn't make any stipulations that you not tell anyone, did he?" Claire flipped to the second page. "Because I would counsel you not to sign a non-disclosure agreement. You should retain the right to tell your son who his biological father is, should you choose to at some point."

Asia's heart dropped. "God, how did this get to be so complicated?" she asked. "I guess when I made the decision to have the baby and tell no one the truth."

"Life's complicated, Asia." Claire reached out her hand to give Asia a comforting pat. "I made a very different decision twenty-six years ago, and gave Noah up for adoption. To be perfectly honest, I wish I hadn't. But I made the same decision not to tell his father. Somehow..." She lifted a shoulder. "The truth will likely get out, sooner or later. So you want to be protected when it does, and you want to be able to be honest with your child."

Asia nodded. "You're right. Does that contract allow me to do that?"

"It appears to." She skimmed the next page. "Nor does it stipulate how you have to spend the money, which would be my other big concern."

"I saw that," Asia said. "He doesn't insist I use the money for college or even exclusively for Zee. In fact, am I mistaken, or does that read like I could take that money and buy a house?"

Claire read some more, nodding. "Yes, essentially, it does, which tells me..."

When she hesitated, Asia leaned closer. "That he's buying my silence?" she guessed.

"No, or there would be a non-disclosure. I think it's an indication that he's trying to do the right thing for you, and Zee. At least that's my initial opinion."

"That's...good." Asia could hear the doubt in her voice.

"But out of character?" Claire asked.

"Not really, not for the man I had a long-distance romance with for well over a year, who I *thought* was a decent guy. But when you find out that 'decent guy' married someone else? His character is in question."

"Of course it is," Claire said. "But was he generally— other than the fact that he cheated on you so brutally..." She gave a wry laugh. "I guess there *isn't* anything other than that fact, but was he good to you?"

"Most of the time." she said. "But he could be quite controlling. He liked to know what I was doing, where I was, who I was with. He had opinions on what I wore or how I did my hair." Even as she described it, she flashed back to sitting in therapy with Nancy, sharing exactly these things about Spencer.

"So now you're scared this is just another way to control you."

"Exactly," Asia said, relieved she understood.

"And in an emotional sense, it does. But in a legal and financial one? It appears to be in your favor." She tapped the page. "You can access the money without incurring any charges in five years, but if you need it before then you have to pay a bank investment fee, which is fair. And taxes, of course. And I would want to include an addendum that you and only you have access to the account, are able to create a new password, and he can't touch it."

She nodded.

"But as far as the money, it's straightforward and clean. Except you can't have it unless you sign the Termination of Parental Rights. You understand that, don't you?"

"You mean I couldn't turn down the money but still sign the termination?" Asia asked.

Claire shook her head, pointing to the long legalese that tied the two together. "This clause essentially says that if you want him out of your life, you have to take the money."

"Why would he set it up that way?" Asia asked.

"He really wants to give you this money, that's why." Claire looked up. "Could someone be pushing him in that direction?"

"Yes. We're trying to find that out. Miles is looking deeper into the people around Spencer. He mentioned to us that he has a friend in the U.K. who is former Scotland Yard and works as an investigator, but he's"—she rubbed her fingers together—"*very* expensive."

"Oh, I bet. Do you think that's necessary?"

"I don't know. I guess it depends on what Miles can find out on his own."

Claire nodded, already eyeing the second document. "And this process, the termination? It might be a little trickier than you think."

"Really? I don't just sign it?"

But Asia could tell from Claire's expression that it was far more complicated than that. "No, you can't just say, 'I relinquish all rights' and it's legal, free and clear."

"You can't?"

"He has to serve papers to you, then file a petition of termination, and a judge has to approve it. He may request a hearing, but that is rare if both parties are in agreement."

"Oh, that is a little more complicated than I thought," Asia said. "How long does that take?"

"Depends on the court calendar, but it could be at least six months."

Asia's eye shuttered. "I want him out of my life before then."

"You won't ever have to see him, it's all done electronically."

"Okay." Asia turned the agreement and skimmed it again. "Oh, man. What should I do?"

"Nothing too quickly." Claire pressed her hands together and reviewed the termination agreement again, then looked at Asia. "If you don't mind, I'd like to share this with a former colleague at my old law firm. She specializes in family law and has handled numerous custodial cases and parental rights dissolutions. I'd like her opinion on this. I just want to be sure there isn't a surprise in the fine print that I'm not seeing. She'll know what to look for and she'll do it pro bono."

"Oh, that's not necessary—"

Claire waved off the offer. "Angela was one of my closest friends in the New York office and I trust her completely. But it might take her a few days to get to this. Do you mind?"

"I don't, although Spencer seemed to be in a bit of a

hurry. But I should be allowed some time to make a decision this big, don't you think?"

"Absolutely. Still, I'll ask her to turn it around as quickly as she can because you need your peace of mind. If she's not in the middle of a trial, it shouldn't be too long. I—oh!"

They both turned when Zee made a soft squawk and opened big brown eyes, his expression melting into a gummy grin.

"Someone's awake," Asia said. "And expect him to be hungry."

"Well, hello there!" Claire wiggled his little sock-covered foot. "Did you finally wake up from your nap?"

He gurgled and looked at Asia, one hand in the air.

"You want that bottle now, my little man?" She stood and unclipped the belt, reaching for him and, for some reason, needing to hold him even closer than usual. Closing her eyes, she pressed a kiss to his curls. "I just want to do what's best for him."

"Of course you do," Claire said. "And I'll do everything in my legal power—which isn't much, since I can't officially practice in this state yet—to help you."

"Thank you." She sat back down then held him out. "Want to practice a bottle for when Katie and Noah give you one?"

Claire's whole face lit up. "Yes, please!"

Asia laughed and handed him over, getting the bottle for her.

"Thank you, Claire," she said as she helped get the baby in place. "I feel so much better after talking to you."

"Of course." Claire chuckled as Zee grabbed his bottle greedily. "And I hope the next contract of yours I review is for the songwriting projects. Congratulations on that, by the way."

"Thank you. We've hardly had time to think about that with all this going on."

"You will."

"Dane thinks this is all just inspiration for our big hit song."

"You never know," Claire said. "And I like that he's looking at it that way."

Asia sat back in her chair and watched the moment, still uncertain about anything that had to do with Spencer, but at least she had good people helping her make the decision.

Asia's boss called just as she headed toward Shellseeker Beach, the sight of Toni Wentworth's name on the screen jarring her from a great mood after a lovely hour with Claire.

She'd put her job on the back burner these last few days. Working remotely did not mean skipping work and although Toni was easygoing and very flexible, when they had a hot prospective recruit ready to close a deal, she wanted Asia's full attention.

She tapped the green button and prayed that wasn't the case right now, because when she'd abandoned her apartment for temporary housing at Shellseeker Cottages, she'd left a lot of her files behind.

"Hey there," Asia said brightly. "What's good, Toni?"

"What's good is that Southside Medical Group in Philadelphia wants to extend an offer for the CFO job to Gregory Kincaid."

Instantly, she slid into work mode. "That's awesome, Toni. Greg's a perfect fit for that management team and everyone's going to be happy." Especially Asia, since that was going to be one healthy commission.

"Agree! But they need a few things to finish the offer letter and contract, and they need them now. Can you drop whatever else you're working on and draft a memo outlining his required salary and perks, and also pull all the recommendations from the last medical group he was with?"

All of that, every ounce of information, was on her desk...in the townhouse.

"Uh, yeah, sure. Any chance it could wait until this evening?" Because that way she could either ask Dane to pick up the files for her, or at least drop off Zee with her mom and come to the townhouse by herself.

Not that she thought Spencer would be lurking in the lot, but she didn't want to take the chance. Because if he saw Zee...he might change his mind about everything. He'd want parental rights. He'd want time with his son. He'd want to bond and connect and...take him.

That couldn't—

"Actually, it can't wait, Asia." Toni's insistence yanked

her back into the moment. "Their HR director is leaving for vacation tonight and wants the offer letter out before he leaves. I can definitely get Brittany to handle this, but she'd get at least half the commission and you did the work."

Asia swallowed a curse.

"It sounds like you're in your car," Toni said, the slightest edge in her voice, as if her patience with Asia's flexible work hours might be wearing a tad thin. "Any chance you can get to your office soon?"

"Every chance," she said without a second's hesitation, squinting into the sun to see the street sign and calculate the drive. "I just had to run a quick errand, but I'll be back at my desk in less than two minutes."

"Good, then you can make this happen. This medical group is a huge account for us and placing the CFO is a big win for you. The offer is well over three hundred for this guy, so your commission is going to be juicy."

Juicy, indeed. That commission was worth the risk of running into her home to write an email. She slid into the left lane so she could make the turn that would lead her to the Tortoise Way Townhouses.

"I'll have that memo done in no time," she promised. "Look for it, and the backup materials, in your inbox in half an hour."

Pulling into the lot, she scanned the visible cars near her townhouse, looking for any that she didn't recognize. A few of the units were short-term rentals for vacationers, so there were always some unfamiliar cars around, but the place seemed virtually deserted on a dreamy beach day like this.

She scooped out Zee, found her keys, and stepped into the cool townhouse only a little surprised that her heart rate had gone up during the short walk to her front door.

Good heavens, she was ready to be done with this. If she signed the paperwork, could she be certain that she'd never, ever have to even *think* about Spencer Keaton again? She didn't have time to get some overpriced former Scotland Yard detective on the job.

Of course, if she was financially independent...

Yeah. Once Claire's friend came back with the thumbs up, she'd sign and move on.

She carried Zee upstairs, dodging his little fingers as he reached for her braids, then eased him into his crib that sat in a sunny alcove near the window.

"Mama has to work, sweet man. Give me just enough time to do a little writing, and then you know what we can do? Count our money on that big commission." She bopped him in the nose with a teething ring, then let him grab it instead of her hair.

"And, of course," she whispered to herself as she walked to her desk, "that *other* big commission...a million buckeroos. Do you want your daddy's guilt fund, Zee-licious one? Or would you rather know his name when you're twelve and confused? Not that he's stopping me from telling you."

Why *wouldn't* Spencer put a stipulation in this whole thing that she never reveal his identity to Zee, or anyone? Did he want to know his son...someday? Want to keep that option open?

She just didn't know. The weight of the decision pressed on her while she settled into her desk chair and flipped open the file, so happy that she'd taken her laptop to the cottage but still had an old-school desktop computer right here for work.

She zipped through the numbers, drafted the email, ended with a flourish, and hit Send.

"And that, my love, is how it's done." She pushed back from her desk, glancing down at her T-shirt, stained from that last bottle he'd had while she burped him at Claire's. "What I need are some clean clothes."

She grabbed a tote bag and filled it with some clean tops and shorts, stashed a few important files and folders so this didn't happen again, and went to the crib to get the baby, but her hands were full. Where should she put him while she got all this stuff in the car?

She should have brought his carrier, then...

Wait a minute. *Why* was she doing this? She had enough hassle trying to work from home with a baby. She didn't need to add hiding from her ex to the list of things that stressed her out.

Did she really have to stay at Shellseeker Cottages because Spencer Keaton had come to town? He'd shown his cards, he'd met Dane, and he hadn't insisted on seeing Zee. She didn't need to cower from the man just because he knew her home address.

Reaching into her pocket, she pulled out her phone and tapped Dane's number, leaning over the crib rail to rub Zee's belly while she talked.

"Hey, Aje. How did it go with Claire?"

She smiled, loving his nickname for her and the fact that he knew what she was doing, and cared. "Pretty well. She's going to run everything by a friend of hers who's an expert in that kind of law. Listen, Dane, I'm thinking..."

"Yeah?"

"Do we have to stay at Shellseeker Cottages? It's a pain in the butt, frankly, and I'm home right now, so—"

"You went home? To the townhouse? Do you think that was a good idea?"

She huffed out a breath. "What's he going to do, knock on the door? We've met him, he's waiting for our response, and I darn near lost half a fat commission because I wasn't at my desk."

"I thought you had all your work stuff at the cottage."

"Not all, but... You really think we should run scared like this?"

He didn't answer right away, then, "It's totally your call, Asia. I'll go where you go."

The words touched her, and made her feel so safe. "Thanks. I've got everything I needed now, so I'll go back to the beach. After you get home from work, we can make a game-time decision."

"Sounds good. Gotta run."

"Bye, Dane. And thank you." Feeling better than she had in a while, she left the files and scooped up her perfect little man, headed downstairs and out the door, locking it behind her.

As she turned, she froze and gasped and stared

directly into the familiar light-brown eyes of Spencer Keaton.

"Oh!" She instinctively cradled Zee closer. "You scared me."

"I'm sorry. I was just about to knock."

"How did you know I was home?" she demanded, stepping away from the door so he didn't have her trapped against it.

"Just taking a chance you might be." He held up both hands as if to show they were empty. "No fan this time, Asia. Did you make a decision yet?"

She swallowed and took another step away, widening her fingers over Zee's little back.

Zee. She realized with a start that this was the first time Spencer had seen him. Was he going to ask to hold him? Should she—

"I don't want to pressure you, but I do need to get back as soon as possible, so I thought, if you had any questions, I could answer them."

"Don't you have any?" she asked on a surprised whisper. Like...didn't he even want to get a good look at his own son?

But his gaze was on her. Locked, in fact, as if he were working very hard *not* to look at Zee.

"I don't have any questions other than how long do you think it will take for you to decide to accept a million dollars?"

She blinked, the amount still so staggering when it was said out loud. "I'm, uh, having an attorney review the documents."

She could have sworn she saw a reaction flash in his eyes, but it was gone so fast only a woman who'd stared lovingly into those eyes for hours on end would have seen it.

"'Kay," he said. "That's fair. Will it take long?"

"Why are you in a hurry?" And why didn't he even so much as *glance* at Zee?

"I need to get back," he said.

"Busy at Innovative Manufacturing?" She wasn't sure why she brought up the job he had her to thank for—maybe because she hoped it was the job pulling him back and not his earthshattering love for his wife. But if he did love her, then—

"I don't work there anymore."

She blinked, drawing back. "Seriously?"

He lifted a shoulder. "I resigned recently," he said.

He'd left that impressive job? And still had a million bucks to spare? That was almost as mind-blowing as the fact that he had yet to even get a peek at his own son's face.

"Then why the rush to get back?" she asked.

"None of your business, Asia."

She bristled and Zee started to lift his head, like he was interested in the voices. She patted his back, searching Spencer's face for a clue as to what she should do. Turn the baby around? Offer to let Spencer hold him?

Why didn't he show any interest in his own child?

"Anyway, I just wanted you to know I am anxious to get all this behind us," he said.

"All...*this?*" She let out a sigh. "Like your child?"

He angled his head. "Asia. Don't make it difficult. I have to go. You know how to reach me, and I hope you will." With a curt nod, he pivoted and started to walk away, but she made a whimpering sound of frustration.

It was enough for him to turn with an expectant look on his face, that glimmer of impatience she knew and hated so much.

"I was just wondering," she said, drawing in a breath for courage. "Why isn't there a stipulation that I don't tell anyone you are this child's father? Even..." She patted Zee's back. "Him?"

"You won't," he said, sounding smug and confident.

"Someday I might. Someday he'll want to know. Are you scared your wife will find out you have a son?"

"*I* didn't know I had a son," he said in a scoffing tone.

"Well, I didn't know you had a wife when he was conceived."

"I didn't." He ended the conversation with a wave of his hand. "I'm being very generous, Asia," he said. "You do with that money and your...*information*...whatever you want. All I'm asking for is a fast resolution. I'm not being unreasonable, just trying to do the right thing."

Was that true? Why couldn't she be sure?

"Goodbye now," he muttered, leaving her standing until she could no longer hear the soles of his expensive shoes on the ground. Then, she heard a car door, an engine, and, finally, silence.

Until her cell rang, startling her. Was it him? Did he want to press the issue?

She managed to get the phone out of her bag and

glance at the caller ID, her heart calming when she saw Miles Anderson's name.

"Hey, Miles. Any news?"

"Nothing you don't already know, Asia," he said. "But my buddy at Scotland Yard has time to do some sniffing around, if you—"

"Yes," she said, speaking on a gut instinct she rarely ignored. "I want to hire him."

"Oh, okay. Good. I'll bring him up to speed."

"When you do, Miles," she said as she leaned against the door, clutching the baby on her hip, "tell him that Spencer Keaton is no longer at his executive position at Innovative Manufacturing."

"Really? That's not what it says online."

"I know. But I just saw him, and he told me he quit. That might be something your guy should know."

"Yes, it might be, though it might not be official. Where did he go for work? Do you know?" he asked.

"No idea." Because, as he'd so clearly stated, it was none of her business.

"Okay, Asia. You stay safe now, you hear me?"

She looked left and right as she walked to her car, making another decision. "I am, Miles. And if you need to see me, I'll be staying at Shellseeker Cottages." The one place she was confident he couldn't find her.

"Good call," Miles said.

It was. She didn't know why, but she knew it was.

Chapter Fifteen

Noah

"He won two Pulitzers? He knew Teddy Roosevelt?" Noah couldn't contain his admiration as they left the small, darkened theater in a group led by an always-skipping Harper. They'd stopped in the middle of the Wildlife Refuge tour to cool off and learn about the sanctuary's namesake, J. N. "Ding" Darling.

"Everyone in this place knows Roosevelt," Sophia muttered, her phone already out to check the oh-so-important posts on social media she might have missed for the last half hour. "Just ask the bald guy who sells the messages in a bottle."

"The bald guy?" Noah shot back. "Do you mean George Turner?"

She finally lifted her gaze from her phone to give him a withering look. "Whatever."

"Did you even watch a minute of that video?" Noah asked, unable to keep the hint of frustration out of his voice. "J.N. 'Ding' Darling was an American hero, and so talented."

"He drew cartoons and they named this *whole* place after him!" Harper announced, dancing on one foot, then the other, proving that the five-year-old had been way more attentive than the seventeen-year-old during the educational film.

"Very good, Doodlebug!" Noah said, giving her flaxen silk hair a tussle. "You're such a good student."

"Then why isn't she in school?" Sophia said. "Come to think of it, why aren't I? Anything would be better than this particular punishment."

Noah glared at her, but DJ instantly took up her defense. "Hey, I know this is a little dull for you, Soph," he said, coming close and putting a hand on his daughter's back. "But think of it as a fun family event."

While she rolled her eyes, Noah and Claire shared a quick, secret look, confirming with each other that this plan had a chance of working. At least DJ saw this outing as they had hoped he would—a time for this disparate family to get closer and do something "normal" and touristy.

Katie and Harper were obviously having a good time, as were Claire, Noah, and DJ. Only Sophia acted like they'd persuaded her to crawl through broken glass and not stroll down tree-lined paths to see shockingly beautiful wildlife in a world-class sanctuary.

But Noah, who'd taken on the camp counselor role ever since they all met up at the main entrance this morning, would not be deterred by a sullen teenager.

"What is fun about it?" Sophia whined.

"The bathrooms!" Harper exclaimed, making them all laugh. But her little face looked so serious, that Noah refused to crack up.

"The learning lavatories were cool, weren't they?" he

asked, remembering how she and Katie had come out of the insanely creative bathrooms after admiring the murals and sculptures of animals and the stall doors wrapped with wildlife imagery.

Laughing, Katie drew Harper closer with a teasing smile. "When nature calls..." she said in a singsong voice, reminding the little girl of the pun that greeted guests near the signs for the bathrooms in the welcome center.

"But this is so much more than cool bathrooms," Claire said, taking Harper's other hand with a loving gaze. "There are also hundreds of species of birds. We can go birdwatching and look for pink flamingos."

Harper hopped like a jack-in-the-box. "Flamingos?" Her voice rose with unbridled excitement. "Yes, please."

"No, thank you," Sophia groaned, still looking at her phone.

"Well, there's a bus tour," Claire suggested.

"I saw the people getting on it." Sophia shot her father a look. "They make you look like a kid."

Noah fought a frustrated sigh, grateful that DJ gave his daughter a warning look. "Come on, honey. Be a sport."

"Okay, then give me a sport to do which is not tour busing or bird watching or going to ridiculous bathrooms."

"How about biking or kayaking?" Noah said, glancing at the brochure that he'd picked up when they walked in. "Or we could go hiking. There are excellent trails."

She shot him a deadly glare, but Harper hopped again.

"Kayaking!" she exclaimed. "I can kayak! Deeley showed me."

"We could do that," Claire said, seemingly happy to have found something that—

"I'd rather eat," Sophia said, finally putting the phone in her back pocket. "I'm famished and parched."

Harper looked up at her. "What does that mean?"

"She's hungry and thirsty," Katie explained. "Are you, honey?"

But Harper's face only registered the disappointment of someone who'd rather do something fun more than eat. But she nodded, silent, and Noah's heart folded in half with love and pride for how mature she was. Way better than the other girl in the group.

"You're a good kid, Doodlebug," he whispered, crouching down to get eye to eye. "Let's have an early lunch, with french fries"—that made her smile—"and then whatever we do next is Harper's Choice. How's that sound?"

"Good," she said softly, some of the exclamation points out of her voice. "I like french fries."

God, he loved this child. He gave her another smile and stood, sharing a look with Katie, whose blue eyes shone with the same love and pride that was filling his heart.

"Lunch it is," he said, waving them along with his folded brochure. "Follow me, fam."

He waited for one last retort from Miss Happypants, like, "We're not your fam," but Sophia was blessedly quiet and cooperative. So much so that after they found a table near the concessions and Katie took Harper to wash her hands, Noah suggested he and Sophia go and get all the food while the rest of them relaxed.

He had to use the time alone with her for a serious talk, or otherwise she was going to implode this day. Plus, he knew DJ and Claire needed some time alone, which Sophia would never give them unless she had to.

"I'll buy," Noah said, leaning into her while they walked. "If you can spend ten whole minutes without taking your phone out."

She looked up at him. "I have money."

"Sophia, come on." He lifted his hands in mock surrender. "What's a person have to do to get through to you?"

Maybe it was his tone, or he'd hit a soft spot, but the hardness left her expression and she managed a smile. Not broad or blinding, but he'd take it.

"Fine. No phone. But I want a milkshake and they're not cheap."

"Deal." They got in the back of the line and waited for a beat, then Noah decided to dive in, because he might not have this chance again. "Can we talk?" he asked.

"Oof. Pushing it, bro," she teased.

"I'll take my chances."

"What do you want to talk about?" she asked, enough curiosity in her voice that he knew she was at least vaguely interested in having a serious conversation with him.

"Our family," he said simply.

Her brows flicked. "Sounds heavy."

"It doesn't have to be, but... Are you so deeply self-involved that you don't realize something's going on with Claire and DJ? Something not good?"

She stared at him, her eyes getting wider, then she spread her fingers and fisted her hand. "I'm sorry, I'm sorry, I'm sorry, but someone is calling me. I feel the long vibrations of a call." She laughed a little. "Please?"

"Go ahead."

She blew out a breath like an addict being given a drug, yanking out the device to stare at it. "Oh my God, it's my sister, Anna, Queen of Stanford. She never calls me. Sorry."

She tapped the screen, whipped around, and walked away with the phone pressed to her ear.

Swearing under his breath, he waited alone, moved to the head of the line, ordered food for six, paid, waited some more, and finally got the order when she came prancing over, looking beyond pleased with herself.

"I'd say you look like the cat who ate the canary, but in this place?" Noah glanced around. "The canaries might divebomb me."

She didn't seem to laugh at—or get—the joke, but that didn't change her expression of pure...joy? Ecstasy? Hope?

"Sophia," he said on a laugh. "Get that other tray and tell me what's got you looking like that."

She scooped up the plastic tray overloaded with sandwiches and fries and let out a long sigh.

"My mother broke up with her boyfriend," she

announced. "And that, my friend, is the best news I've had in weeks."

Noah considered that, holding onto his tray full of food and walking back to the table, accepting that his heart to heart with Sophia would have to wait.

"That's good. I guess." Maybe not for her mother, but since when did Sophia care about a little thing like her parents' well-being?

"Are you kidding? It's great! Now Dad and Mom can get back together."

He stopped so dead in his tracks, a fry tumbled to the ground. "What?"

"Oh, come on. Do you think you're the only one who secretly hopes their parents get back together?"

He stared at her. "I had no idea that was a possibility." And, he was certain, neither did his mother. How would Claire feel if she heard this?

"It's as much of a possibility as your parents getting together," she shot back.

"Except we're talking about one of the same parents. Does DJ *want* to get back with your mom?" Because Noah was pretty sure he was a heck of a lot closer to Claire than the woman who'd divorced him in California on the grounds that he spent too much time at work.

"But mine came first," she said, her voice as weak as the argument.

"Not technically, but I don't think that's what's important."

"You know what's important?" she demanded.

He stared at her, waiting for a typical Sophia

pronouncement, like, "My happiness is important and that's all that matters."

"Tell me," he said when she didn't.

"That my dad is happy," she said, surprising him with the closest thing he'd ever seen to empathy in her.

"Well, I guess..." He blew out a breath.

"He's your father, too," she reminded him.

"He is, and I want him to be happy, but..." He looked across the crowded outdoor dining area, spotting Claire and DJ next to each other at a long picnic table. DJ was on the phone—reminding him of Sophia—and his mother looked off into the distance, a sad expression on her face.

Right then, he had to admit, neither one of his parents seemed particularly happy.

"No buts," Sophia finished. "He needs to be happy, Noah, and as much as you and Claire have pushed and prodded and convinced him he belongs here, the truth is, he's a California guy with a family out there who used to be happy and whole and...well, a family."

He just looked at her, trying so hard to see this from her perspective. It wasn't that hard, honestly. Ever since he'd met DJ, Noah had known he was competing with the Fortunatos of California.

"So you think he's going to go back and...and try again with your mom?" Even as he said the words, they hurt. Not his pain—he'd lived with a sense of abandonment since the day his parents didn't come home from work at the World Trade Center, and he'd been too young to understand anything except that they were gone. The hurt he felt now was for Claire, who wanted a family as much as—if not more than—he did.

"I'm going to do everything possible to make that happen," she said.

He felt his jaw loosen. "Sophia. He's in a relationship."

She lifted a shoulder and a matching eyebrow. "May the best mom win."

She took off to the table, a bounce in her step he hadn't seen all day. Maybe ever.

What was he going to do? Everything possible to make *something else* happen?

"French fries!" Harper came skipping toward him, greedy hands outstretched, reaching for food but having no idea of the hold she had on his heart.

And just beyond Harper's happy face, he saw his mother and remembered that the whole idea of today was to form family bonds. Too bad he didn't have a chance to explain that to Sophia, who was on a mission to break them.

Despite leaving it all on the Ding Darling court of birds and gators, Harper couldn't or wouldn't crash on the way home, so Noah didn't bring up anything about his conversation with Sophia on the way home after the long, hot day.

Instead, Harper chirped about the stuffed iguana Claire had bought her at the gift store that she named

Iggie and pronounced her new forever best friend, and Katie peppered her with questions.

As they talked, Noah looked up into the rear-view mirror and caught Harper's angelic face and joyous expression and wondered...would she be brooding, surly, opinionated, and selfish when she was seventeen?

"Never," he murmured to himself.

"Never what?" Katie asked, always in tune to his moods.

"Tell you later," he said.

"Tell her what?" Harper asked, confirming what he already knew—the kid never missed a beat.

"Tell her...a story about Iggie the Iguana who...got lost in the bathroom drainpipe at Ding Darling Wildlife Refuge," he replied.

"Tell me that story!" she demanded in her high-pitched voice, holding Iggie up. "Tell us both!"

"It'll be your bedtime story," he promised, hoping that would be soon. He really needed to unload to Katie.

"I'll get her bathed and in PJs," Katie said. "You can whip up some scrambled eggs and toast for her, and then after she has a little dinner, it's bedtime story."

"Yay!" Harper sang. "Did you hear that, Iggie?"

As she nattered on to her toy, Katie reached over the console and whispered, "Then you can tell me what's got you in knots, Noah Hutchins."

He just sighed and smiled, falling even a little deeper in love with the woman who knew him like no other.

An hour later, the three of them were lined up on Harper's bed—with Iggie, of course—while Noah put his storytelling skills to work. After the inspiration of the refuge, however, he easily spun a tale about a hapless volunteer iguana who'd come all the way from South America to work at the world-famous refuge, only to accidentally take a visiting dignitary—Princess DoodleHarp—down a drainpipe, deep under the sanctuary.

There, they launched on an adventure as they tried to make it to freedom, based on all the animals that had captivated Harper that day. There was the delightful flamingo named Dancer, who pirouetted her way through the refuge to alert the keen-eyed black-and-white warbler, who sang for help. And they rode the turtle over a river, and came face to face with Deadly Diamondback, a snake of a villain, and finally were saved by a misunderstood alligator who had no bite but a big heart, and his chubby manatee friend named Buddy.

By the time he finished, Harper's eyes were heavy, his plotting had run out of twists and turns, and Katie gazed at him like *he'd* saved the day, not Buddy and Alphonzo the Alligator.

"You're the one who deserves a Pulitzer," she whispered as they tucked Harper in for the night. "Will you give me one good reason why you don't write a children's book?"

He opened his mouth to give many, but none would come. "I...don't know. I never tried."

"You just did!" she exclaimed. "And it could be a movie. I was enchanted, and so was your audience of one."

"I put her to sleep," he joked.

"That was the job. And I'm serious," she added as they turned out the light and stepped into the hall. "That was a great story."

"Glad to hear it, but..."

"But you need to sit out on the patio with me and a bottle of wine, am I right?" she asked.

He pulled her in for a hug. "So right."

"Go out there now," she said. "I'll be with you in a sec."

He followed the order, sitting on a rattan chair and leaning his head back to think about the day's problems, but the story kept spinning in his head. A cast of... animals? A happy ending? A life lesson or two woven into a classic, timeless tale and told in simple language?

Maybe he *could* write a children's book. Maybe...he *wanted* to.

"All right, then." Katie breezed out carrying a small wooden tray with open wine, two glasses, and some cheese and crackers. "Light dinner, long talk."

"I love you," he said simply, the declaration coming straight from the heart.

She smiled at him. "I love you, too. Is that why you're sitting in the dark with a big ol' grin on your face? Here I thought you were miserable."

"I am. Well, was. You change everything, Katie."

As she poured wine, she looked over at him, her blue eyes warm. "And I haven't even tried."

"You don't have to." He took the glass of wine she offered, waited until she had hers, then held his up. "To

Iggie," he said, getting a surprised look. "Who might just be the hero I needed to break my writer's block."

"Noah!" She dinged his glass. "I'm serious about the children's book."

"So am I," he said, surprising himself with the vehemence in his voice. "So that means the day wasn't a complete disaster."

"Disaster?" She sat up. "I mean, there was some stress here and there, but I thought it was a blast. Harper was in heaven, and Claire and DJ seemed to do very well, since I know that was kind of why you wanted to go. Was it Sophia? Did she take her face out of her phone long enough to upset you?"

"Yes," he said simply, then closed his eyes.

"What? When?"

He relayed the news about DJ's ex-wife breaking up with her boyfriend, and Sophia's determination to get him back to California and reunited with that now-available woman.

"And you think there's an actual chance of that happening?" Katie laughed lightly. "First of all, he loves Claire. Second of all, that marriage ended for a reason. What makes her think that would work? And third, she's nothing but a drama queen looking for attention and she sure got it. You need to relax, Noah."

He knew she was right on every count, but... "I guess I don't trust him."

"DJ? Is he flirtatious or has he ever done anything that makes you think he'd be unfaithful to Claire?"

"No, no. I mean I don't trust his 'live in the moment'

and 'do what feels good' attitude. There's nothing to keep him in one place. And I guess that's at the root of what worries Claire. I told you she and I talked about it."

Katie nodded. "You can't fix whatever's wrong in their relationship, no more than Sophia can break it apart. That's for them to handle."

"I know, but..." He gathered his thoughts, which were all over the place. "I feel responsible for them."

"You aren't, but why do you feel that way? I mean, other than the fact that you're a fundamentally good guy?"

"They wouldn't have met if not for me. Met the second time," he clarified. "I want it to work out. Claire wants it to work out."

"It still might," Katie said, but there was enough hesitation in her voice that he looked at her.

"Even you doubt that," he said.

"But not because DJ's ex-wife is suddenly available," she said. "More because they didn't say a lot to each other today. What they did was kind or nice or certainly civil, but I didn't feel much electricity."

He gave a soft grunt. "I'm so disappointed," he admitted. "In my father."

"Well, now I can give some advice." She reached over. "I'm an expert on fathers who disappoint. The thing is, I don't think any parent wants to let a kid down on purpose. We just do the best we can. I'm sure I'll disappoint Harper somewhere along the way."

"Doubtful," he said, staring out into the darkness, watching headlights travel down the main road that was visible at night. "Should I tell her?" he asked, struggling with the issue that had been pressing on his heart all day. "Should I tell Claire that DJ's ex-wife is somehow free and back in the picture?"

"No," she said without a bit of hesitation.

"Don't you think she should know?"

"The ex is *not* in the picture, for one thing. And consider the source, Noah. That phone call could have been about something else, or she could be speculating, or her mother and her boyfriend had a fight and they're already back together. You have no idea, but what we do know is DJ has shown no signs, ever, about wanting to get back with her. You're letting Sophia, the original drama mama, dictate your mood."

He let out a breath as if he'd been the one to make the speech, turning to her. "You're so right."

"I am," she agreed. "And you're worrying for no good reason."

"It's a good reason," he countered. "It's really hard letting go of my stupid 'I finally have a family' dream."

"Why let it go?"

"Because if they break up—"

"You *still* have a family, even if it's not traditional," she insisted. "You have Claire and you have DJ, they just might not have each other."

He nodded.

"And you have us," she added on a soft whisper. "Your two favorite girls."

He turned to her, hearing something in her voice that

just reached in and grabbed his heart. "You are my favorites."

"And we love you."

He smiled, the words like a balm. "I know."

"And all you have to do is say the word, Noah Hutchins, and we could make it legal."

For a moment, he wasn't sure he'd heard her, she'd spoken in such a husky whisper. But he knew from the intensity of her gaze that he'd heard and heard right. "Legal, huh? Funny, my mom's a lawyer..."

She laughed softly and angled her head. "I'm just sayin'."

"What are you saying?" he asked after a short beat.

She lifted a shoulder. "Only that...I'm ready."

"Are you?" He sat up a little bit, then leaned closer. "Because I wanted to write that book and get all my finances in order, and maybe figure out..." His voice trailed off as he took in the sweet, inviting way she looked at him. "Or not," he finished. "Maybe I should just seize the day, like DJ would say."

"Maybe you should."

He brought her hand to his lips, silent as he considered just how much he wanted to marry her, and how it felt to know she wanted that, too.

"All I'm saying is you don't have to dream about a family, Noah. You have one right here and we love you very, very much."

He pressed her knuckles to his lips, his brain already spinning over when, where, and how he could ask her. He wanted it to be somewhere amazing and romantic and, yes, he wanted Harper to be there. His family, too. He wanted their engagement to be a beautiful event.

"Katie." He gave her one more kiss. "I don't know what I'd do without you."

"And I'm telling you that you don't have to find out."

They sat quiet in the dark for a long time, and with each passing minute, Noah's stress lifted more, replaced by a new certainty about his future.

Chapter Sixteen

Claire

"Take that, civil procedure!" Claire smashed the Send key to submit her practice test, dropping back on her chair with a noisy exhale. Checking the clock, she gave a small fist pump and watched the red "Practice Test Submitted" message flash on her screen.

That was all she needed to do today, leaving her time to spend with DJ, if he was still here.

As had been the case for a few days—more, if she was being honest—an intangible but undeniable coolness had settled between them since the day at the wildlife refuge.

Her plan to "bring the family together" had worked well enough, but they seemed fractured again.

Pushing out of her seat, she opened the bedroom door and listened for any conversation or sounds but she didn't hear anything. Sophia was at school, she was certain of that, but where was DJ?

She walked into the kitchen, glancing around, then caught sight of movement out by the pool, where he was pacing, phone to his ear. He seemed intent, listening, then talking with his one free hand moving as it always did when he wanted to make a point, then he laughed.

Who was he talking to?

After a minute, he dropped onto one of the chaises, dragged his fingers through his hair, and said something, and whatever the response, it brought a huge smile to his face.

If she didn't know better, she'd swear he was...

A chill wormed its way into her chest as she stared at him. Could he...would he...was he talking to *another woman?*

No. DJ wasn't a cheater.

But there were all those hours at Luigi's, only to...not buy the place. And plenty of times he just disappeared without too much of an explanation. He'd spent darn near as much time as Sophia on the phone texting yesterday, without making any attempt to tell Claire who he was talking to.

She brought her fingers to her lips and suddenly felt incredibly...naïve. And blind. And stupid. And...*no.* She couldn't believe he would do that to her. She couldn't.

Without giving herself time to think about it, she walked to the sliding glass door and pushed it open. Instantly, he looked up, and yes, that was guilt all over his handsome face.

"Hey, I gotta run," he said into the phone. "Catch you later. Yeah, yeah. You bet."

He practically stuffed the phone in his cargo shorts pocket as he stood, his expression changing to something more serious and even a little...scared?

Oh, no. Could she take infidelity? Yes, she would survive and move on. But she so didn't want to.

"How'd it go?" he asked. "Did you nail the test?"

She nodded, coming outside without even closing the door behind her. Let the AC waft out—she might need to make a quick getaway if he broke her heart. "With six minutes to spare," she told him.

"There you go, Counselor. Well done." He took a few steps closer, searching her face. "You look like it took a toll. Was it taxes? Torts?"

"Civil procedure."

"Ugh. I don't know how you do it."

She shrugged. "Who were you talking to out here?"

"Oh, um..." He looked completely flummoxed. "Just someone...someone."

Really? He couldn't even come up with a lie? She gave a dry laugh. "Someone I know?"

He shook his head, his always tanned skin paling. "No, just a person. A pizza...person."

Was he serious? "Ah. But not Luigi."

"No, no. But she knows Luigi, which is how I..."

"She?" There weren't a lot of women in the pizza-making world, she thought with a thud in her gut.

"Yeah, yeah." He blew out a breath, far too self-aware not to realize how guilty he sounded. "Anyway, what's up for today?"

Seriously? He was going to carry on an affair under her nose, stutter and lie about it, then casually ask about the day ahead?

"More studying?" he asked when she didn't answer.

"Maybe. What about you? More long chats with women?"

"Claire!" He tried to sound put out, but even he had

to give a guilty chuckle. "I guess I know how that sounds, but..."

"It sounds like you're talking to a woman. Should I be jealous?"

For a long time—way too long—he just looked at her, a weird, unreadable expression in his dark eyes. "Jealousy is for the insecure, Claire. That's not who you are. Not a woman who aces a civil procedure bar exam with six minutes still on the clock."

She crossed her arms and swallowed hard, not wanting to have this conversation, but...no. No. She was *not* her mother, a woman whose husband had actually *married* another woman while they were still married. Forget her father's stupid guilt-charged reasons for committing bigamy, the legacy of women who let men walk on them ended with Claire.

"Who is she and when were you going to tell me?" she asked in a voice generally reserved for cross-examining guilty witnesses.

He blinked, probably more at the tone than the question. "Her name is..." He made a face. "I'm not really ready to tell you."

"What?" she choked the question. "That's too darn bad, DJ. I'm ready to hear."

"I haven't made a decision yet, and until I do, there's no reason—"

"A decision?" She took a small step backwards, the words slamming her. "To do what? Leave me?"

He didn't answer, but stared hard. "Claire, I wanted to..." Another drag of his hand through his hair, another noisy put-upon sigh, and with each passing second, she grew colder inside.

"You're seeing someone else? I just can't believe—"

"No! Oh my...that's what you thought?"

She gave a mirthless laugh. "Yes. What else would I think?"

"Oh, Claire!" He dropped his head back and actually guffawed. "You really don't know me at all, do you?"

Relief washed through her so hard she almost swayed. "You're not cheating on me?"

"No!" He reached for her, but she stiffened, still not ready to melt into his arms. "Claire, I adore you. I love you. I would not in a million years even look at another woman. You know me better than that."

But did she? "Then why do you seem so guilty after talking to a mysterious woman who's left you with a decision you're not ready to share?"

"I seem guilty because...I *am* guilty. But not of cheating on you," he added quickly.

"Then of what?"

He took her hand and tipped his head toward the table, then pulled a chair out for her. "I guess the universe is telling me it's time to come clean."

"The universe and the woman you live with," she said dryly, falling into the chair and watching him slowly take his.

"I'm just not sure the timing is right."

"Make it right."

He drew back. "You are very mad at me."

"You've been distant," she said. "You've been absent.

You've been distracted and preoccupied and didn't even care too much when your daughter stole my car."

"She didn't...okay, okay. I was really in the middle of it that day."

"In the middle of what?" she asked. "You were making pizza at Luigi's and...weren't you?"

"I was, but it was more than that." He settled into the chair, letting his eyes close. "I was auditioning for the opportunity of a lifetime."

"Auditioning? For what?"

"A friend of Luigi's—the woman I was just on the phone with—happens to have recently taken the top marketing job at a fairly new company making high-quality but extremely affordable home pizza ovens. The company is called Cornicione."

"Cornish..." She frowned. "I thought it was what you call the rim or the crust. You're always talking about having the perfect corn...ish...own." She pronounced it phonetically, having heard the word dozens of times but never seen it spelled out.

"'That's right. And this company, which is heavily funded and quite possibly going to go public in the next year or two, took that word for their name. It's brilliant, if you ask me," he added with a smile.

"What about them? What are they auditioning you for?"

"The chance of a lifetime," he said, that old passionate spark making his dark eyes twinkle. "They are going to select one *pizzaiole*—and, man, you should hear some of the big names they are considering—to do pop-up pizza events..." He took a deep breath and rushed out the rest. "All over the world for the next two years."

All over the... "Oh," she whispered, letting that hit her in the heart. "But, wow, DJ. They're talking to you about that? That's pretty amazing."

It was a whole lot of other things, too, but the honor couldn't be ignored.

"Yes!" His face lit up. "Can you believe it? Luigi got me in the running when he turned them down, and she knew my name and reputation. So she came for a few days and—"

"And you didn't tell me?" A new level of disappointment grabbed at her throat. "Why not?"

"You were busy and I didn't want to worry you and..." He shook his head. "I'm lying. I didn't want you or anyone to talk me out of it. And I knew you would."

"No, I wouldn't."

"Claire, I'd be leaving with essentially no breaks. Traveling the world from one end of the globe to the other." Even as he said it, she could hear the lust for that life in his voice. "And I don't know if I'd ever..."

"Come back," she finished for him, the words lodging in her throat. "Noah will be sad," she finally whispered.

"Not if he comes with me. And you, too."

She stared at him, speechless. "You think we can just up and travel the world with you?"

"Doesn't it sound amazing? More than two months in Italy, to start with, which is where they're kicking off the campaign, for obvious reasons. Every beach and town up and down the boot. Then France, Germany, Spain, all over. Europe is the first seven months, then it's off to South America, the Far East, Australia, and…" He caught himself and took a breath long enough to read her expression. "You don't want to go."

"I don't." She shook her head. "It's not what I'd planned. And Noah?"

"What could stop him?"

"Um, Katie?" She couldn't believe he didn't realize that. "Are you completely unaware of how in love he is?"

"Pffft." He flicked his wrist. "He's so young, for crying out loud, and he should know better than to get tied down to a woman and her kid. The real hang-up is going to be cash. Cornicione has a huge budget…for the talent and culinary producers and PR people and advance people and…all the people," he said on a laugh. "But we'd have to pay for you and Noah to go. Still, I think—"

"Stop." She held up her hand. "Just…give me a second, okay?"

He obliged, taking a breath, then turning his phone over to read it. He started to respond to a text, but she leaned forward.

"DJ. Talk to me."

He put the phone down. "You said you needed a second."

"You said you wanted to live your life by being in the moment," she volleyed back. "Be in *this* one."

He had the dignity to look chastised…for about three seconds. "Claire, I'm sorry. I'm pretty flipped out and excited about this. It's a dream for me. And you know what my favorite philosopher, Paulo Coehlo, says about a dream."

She didn't know, but she'd heard enough quotes from the guy. "I should probably take a guess. Dreams are...like air? Everyone needs one?"

"Close. 'Dreams provide the nourishment for the soul, just as a meal does for the body.'" He pointed his finger in the air like a teacher making a point. "And he also says, 'Fortunate are those who take the first steps.' And, 'A life without a cause is a life without effect.' And—"

She stopped him. "I get it. But did he say anything about leaving the people you love?"

"Claire, I simply never dreamed you wouldn't want to go."

Really? She wasn't sure that made sense. "Then why didn't you tell me about it until now, when I essentially forced the issue?"

"I was waiting for them to sweeten the offer, of course. I did assume that you'd jump at the chance to see the world this way."

She felt a frown pull. "For two years?"

"What could be better, Claire? We'll have so much fun and so many experiences!" His enthusiasm made his whole face light up again. "It's like a two-year honeymoon."

She blinked. "We're not married."

"We could change that...or..." He narrowed one eye, pretending to analyze her expression. "Not. It doesn't matter. We go as a team, and if Noah would rather hang here on this island and work his jobs and…whatever he decides is fine. But you? I'm counting on you, Claire."

She angled her head. "I'll be honest, too, DJ. Nothing about traveling around Europe for months on end to go to pop-up pizza events truly appeals to me. The fact is, I've been having fun studying for the bar. I'm excited about starting my own practice and was hoping we could…buy a house."

"Buy a…" He huffed out a breath. "No house for me. Ever. I'll never be that tied down to a mortgage or a responsibility."

Did *she* fall into that category of "responsibility"? Did Noah?

"I guess I always knew this," she said after a moment. "You've never hidden who you are or how much you want to be free to follow your passions."

"No, I haven't."

"I just hoped that…" Her voice cracked, but she finished anyway. "That I'd be your passion."

She longed for him to reach for her and tell her she was everything to him, but he didn't. He didn't move at all, but looked at her with a little sadness, a little pity, and a whole lot of apology in his eyes…silent.

Unless she counted the sound of her heart breaking, which was deafening right at that moment.

"Oh, DJ. You've made your decision. You're struggling with how and when to tell your family."

"That not entirely true. Holly Kirkman, the VP of marketing, just increased the offer with stock options and I haven't said yes or no."

"I didn't think you were a man driven by money."

"I'm not," he said quickly. "I'm driven by passion. Mine, which is outsized for this product and idea, and other people's for me. Holly and her team want me, over some very big names in the pizza world. That means a lot."

Maybe, Claire thought as she listened, *she* didn't have enough passion for *him*. Her life was simple, as were her needs. She wanted her family unit close and safe. She wanted harmony in her home and heart. She wanted to love her job and do it well, and to enjoy this detour to Sanibel Island that life had sent her.

None of that was outsized enough for a man like DJ.

She leaned back as the power of that realization hit her, and suddenly, she felt oddly...relieved.

"I understand," she said softly, then added, "I don't think Noah will, though. When are you going to tell him?"

He made a face as if he didn't even want to have that conversation. Had he really expected Noah to go—on his own dime?—or had he hoped that Noah would want to stay?

"Gimme a few days," he said. "I have to iron a few things out and maybe I can get them to throw in some free family travel as a bonus. I'll find the right time to tell him and Sophia."

"She doesn't know?" For some reason, that surprised her. They seemed so close.

"God, no. But she's been making noise about going back to California, so I hope..."

"You hope she does," Claire finished, making him grimace.

"Not exactly, but it would be easier all around. I doubt she'd want to stay here if I'm—if *we're*—gone." He leaned forward. "Don't write off the idea, Claire. Please?"

Claire nodded, suddenly feeling deeply...unsettled. Not upset, not depressed, not even brokenhearted. Just troubled.

"And let's not mention it to Noah until I find the right time and words, okay?" he asked.

"Of course." She pushed up, already knowing in her heart exactly how she wanted to handle this. She couldn't get to Shellseeker Beach fast enough to share all of her feelings with Eliza and Teddy and get it all figured out.

"Hey." He finally reached for her hand and held it tight. "I love you, Claire. I want you to know that."

"I know you do." She smiled. "You just love pizza more."

He shook his head. "I want you to come."

"And if I don't?"

"Then...it might be time for this season of my life to change," he said. "I felt exactly like this when I came here, and now...it's time to start the next adventure. It's who I am now."

Now? She looked hard at him, remembering the man who broke up with her on his graduation day at Fordham University, a boy itching to start his next adventure, unaware she carried his child—not that her pregnancy would have changed his plans.

This was who DJ Fortunato had been, no matter if he

couched it as "a new career" or "a bad divorce" or his "latest passion."

This man was a leaver, and, deep down, she'd always known that.

"You okay?" he asked tenderly.

"I'm fine," she said, and meant it. "It's Noah I'm worried about."

He nodded. "I'll do my best to minimize the impact."

And the rest of them—Katie, Claire, Eliza, Teddy, even Harper—would pick up the pieces.

Chapter Seventeen

Eliza

After walking the newest guests through Junonia and getting the family of four set up for their week at Shellseeker Beach, Eliza strolled back through the property with her mind fully on the business of running *this* business.

Those guests were in, another family arrived in a few hours, and still one more would be in from Pennsylvania, and not expected to arrive until very late tonight. She'd promised to wait up for them so they could sleep comfortably in Cantharus, which she knew Katie had just finished cleaning.

But she wanted to stock the fridge with water for both those cottages, and maybe get some of the prettiest flowers from Teddy's garden to put in vases in the rooms. Water later, flowers now.

She continued through her mental checklist as she walked toward the garden to enlist Teddy's help, but when she rounded the path and caught sight of the tea hut, her smile grew.

Teddy and Claire were sitting side by side at a table, deep in conversation.

"There's my sister," she called as she approached,

never tired of saying that word. *Sister*. Who knew she'd ever have one, especially one she treasured so completely?

When Claire turned and waved, Eliza's heart dropped as she could instantly see something was wrong.

"Hey." Eliza reached the table and looked hard at Claire, knowing that a stranger wouldn't notice, but there were shadows in her dark eyes, and her usual smile was absent. "Bar exam studying got you down?"

"I wish," she said, slumping in the chair. "Got a minute to hear my tale of woe?"

"More than a minute." She dropped into one of the other rattan chairs, looking at Teddy, who had a tea in one hand and Claire's hand in the other.

"She's blue, and that's not just her aura," Teddy said.

"I think DJ's leaving, and for good this time," Claire announced.

"What?"

She scooted in and listened as Claire described the conversation she'd just had with DJ, and each word made Eliza feel worse. How would she feel if Miles up and left for years to follow his passion?

She wouldn't like it at all. Maybe that would be the moment of clarity she longed to have, but she honestly didn't want to find out that way. She pushed her own issues out of her mind and listened to Claire, peppering her with questions and adding lots of support as she shared.

The other question that echoed in her heart was more

immediate and worrisome: would Claire leave for two years?

"He might not go," Teddy said when it seemed that Claire had told them everything.

"It sounds like he's leaning toward it," Eliza said.

"He's going," Claire assured them.

"Are you?" Teddy and Eliza asked, their perfect unison making them all laugh.

"I..." She shook her head. "I can't even fathom living on the road for years, my whole life revolving around... events. I love that he wants me to go, but I can't believe he ever really thought I would. Maybe, but I'm just not excited about the idea."

"Then he'll go alone?" Eliza asked. "How do you feel about that?"

Claire bit her lip, considering her response. "Surprisingly, I'm not that upset."

Teddy and Eliza shared a look, then Teddy asked, "You love him, don't you?"

"I do. But I've always known deep in my heart that this could happen. I'm truly relieved it's not another woman, but never expected to lose a man to dough and cheese."

Eliza smiled at that. "Would you keep your relationship alive long-distance? I know, I know, I'm jumping the gun with these questions."

"No, they're fair questions. I don't know." She let out a sad sigh. "I've always known that you can't truly hold on to a man like DJ, with his 'live in the moment' philosophy. Moments change, and that's just not stable enough for a woman like me. But..."

"But what?" Teddy pressed.

"Well, now I've been in this relationship, and had this little family experience, and I've really loved it," she admitted. "I honestly didn't know how much I was missing something like that—a man in my life, a family around the table, even grown."

"You deserve that love, Claire," Eliza said, her heart squeezing with just how much she wanted her sister to have all that she wanted.

"And you shouldn't compromise," Teddy added.

"I know." She looked down, running her finger over the table as she thought. "I'm not going to be like my mother, who looked the other way when her man hurt her."

Teddy, who'd lived with and loved that same man, sighed audibly. "I respect that, Claire. More than you know."

"Thank you," she said. "And honestly, I'm not worried about me. I might not love the idea, but I'm much more concerned about how Noah will take this. The kid was abandoned by me—"

"You gave him up for adoption into a loving family," Eliza corrected. "That is not abandonment."

Claire conceded that with a tip of her head. "Then those parents died. He's spent his life hoping and searching and dreaming of a real family and now, he has it. Then..." She let out an unhappy groan. "Should I tell him before DJ does? Kind of ward off the shock?"

"I don't know," Teddy said. "DJ asked you not to."

"He did," Eliza agreed. "But I do understand the temptation. I never keep anything from Livvie. Dane?" She laughed. "I guess sons are different, because I don't tell him everything."

"Oh, speaking of Dane!" Claire snapped her fingers. "On the way over here, I got a call from my friend who looked at the contract for Asia and Dane. She cleared it with five stars. I want to tell Asia she can sign it without worry there's something in the fine print."

"She's at Slipper Snail," Eliza said. "I just saw her when I was over there."

"I'll go tell her now, but..." Claire dropped her chin into her palms. "I still have to decide what to tell Noah, if anything."

"You can tell him something now," Teddy said, surreptitiously pointing toward the beach. "Here comes the son," she sang.

They turned and caught sight of Noah jogging on the sand, his gaze on them. He lifted a hand in greeting, making it clear he was on his way to the tea hut, as he often was when they were gathered here.

"But he's not scheduled to work right now," Teddy said, glancing behind her at the small structure. "I'm covering for him, though it's been slow."

Claire's face slowly lit up as she watched him approach, the love she felt for this young man palpable.

"Whatever you decide," Eliza whispered, putting a hand over hers, "it will be right. Nothing will tear you and Noah apart, I promise."

Claire flashed her a grateful smile just as Noah reached them.

"Hello, beautiful ladies who spend a lot of time at this table," he joked, his whole face bright and handsome. "May I join you?" He didn't wait for permission, pulling out the fourth chair at the table and sitting down.

"You are always welcome, my darling," Claire said, beaming at him. "And you look so happy."

"Good day in rentals. Deeley just got back from the other location, so I got a break."

"And a break makes you that happy?" Eliza teased. "Then my son-in-law is working you too hard."

"Nah, that's not what has me on a cloud." He looked from one to the other, then settled on Claire. "I need advice and help."

"Oh?" She sat up, looking pleased. "Happy to provide both, aren't we?"

Teddy and Eliza agreed, inching in to find out what he wanted.

"Okay," he said, huffing out a breath. "I've made a huge decision. Oh, and it's secret, so..." He tapped his lips.

"We're sealed," Teddy joked, zipping her lips.

"I'm going to pop the question."

The three of them let out a hoot that Katie probably heard no matter where she was on the property, making him laugh and shush them.

"Oh, honey." Claire reached for him. "I couldn't be happier for you and Katie."

"Thanks, Mom. I really want it to be a special

surprise for her, and for Harper, who I want to include. And after seeing Deeley's proposal to Olivia, I know that I want my family right there to witness it."

Then he better move fast, Eliza thought, knowing that DJ could head off for new adventures sooner rather than later. Claire had enough concern in her eyes that Eliza knew she was thinking the same thing.

"I thought maybe we could do something like we did at the refuge," he said. "Just us, you know, but somewhere special. Not just on the beach or in the gazebo, but somewhere the pictures would be amazing."

"How about on Miles's boat?" Eliza suggested. "At sunset? Gorgeous pictures, water everywhere, and I know he'd make it a really special event."

"Oh, I like that." He lifted his brows in question at Claire. "Good idea? You and DJ and Sophia, Katie and Harper." He angled his head toward Eliza and Teddy. "Any more and we'd sink."

They laughed and assured him they understood.

"I love it," Claire said. "Do you want me to tell DJ and Sophia—"

"No, let's surprise them," he said. "I don't know if I could trust Sophia not to say something. I'm sure you can convince them to take a sunset cruise in the next day or two, right?"

"Oh, that soon?" Claire asked, and Eliza knew why.

"Yep. I already have a ring." At their reaction, he laughed again. "Trust me, I've known for a while I wanted to do this. Like, about five minutes after I met her."

Eliza smiled, thinking of the statement as the others asked some questions about the ring and how surprised Katie may or may not be.

I knew about five minutes after I met her.

So, Noah had clarity. Even Claire had it, although it went in the other direction. Why was Eliza so uncertain? Because she didn't plan on marrying ever again. That was what was stopping her. Wasn't it?

Maybe it had nothing to do with getting married again. Maybe it had to do with...Miles.

THE NEXT DAY, while making her rounds of the cottages and chatting with staff and guests, the thoughts about her elusive "clarity" still plagued Eliza. She knew what she had to do—talk to Miles. They had to have a heart to heart, but what would she say?

I'm waiting for a lightning bolt.

That would sound insane. Maybe she could talk to him about letting go of the whole marriage idea and just enjoying each other's company. She didn't want to break up, not for one minute. But—

Her thoughts were interrupted by a text from Teddy announcing a "big surprise" and telling Eliza to come back to the beach house, stat.

She did, taking her time to mentally have that conversation with Miles, but looking up to the deck when she heard laughter and a familiar voice.

"Is that Mia Watson?" she called, a smile breaking

when she saw the familiar caramel-colored hair of the editor for *The Last Resort.*

"I come bearing a magazine with the most awesome cover!" She waved a glossy magazine in the air. "Come and see, Eliza!"

She hustled up the steps, her heart lifting even more when she saw Alec Dornenberg, the son of one of Shellseeker Cottages' longest-running guests, sitting on a chaise in the corner.

"Oh, you're both here," Eliza said, hugging Mia and then Alec when he stood.

"We've been traveling together a bit," Mia said on a laugh, her eyes shining as she looked at the man she'd met as a teenager on Shellseeker Beach and "rediscovered" here last month. All these years later, the romance had obviously bloomed brightly. "Look! Shellseeker Cottages made the cover of our Hidden Gems issue!"

"Wait until you see the spread, Eliza," Teddy said excitedly, zipping through her own copy. "We're going to be booked for the next decade!"

"Oh, wow, look at this!" Eliza gasped.

The magazine cover featured the view from one of the cottages, with the patio deck in the forefront, sweetly decorated with seashells and some coastal lanterns, the view endless to the turquoise horizon. "This is stunning, Mia!"

She beamed back at Eliza. "And wait until you read the writeup!"

"I'm reading it," Teddy exclaimed. "Listen to this: 'When you wake up in Shellseeker Beach, the world is bathed in the golden light of morning, reflected off the millions of treasures in the sand and the miles of water in the Gulf. The day unfolds with hours of sunshine, salt-water, and shell seeking, but it's the sunsets from the exquisite gazebo that provide the perfect moment of every dreamy day.'"

"Oh my gosh!" Eliza pressed the magazine to her chest. "You're such a good writer, Mia!"

"I keep telling her that," Alec chimed in. "Every word is as beautiful as she is."

"Aww. Listen to him. You guys are..." Eliza didn't know what to call them. Reunited after more than twenty years, obviously together, but was it serious?

"We're..." Mia laughed as she and Alec put their arms around each other and shared a warm and loving look. "Should I tell her?" she asked.

"Hey, if it was up to me, I'd shout it from the rooftops, but you're the one worried that people think we don't know each other well enough to be engaged."

"What?" Eliza asked in unison with Teddy, who rose from her chair.

"You're engaged?" Teddy asked.

They laughed and Mia bit her lip and held up her left hand. "I know it's crazy and we've only been dating a month or so, but..."

Alec beamed at them. "A month? I've been waiting for this girl to come back into my life for more than twenty years. I couldn't see living one more without her. When you know, you know, right?"

Eliza's heart dropped a little, even as she exclaimed

her congratulations and hugged both of them several times.

When you know, you know.

Why didn't she know?

"In fact, one of the reasons we're here is to see if we could reserve Junonia and the gazebo for a wedding in a few months," Mia said. "As you know, that gazebo is where we had our first kiss when I was thirteen."

Another chorus of cheers and a round of more hugs, as this news had to be celebrated.

"Oh, let me get the reservation book," Teddy said, starting to go inside, but Eliza snagged her arm.

"I have the electronic version right here on my phone," she said, making Teddy roll her eyes.

"I like the book," Teddy said with a sly smile. "But Eliza is dragging me into the twenty-first century whether I like it or not."

They laughed some more, heard all about the engagement, and found a perfect date for the newlyweds. But through it all, there was a weight on Eliza's heart that had been growing and growing. When Alec and Mia took off to go walk to the gazebo, Eliza turned to Teddy.

"Listen, I have to—"

"Talk to Miles."

Eliza blinked, then laughed. "You're not a mind reader, Theodora. Is my aura the color of a panicked woman?"

"Eliza, don't panic." Teddy reached for her, and even before her tender, healing hands were on Eliza's shoulders, everything was a little bit better. "No, I'm not a mind reader. But I saw your expression when Mia said she was engaged, and yesterday, when Noah announced he wanted to be. And even when Claire said she'd come to a decision about DJ. You want..."

"Certainty," Eliza whispered. "It's all I want, Teddy. I don't want to string him along, but I don't want to give him up, and I don't want to..."

"Marry him," Teddy said.

"I don't want to marry anyone," Eliza replied. "If I did, it would be Miles, in a heartbeat. But I'm just...struggling."

"I know you are. Go talk to him, Eliza. Now. Don't waste another minute."

"I have too much to do right now, including look at this magazine." She fluttered the publication. "Which is going to every travel agent in the country and beyond!"

"Eliza." Teddy looked at her, eyes filling. "You have changed everything here, you know that?"

"What do you mean? A little upgrade here, a renovation there, and an electronic reservation system?" She grinned. "The heart and soul of Shellseeker Cottages is still you, Teddy Blessing."

"But you're leaving your mark, and it's a better place because of it. I was telling Dutch last night."

She choked. "Excuse me?"

"Sometimes," she whispered, "I walk by that box of ashes and feel like I have to take them somewhere. Until I do, I'll keep talking to him."

"Is that so bad?"

She shrugged. "I don't mind, but I am starting to worry that he's not resting."

Eliza didn't buy that, but she remembered the dilemma of not knowing what to do with Ben's ashes. "Let me think about how to get him in the air, Teddy, to meet his last request. And while I do, I'll call Miles and see if I can have dinner with him tonight."

She didn't have a chance to call until Mia and Alec left, then a new couple had been checked in, and through it all, the phone didn't stop ringing for reservations. The online version of *The Last Resort* had been posted and they were busy.

Finally, she settled onto a bench in the garden and dialed Miles's number.

"Hey," he said, as brusquely as she could remember. "What's up, E?"

"You okay?" she asked.

He didn't answer right away, then said, "Swamped. And I'm taking Claire and DJ and their whole gang on a boat ride tonight, remember?"

"Oh, that's tonight? For some reason, I thought it was later in the week."

"It was going to be, but Claire texted me and asked if we could move faster."

Of course, because DJ wanted to take off for his next adventure.

"Sorry to sound rushed," he said. "Are you okay?"

"Yes, yes, I'm fine. I was calling to make a dinner date with you, but maybe tomorrow?"

"Of course, but..." His voice trailed off again.

"Miles? Is everything all right?" she asked, wondering if he somehow sensed that she wanted to talk seriously about their future as a couple.

"Holy...wow."

"What is it?"

"I...don't know exactly. I just got an email from my Scotland Yard guy and, whoa, I have to talk to him."

"About Asia?" Eliza asked.

He didn't answer, but she heard the computer keys clicking. "Yes. He said he found something interesting, but..." He was quiet for a moment, no doubt reading. "I'm not sure what to make of this, and it's kind of late in the U.K. to call him, but I'm going to try right now before my passengers show. I have to run, but yes to dinner tomorrow."

"Okay, see you then." She disconnected the call, leaving her sitting in the garden, holding her phone, the echo of his voice in her ears.

She sat very still for a long time, waiting for that lightning bolt, that elusive clarity, the answers from the universe around her or God above.

But none of that happened, so all she could do was sigh and get back to work.

Chapter Eighteen

Noah

"You nervous?" Miles asked with a teasing smile when he opened the door to let Noah in before the boat ride.

"Petrified," he admitted, crouching down to give some love to a barking Tinkerbell. "I came early to help you get the boat ready."

"For which I'm eternally grateful. I have had a wild day and prepared some food and drinks, but if you want to go out there and get her cleaned up, covers off and cushions up? Knock yourself out. I'm trying to reach someone overseas, then I'll join you."

"Aye-aye, Captain." He gave a mock salute as he stood. "And thanks, Miles. I know you're busy, and I could have waited another few days."

"Your mom was in a big hurry," he said, stepping back to let Noah in.

Noah chuckled. "I think she's afraid I'll change my mind."

"Will you?" Miles asked as they walked into the house.

"Not unless I lose this ring." He tapped his front pocket. "Otherwise, I'm ready to hit the knee."

"Well, don't take a swim and kiss that ring goodbye," he joked, giving Noah a nudge. "Cooler's in the kitchen. Keys are on the counter. I'll be out there in a few minutes."

While he set up the boat, Noah practiced what he wanted to say to Katie—and Harper— and with each passing second, his heart hammered a little bit more. He wanted this to be perfect for her, and for his soon-to-be-daughter to understand what it meant. For his mom and dad to be part of it, no matter how strained they seemed, felt so perfect. And Sophia? Well, she'd take pictures and provide some snarky commentary after he popped the question. Having them there was one more "family event" that he hoped would bond them together.

Just a few minutes later, Miles jogged down the dock, with Tinkerbell right beside him.

"That was a quick call," Noah said.

"I had to leave a message," he said. "But that's fine. I can talk to him tomorrow. Everything good on board?"

"It's—"

Tink started barking, running back to the house as the sliding door to the house opened and the rest of the passengers arrived. Noah saw Harper, who was skipping around with her usual delight in life, and Sophia, who had her face in the phone. Consistent, if nothing else.

Claire and DJ weren't talking, though they walked next to each other.

All of them simply disappeared when his gaze landed on Katie. She'd taken her ponytail out and her wheat-colored hair spilled over her shoulders, a pink sweater bringing out her creamy complexion.

Laughing as she watched Harper and Tink, she seemed to radiate joy and stability and hope and happiness.

"She looks good," Miles murmured to him, following his gaze.

"I can't wait to make her my wife," he admitted, glancing at the other man.

The words had an impact, he could tell, as he noticed a distinct flash of emotion in Miles's green eyes. "Not gonna lie, kid. I'm jealous."

Noah drew back. "Eliza?"

Miles just laughed. "Some women, like fish, are just impossible to reel in."

"Don't know until you drop the line, Miles."

"So true." He gave Noah a broad smile. "But you are, and I'm really happy for you."

"Thanks, man. And thanks for providing the perfect backdrop."

"My pleasure."

"Noaaaahhhh!" Harper came prancing down the dock, making Tinkerbell bark at a kindred soul.

Noah hopped onto the dock to greet everyone, trying to act like it was just another fun, easy family outing...and not the most important day of his life thus far.

Claire's eyes were brimming with emotion when they hugged.

"Don't give me away," he whispered in her ear.

She responded with a squeeze, smiling as Harper

gave Tink a belly rub, with Katie taking a few pictures on her phone. Claire gestured for DJ to join her and they walked to the boat, leaving Noah and Sophia on the dock together.

"Hey, Soph," he said to his sister.

She looked up from the phone. "How long are we going to be out here?"

"Oh, come on," he said, narrowing his eyes. "I'm gonna need you tonight."

"For what?"

He was half tempted to tell her, hoping that having her in on his plans could get her cooperation, but...she could just as easily use her knowledge for evil instead of good. She could cause problems, or "accidentally" mention it to Katie, or just wreck the night out of spite. He simply didn't understand his half-sister, and now wasn't the time to try.

"To keep things light and fun."

"Me?" she scoffed. "Fun's your kid's department."

He glanced at Harper, who was clinging to Tink's collar and letting the dog lead her to the boat with much shrieking and laughter. His kid.

Well, she was about to be, he hoped.

"Just stay off your phone and be..." He almost said "engaged," but caught himself. "Involved in the conversation."

She rolled her eyes. "I'll do my best. What's Dad's deal, anyway? Do you know?"

"His deal?" He looked over his shoulder at DJ. "What do you mean?"

"Something is so up with him. I heard him say something about 'not announcing' to Claire, so I was wondering if you knew." She made a face. "Hoping he's announcing he's moving home to California."

Or announcing something else. Maybe Claire had told him that Noah was going to propose tonight? "I don't know. Just do me a favor and...be nice."

"Nice is my middle name." She blew past him to the boat, leaving just one more person for him to greet. The one who mattered most.

Katie reached her arms to him, her hair fluttering in the breeze.

"You look beautiful," he said, pulling her close to him.

"So do you." She patted his shoulders. "Cotton sweater and khakis. Very Ralph Lauren, Noah."

He laughed, probably sounding as nervous as he felt. "And here I was going for J.Crew." He slipped his arm around her and started walking them toward the boat.

"Noah." She slowed down and looked up at him. "Are you okay?"

"Yeah, why?"

"You're shaking."

He managed a smile. "My sister makes me nuts," he lied.

"Don't let her. Stay with Harper and me all night. We love you the most anyway."

"I know you do." And he also knew he was doing the right thing. All he needed was the perfect moment to make it happen.

THE RING WAS BURNING a hole in Noah's pocket as they cruised through the Sanibel canals, around the lighthouse, and into the open Gulf. He certainly didn't want to pop the question when they were underway, making a wake with the loud engines. He stayed on the banquette, with Katie on one side and Harper on the other, and Tink on Harper's lap.

"Why don't you have to wear a lifejacket, Noah?" Harper asked, tugging at the clasp of the bright red one she wore.

"Because I'm old and I can swim."

"I can swim," she shot back.

"Harper," Katie leaned in to look at her. "It's not an option, okay?"

"Tinkerbell doesn't have to—"

"You wouldn't catch me in one of those things," Sophia said, looking up from her phone across from them. "And I *can't* swim."

"You can't?" Harper's eyes popped. "You never took lessons? What if you fell in the pool?"

"Someone would save me," she said with cavalier ease.

But Noah had spent enough time in their home pool to know she wasn't lying, and always stayed in the shallow end.

"I wanted you to have lessons," DJ said, "but that was your mother's department and she didn't follow up."

"Don't diss Mom, Dad. She was a great mother and a wonderful lady. She still is, you know."

"I know," he said, seeming oddly disconnected or preoccupied.

"Opinion from the crew," Miles called from the helm, glancing at Noah. "How does this look to drop anchor?"

Noah knew why his opinion mattered, and was grateful to Miles for asking. Looking around, he gauged the position of the sun, the backdrop of Sanibel and the coast, and the colors of the sky and water.

"I think this is perfect," he said.

"Really?" Sophia made a face. "Let's go out further. I like when the boat goes fast."

"I like it right here," Miles said, lowering the throttle to quiet the engine.

For a moment, the boat bobbed in its own wake and Noah took a deep, calming breath.

Now? Should he just stand up and say it? Should he wait? Sweat prickled his neck and he wiped a clammy hand on the leather next to him.

"Dad, have you talked to Mom lately?" Sophia asked, her question cutting through the peace of the moment with an edgy demand in her voice.

Really? Now, Sophia? She was going to start her lame "get DJ back with his ex" campaign now?

He glanced at his mother, curious to see if she knew anything about that project, and he couldn't help but notice there seemed to be an invisible barrier between DJ and Claire. The family outing idea hadn't really brought them closer. If anything, they seemed more distant.

Then DJ leaned a little closer to Claire, instantly making Noah feel better.

"Look at that, Claire," he said softly, pointing to the horizon. "That's the edge of the world."

Sophia snorted. "Uh, if you're a flat-earther, Dad."

To his credit, he ignored the comment, his gaze split between the view and Claire. "Don't you just want to go there?" he whispered. "Wherever it leads?"

Noah frowned, not sure what that meant, but his mother actually sighed uncomfortably. "Honestly, it's pretty to look at, but I'm fine here."

DJ searched her face, as if she'd said something different or deeper.

"I respect being fine here," he said. "But how can you not have some part of you that wants to...go?"

"Because I don't want to go, DJ. I don't want to." Claire seemed to grind out the words with low-key anger behind them.

He must have heard it, too, because Noah's father flinched at the statement. "Your mind is made up, Claire?"

Wait a second. What was he talking about? What were *they* talking about?

Claire's eyes shuttered. "Not now, DJ."

"Why not now?" DJ demanded. "What's better than now? Now is all we have, Claire!"

Noah sat up straight, but Sophia leaned forward.

"Does someone want to fill the rest of us in?" she demanded.

"No," Claire said. "It's nothing."

"Not nothing," DJ fired back, heat in his dark gaze. "How can you say that, Claire? How can something that's everything to me be nothing to you?"

"Maybe she doesn't really care about you," Sophia chimed in, ignoring the looks that everyone gave her. "Hey, whatever. I'm serious, Dad."

"So am I, Claire," he said, his tone rich with meaning that was, sadly, meaningless to Noah.

He glanced at Katie, who seemed just as confused, but she slid over him to get next to Harper, putting a protective arm around her daughter as if she expected a physical fight to break out.

Really? Now? Moments before he was going to propose?

Claire understood. Her expression was sheer misery as she shot him an apologetic look.

"Claire?" DJ pressed. "You didn't answer my question. How can my everything be your nothing?"

"What are you talking about, DJ?" Noah finally asked.

"Does it matter?" Sophia popped to her feet. "Clearly these two have nothing in common, and it's about time we talked openly about it."

"Sophia." Noah and Claire chided her in perfect unison.

"We need to talk!" Sophia insisted. "Isn't that what these stupid outings are all about?"

Harper looked up, eyes wide. "We don't say 'stupid,'" she whispered.

"Come on," Katie stood with her. "Let's go below and

play cards. Let everyone talk and have a grown-up discussion."

"They're having a *fight*," Harper announced in her uber-serious way that stated the obvious. Normally, it was precious and funny, but nothing was funny about this. Nothing.

"Good call," Miles muttered from the bow as he hauled the large metal anchor out of its case and lowered it to the water.

"Just come with me, Harper." Katie shot Noah a look with nothing but abject confusion in her eyes, but he just gave her a secret nod, thanking her for taking Harper away from this.

Except *this* was supposed to be his marriage proposal.

Frustration crawled through him, and it took one look to know Claire felt the same way.

"Claire, I don't want to bury this anymore," DJ said. "Let's talk."

"Not now, DJ. Not tonight," she pleaded with him. "This was supposed to be special."

"It would be a hell of a lot more special if I could announce the biggest news of my life," DJ's voice rang out so loud Tinkerbell barked and put her ears back.

"What is that?" Sophia demanded.

"DJ." Claire put a hand on his arm, her expression pained. "Not tonight. Please, *please*."

Noah couldn't agree more, but he watched in shocked silence, somehow sensing deep down that his knee wasn't going to hit the deck and that ring wasn't coming out of his pocket tonight.

"Now is all we have, as you know," DJ said, standing up like he was Socrates making a speech.

Really?

"Dad, out with it already," Sophia insisted. "What are you talking about?"

He put his hands on his hips, bracing his feet wide, looking from one to the other until his gaze landed on Claire. "I've made my decision," he said. "Have you made yours?"

"DJ, this night wasn't supposed to be about you," she said softly. "Can we please just—"

"No!" Sophia demanded. "I want to know what's going on. Do you know, Noah?"

"I have no idea, but I'm with Claire. I'd really rather—"

"Well, I'd rather say my piece." DJ took a deep breath, then blew it out. "I'm taking the position as the face of Cornicione, a pizza oven maker, and for the next two years, I will be traveling every inch of the globe to do pop-up pizza events in exotic and faraway places."

Noah stared at him, blinking. He was leaving? For two years?

"Daddy!" Sophia wailed. "You can't be serious!"

"And I've asked Claire to go with me. And you, Noah—"

"I thought you didn't know about this!" Sophia flung the words at him.

"I don't. I...don't know what you're talking about, DJ. No one ever asked me to do anything."

"Well, I'm asking you now. You mother won't go.

She'd rather stay here and *be a lawyer*." He rolled his eyes, making his thoughts about her chosen career painfully clear. "She'd rather write briefs and torts than come with me and see beautiful places and meet wonderful people. But would you go, Noah?"

Would he go... "Where?"

"Everywhere! Anywhere! Positano and Paris! Mexico City and Morocco! New Zealand and Santorini and Sydney and Spain! I'm going, and I want someone from my *family* to go with me!"

He wanted Noah to go on that trip and...leave Katie? And Harper? And the life he'd built here? To go make pizza for strangers?

"I'll go!" Sophia practically jumped, her body making the boat rock. "Maybe Mom will go, too. You want a family, Dad? You have one, remember?"

"You're going back to California, Sophia, and I don't want your mother on this trip."

"What?" The single syllable seemed to bounce over the water and make Tinkerbell sit up like she needed to protect someone. "What is wrong with you? Why are you doing this? I want to go! Forget Mom, but I am not going home without you!"

"Whoa, whoa, *whoa*." Miles walked right into the fray, stern face on, hands raised. "This is your Captain speaking with an order: calm down, lower your voices, and stop fighting this minute."

Sophia choked. "Calm down? When my dad is going to abandon me again? How many times, Dad? How many times can you just walk away?"

Claire let out a moan, and Noah immediately went to her. "'Sokay, Mom," he said softly, sensing her distress.

"It's not okay, Noah," she ground out, her gaze narrowed at DJ. "This isn't fair to you. To any of us."

"Life isn't always fair!" DJ bellowed.

"Daddy!" Sophia cried. "You can't leave again! You can't. I'm going—"

"Stop." Miles put a hand on her shoulder as if he could still her. "I'm going to get us underway and back home, and you can take up your family feud on solid ground. I don't like this."

"*You* don't like it?" Sophia demanded, shaking him off. "I am constantly being abandoned! Left behind and ignored." She spun around and pointed a finger at her father. "By you!"

"Sophia, you need to settle down," DJ insisted, finally looking chagrined by the whole scene.

"No, I will not settle down. I came here to bring you home, Dad. Mom's free from that horrible man and I know she'd take you back! Please come home!"

DJ's eyes widened, looking horrified, and, still under Noah's protective arm, Claire sat up.

"You came here to bring him home?" she asked on a jagged whisper.

"I wasn't going to give up without a fight," she shot back.

"Sophia, sit down." DJ tried to guide her to the leather seat, but she jumped up and down like a toddler having a tantrum.

"Stop it!" Miles ordered from the bow, holding the

heavy anchor he'd just pulled from the water, making Tink bark again at her master who no doubt never raised his voice.

"I don't want to stop it!"

He gingerly placed the anchor on the deck instead of storing it, visibly fighting for control. He straightened and walked to her.

"You will stop it, or you will go below and stay locked in there until we are at the dock."

She curled her lip. "You can shut up, because my dad would never let me be locked in anywhere."

"Don't tempt me," DJ scoffed.

Her eyes flashed with fire and fury, so apoplectic words couldn't come out.

Claire leaned into Noah with a groan. "I'm so sorry, honey," she murmured. "I know this wasn't what you wanted tonight."

"No, it wasn't."

"What about what I want?" Sophia cried, clearly not so upset she couldn't hear the comments from the peanut gallery.

Noah stood slowly. "Will you please give it a rest and think about someone else for a change?"

"Sure! Sure I will. You want me to give it a rest? How about a permanent rest? How about I just be done with it all so you can go on about your lives and off to...to... Morocco or whatever."

"Soph—"

She didn't listen but launched herself toward the bow, moving with remarkable grace and purpose, fast enough that no one could react and yet, somehow, it still all unfolded in slow motion.

At the railing, she leaped into the air, twisted her body in a spin, and threw herself into the water with a noisy splash.

"Sophia!" DJ yelled, running after her, but Noah was faster, throwing himself toward the bow with one thought: *she can't swim.* Just as he sucked in a breath to jump in, a strong hand clamped onto his arm.

"The ring," Miles muttered before flinging himself in front of Noah and diving straight in toward the bubbles in the water.

Tinkerbell started to follow with a stream of desperate barks, but Noah grabbed her just in time to keep her from jumping into the chaos.

Claire joined them, clutching Noah frantically as they watched.

Miles managed to get hold of Sophia, but she pushed him off. What was wrong with that girl? She flailed and flung, barely gasping for a breath, then sinking below the dark surface again. Miles came up, sucked in air, then dove down again.

"Should you go in?" Claire asked.

"I will," DJ said.

But just then, Sophia popped up, nothing but hair and an open mouth, her hands grabbing at the air in desperation.

"Soph!" DJ fell to the deck to reach down to her, but she didn't see him, panicking and screaming for help.

Miles popped up next to her, getting a grip, just as

her hand curled around the anchor line, a huge loop of rope hanging near the water.

She got hold and pulled so hard and so fast that the anchor tumbled off the deck while Noah dove for the rope, but he wasn't fast enough.

The anchor slammed into the water, inches from a screaming Sophia, disappearing right where Noah could have sworn Miles was. Cursing, he managed to snag the line, praying it hadn't hit Miles, yanking the beast out of the water.

"Help me!" Sophia demanded.

"Hang on." Noah pulled and pulled to get the anchor out of their way, knowing it was the most dangerous thing on the whole boat. He managed to get it up and onto the deck, just as Sophia got hold of DJ's hand and he pulled her up.

Suddenly, Claire let out a harrowing scream that made every hair on Noah's body stand on end.

"Blood! There's blood! There's blood in the water!" she hollered. *"Where is he?"*

Noah dove head first into the water, not taking one second to think about anything—not the engagement ring, not his life, not anything—except Miles.

Chapter Nineteen

Eliza

She'd lost all concept of time, so Eliza had no idea if it was morning, noon, or night when the nurse let Claire into the tiny windowless room where Miles clung to life in a medically induced coma.

"Hey," Claire whispered, quietly crouching next to Eliza's chair. "How about you take a break? Eat something or get some sleep? You've been in here all night and half the day."

Had she? It didn't matter. She wasn't leaving the man who lay utterly still, his head wrapped in bandages, his body wired to IVs and monitors, a ventilator tube down his throat, his chest rising and falling with breaths he wasn't even taking on his own.

"I can't leave him," Eliza rasped. "I...can't."

"Oh, baby." Claire put her arm around Eliza. "I'm so sorry. We all are."

"I love him," she whispered, her voice actually hurting her throat, having been ripped by sobbing tears for so long. "I can't lose him, Claire. I love him."

"I know, baby. I know." Claire rubbed her back. "You've been here a long time, though. And they won't let me stay for more than a minute, which is all I need to get you out for a break. I think you should eat. Get some air. Walk around. Have you even gone to the bathroom?"

All Eliza could do was lift a shoulder.

"Livvie's outside, and Teddy," Claire whispered. "Deeley's on the way to the airport to get Janie and her husband."

"Oh. *Oh.*" She blinked, vaguely remembering asking someone to contact Miles's daughter. "And his son?"

"Pulling some military strings to be here in a few days," Claire said.

"Okay." Eliza ran her hand through her hair, trying to think clearly. "And everyone else is...here?"

"Well, this is a different kind of waiting room than when my mom had her surgery." Claire glanced around the small ICU room. "So only a few of us can be here. Everyone else is at Shellseeker Beach, holding down the fort. Camille and Buck are on their way back."

"I'm so grateful Buck called the hospital and got me in here," Eliza said.

"My new stepfather, throwing his multimillionaire weight around again."

Eliza almost smiled at that. Almost. But then another wave of nausea rolled through her. Or maybe that was hunger. "I could eat...maybe. But I don't want to miss a doctor."

"There's nothing to do until they make sure his brain doesn't swell. If that doesn't happen, they'll bring him out of the coma and..."

Eliza closed her eyes, remembering what the doctor

told her. "No one has any idea how he's going to be after that anchor hit him in the side of his head. He could be..."

"Anywhere from unresponsive to just about normal."

The doctor's words echoed constantly in her head.

"He'll be fine," Claire insisted. "Thank God that thing didn't break his skull."

Eliza shuddered, knowing no one could have survived that. But even this was catastrophic.

Claire rubbed her back with warmth and reassurance. "With this accident, he'll be a little slower, a little scarred, but he's going to be fine."

They didn't actually know that, though. There was a lot of leeway in the word "fine."

"Or he could need twenty-four-hour care for the rest of his life," Eliza added, groaning at the thought. "He could have no motor skills, a severe loss of memory, or even no ability to speak, eat, or...live." Her voice cracked. "We won't know until he comes out of this coma."

"Eliza." Claire added some pressure to her touch. "He's going to be *fine*. We will not stop thinking that. But you won't be if you don't get some air and food. Please?"

"Will they let me back in?"

Claire gave her a look. "If not, we will invoke the name of Abner Underwood and all doors will open. Come on. Please?"

Eliza let Claire pull her up out of the seat. "What if he wakes up while I'm gone?"

"He can't," Claire said gently, trying to guide her away. "They have to bring him out of the coma."

But Eliza stayed close to the hospital bed, looking at

Miles, his eyes closed, his skin sallow, his head wrapped in a thick bandage. She ran her hand over the blue hospital gown that covered his arm.

"I'll be back soon, dear Miles," she whispered. "I promise. I won't leave you, honey. I won't. Not ever."

Tears welled as she let Claire lead her out, down a hall she didn't even remember entering, through double doors to a very undersized family room where Olivia and Teddy practically leaped up from their huddle when she walked through the door.

"Mom!" Olivia folded her in an embrace, rocking her a little, squeezing a lot. Teddy joined them, wrapping the two of them in her loving arms.

"I'm fine, really," she assured them.

"I'm going to disagree," Teddy said, patting her back.

"I'm sure my aura is dark and sad." Eliza gave her a smile, only half joking. "I wish you could go in there and feel his. Maybe it could tell us something."

"I don't have to," she said. "He knows you're there, and that's all that matters."

"Do you think?" Eliza asked hopefully. "I do so wish he knew I was holding his hand, talking to him, praying for him."

"He knows," Teddy said with the utmost confidence. "I've heard many coma patients can hear."

As much as Eliza wanted to believe Teddy was right, she knew that silent, still, sleeping man wasn't aware of anything.

"Come on," Olivia urged her. "There's a coffee shop

with outdoor seating. Katie and Noah are there, waiting for you."

"Is Noah okay?" she asked as they walked. The last she'd seen him, when the Coast Guard was wheeling Miles into the hospital where she met them, the young man had been a wreck. His clothes were still soaked, his tears still fresh, some blood on his hands from the efforts to help Miles once they got him back in the boat.

Next to her, she felt Claire stiffen.

"Is he?" Eliza demanded.

"Let's just say it wasn't the best day of his life, and that's exactly what he—and I—headed out on that boat hoping to have."

They were right about one thing—she needed air. Almost immediately after stepping into the sunshine, Eliza's head cleared, enough that she could ask questions about everyone else involved.

"How is Sophia?" Eliza asked, knowing the terrible accident had happened after the impulsive teenager had apparently decided to jump in the water and needed to be saved.

"Traumatized," Claire said. "DJ's stayed with her from the minute it happened. His ex wants to fly out here and get her."

"And he's leaving on his big trip?" Eliza asked, bits and pieces of "normal life" falling into place.

"I don't know, or care."

Eliza glanced at her sister, not sure she'd ever heard her use that dismissive a tone. "Oh, Claire."

"I don't," she said. "And this isn't about me or Sophia

or DJ. This is about Miles, a dear friend and the man my sister loves." Her voice wavered with pain and frustration. "I couldn't feel worse about any role I've played in this."

"You haven't played a role."

Claire slowed her step. "You're not mad at me, Eliza? For taking my family on that boat? Because if we hadn't..."

"Stop!" Eliza put both arms around Claire and pulled her into a surprisingly strong hug, considering she hadn't eaten or slept for so many hours. "I love you. You had nothing to do with this accident, and if it weren't for your son, Miles could have died."

Claire let out a whimper as they hugged.

"Come on," Olivia gently prodded them down the street. "There's Noah, and Katie. Let's hug it out over coffee and a sandwich."

They did, giving each other long, emotional, teary hugs while Olivia brought them all coffee and food, and tea for Teddy. They gathered around a table under an umbrella, mostly quiet, but connected in their grief and regrets and worry.

"How's Harper?" Eliza finally asked, not able to even take a bite. "This must have been just awful for her."

"Thank you for thinking of her," Katie replied. "It was tough. I managed to keep her below deck, but she caught sight of blood. The Coast Guard was wonderful with her. She's staying with my sister, who's taking great care of her."

Eliza nodded. "Good, that's good. And..." She looked around. "Where's Dane?"

"He's helping at Shellseeker Cottages," Olivia said.

"I had to be here," Teddy said. "And we had a whole bunch of turnover and new check-ins."

"Roz is handling housekeeping and helping, too," Katie added.

Again, Eliza nodded, her brain so foggy and broken, she couldn't even worry about the resort. "And Deeley's getting Janie," she said, sounding a little like a zombie. Then she sat up. "Oh my gosh, where is Tinkerbell?"

"With Harper and Jadyn," Katie said. "Tinkerbell doesn't want to leave Harper's side, and that's actually been a blessing."

Eliza sighed in relief. "Thank you. I completely forgot about her."

Olivia put her hand on Eliza's arm. "We got this, Mom. There's a village, remember?"

"Thank God for that," she said on a ragged voice. "And while anyone is talking to God, please have Him save Miles." Tears threatened again as her heart pinched with fear and worry. "He's too young and amazing and loved and..."

With the tears came more hugs and words of love and support, so much that it almost overwhelmed her. After a few minutes, Eliza ate a little, and some questions rose in her mind.

"I still don't quite understand what happened on the boat," Eliza said, putting down her sandwich. "I know Sophia pulled the anchor, but Miles always stores that.

He'd *never* leave the anchor loose on the bow. He's so particular about that anchor."

Noah and Claire, the only two eyewitnesses to the event, exchanged a look.

"There was, uh, some drama unfolding," Claire said.

"Be real, Mom. Sophia went off the rails." Noah rolled his eyes. "The whole thing was a huge play for attention and, well, she got it. And I'm furious."

Eliza could feel Claire's discomfort as she shifted in her seat. "He's not wrong," she said softly. "Basically, Sophia had a temper tantrum and..."

"Decided to jump in the water?" Eliza finished when Claire didn't.

"She can't swim," Noah said stiffly. "She was threatening to kill herself."

"What?" Eliza drew back in shock. "Why?"

"Because she was trying to do what she does best," Noah grumbled. "Get her way by being a spoiled brat. And her father darn near tried to help."

"What are you saying?" Eliza asked. "Did he push her or something?"

"No, no," Claire said quickly. "But..."

Again, looks were shared and words weren't spoken.

"Annnnd...what aren't you telling me?" Eliza demanded.

No one spoke for a minute, then Claire leaned in and put her hand on Eliza's. "DJ didn't want to call the Coast Guard. He didn't want anyone to know that Sophia had jumped in the water and pulled the anchor off the deck. He thought we could get him home and to a hospital—"

"He wanted to protect her over Miles?" she nearly choked on the question.

Claire's eyes shuttered. "It doesn't matter. He lost that battle." She shifted her attention to her son. "And Noah won."

"Might have cost me a relationship with my father," he said glumly. "But I honestly don't care. Miles is more of a father to me anyway."

"Oh." Eliza fell back in her chair, letting this sink in.

"But we did contact the Coast Guard immediately," Claire said. "Miles was airlifted, along with Noah—"

"I wasn't about to leave him."

"—and they got the boat back to his house since none of us could possibly handle that," Claire finished, her expression one of pure anguish. "Eliza, I'm so sorry. I feel wretched."

"You don't have to, but I'm sure..." She sighed. "I'm sure this broke a relationship or two."

"Those relationships were already cracked," Claire said.

"Have DJ and Sophia come to the hospital?" Eliza asked.

"He's stayed home with Sophia," Claire said glumly. "She wants to go back to California and he's hashing it out with her mother, who might come to get her. Or he might take her. I honestly don't know since I've hardly spoken to him."

"What a tragedy," Eliza murmured. "I can't believe it all fell on Miles, who only wants to help people." She groaned a little, slipping back to their last conversation, a brief one on the phone when they planned to have dinner. "We were going to talk and...and..." She sat up and blinked as something else Miles said popped into her head. "Oh my gosh, did Asia sign the papers from Zee's father?"

"She might have," Claire said. "I gave her legal clearance before we even went out on the boat. There were some minor edits recommended by a family law attorney. Why? What is it, Eliza?"

Eliza pressed her temple, trying to remember that conversation. "Before he went on the boat, Miles said he got an email from the investigator in the U.K. that was... interesting? Intriguing? I don't recall, but it was enough that he wanted to call the man even though it was late."

"He had to leave a message," Noah said. "He mentioned that call when we were getting the boat ready."

"Maybe Dane and Asia could call the investigator, in case it's something she should know before she signs." Eliza gave a questioning look. "Did he lose his phone?"

"If it was in his pocket, it's probably gone," Noah said.

"Sometimes he tucks it into the chart holder at the helm," Eliza said.

"I can go look," Olivia said, standing up to go. "Do you have a key to his place, Mom?"

"Yes, yes, in my bag. Do I have my bag?"

Teddy smiled and lifted it. "It's right here. I grabbed it when we flew out the door to the hospital last evening."

Eliza barely remembered the blurry moments, only a

frantic phone call from Claire and the wild ride to the hospital with Teddy, determined to get there when Miles did.

As she clipped Miles's house key to her own, Olivia said, "I'll call Asia on the way over there and see if Miles called her before they went out on the boat. I'll tell her not to sign anything, then look for the phone."

"What if it's gone?" Eliza asked.

"Then maybe Dane can poke around Miles's office for the guy's name and number." Olivia bent over and kissed Eliza's head. "I know you want to go back with Miles, Mom. We got this. Don't worry."

Eliza looked up at her, then at the other beloved faces around her, a flutter of hope and optimism in her heart. "Amazing how we come together, isn't it?"

"That's what families do," Teddy said, taking her hand and giving it a squeeze. "Now you get back up there and tell Miles we love him and can't wait for him to be our Captain again."

She felt her eyes close, Teddy's optimism feeling terribly hollow right then.

But no matter how together this family was, how much positivity and support and care they provided, no one could assure her that Miles would wake up on the right side of the spectrum between *unresponsive* and *just about normal*.

Still, she loved them all, and was so grateful to be surrounded by this amazing found family. She knew she'd need them all in the days to come.

Chapter Twenty

Asia

"Now?" Asia pressed her hand to her chest at the tone in Spencer's voice, the unexpected call yanking her from her day of work, ignoring the ding of another text as she tried to process what he was saying.

"I have to leave for London tonight. I'm not going back without the paperwork signed."

There it was. There was that dreadful, demanding tone she used to hate. The one that put her on edge and had so much control over her.

But he didn't control her anymore.

"There's no comfort in control, Asia."

Nancy's voice played in her head as she took a breath and lined up her arguments. "You were quite clear that I had a few more days, Spencer."

"And I was quite clear that we're running out of time, Asia."

"You're running out of time, not me," she shot back.

"Then the deal's off the table. I'll find another..." His voice trailed off. "Another way to meet my obligations," he finished.

She squeezed her eyes shut, wishing she didn't want a million dollars from him, but...

She looked at wee, sweet Zee snoozing in his playpen. That much money was a huge security blanket for her baby. Forever protection that he needed and she deserved.

"So?" he prodded. "Today?"

Today? With Miles in the hospital, it felt like their whole world had come to a screeching halt. Dane was distracted and worried about his mother, helping her at the resort, and even her parents were in crisis mode when they weren't on their knees in prayer for their friend.

"Look, we've had a tragic boating incident and—"

"I honestly don't care if the *Titanic* sank, Asia. I'm out of time, and I've been more than fair. You've had a week to consider the offer, time to run the contract by lawyers, and there's not a single stipulation that isn't in your favor. I'm giving you a million bucks, for crying out loud. What more do you want, Asia? It's for your child."

The last two words punched.

"He's your child, too," she said, leaning over the side of the playpen where Zee slept. "Not that you'd know it by the way you *don't* look at him."

A long silence, followed by a sigh, was his only response. She grimaced, waiting for what would come next.

"And why do you think that is?" he asked in a quiet voice.

"Because...you don't care?"

"Maybe it's because I *do*," he volleyed back. "That's my son in your arms. My son! Do you think I might not look at him because if I see myself in his face, I might not ever be able to let him go?"

The words pushed her onto the bed, nearly making her whimper.

"I do care about him, very much," Spencer added. "Why do you think I've done this? I'm giving you one million dollars to use to take care of him. What else do you want? For me to ask to hold him? Fall in love with him? Imagine...what it could have been like if...if..."

"If you hadn't met and married another woman," she finished for him.

"Ahh, now I get it. Is that what you want, Asia? An apology? For me to grovel and beg your forgiveness and tell you what a mistake I made?"

She didn't answer, mostly because her heart was pounding and she didn't trust her voice. Anyway, the answer would be, "No," because she was long, long past wanting him to plead for her forgiveness.

"Fine. I'm sorry!" he growled. "Does that make you feel better? I'm very, very sorry, so please accept my apology and my million dollars and let me pick up the pieces of my life."

She made a disgusted face, a little sickened by his over-the-top tone and attitude.

"Meet me at the Lighthouse Café again," he said, not waiting for her to answer. "In the parking lot behind the ice cream store next to it."

"Why there?"

"Because I want to get in and out as fast as possible

and I have a plane to London to catch. No coffee, no chitchat. An hour, Asia. Bring the paperwork signed, and the deal will be done."

She swallowed, wishing she didn't doubt him so much. "I'm not sure if I should—"

"And bring our baby," he added. "I'd like to, um, yeah. Just for a moment, I guess, I'd like to hold him."

With that, he hung up and she dropped onto the closest chair, trembling.

A few minutes later, she found Dane on the Shellseeker property and relayed the whole conversation —all but the last sentence—to ask him to come with her.

"I know you're busy filling in for your mom and Teddy—"

"You're not going alone, Asia," he said. "That's out of the question."

"I can, but...I'd like you there."

"Of course." His frown deepened. "You're sure? You signed the paper?"

"I did, but it's meaningless until I give it to him."

"Can't you scan it and email?" he asked. "Why the in-person meeting?"

She couldn't really answer that, except for his final request to bring the baby. "I don't know, but maybe it's a legality or something." She swayed as she stroked Zee's head in the carrier wrap around her neck and stomach. "Can we leave now?"

"Yes, but didn't you have Miles hire that Scotland Yard guy?"

She shrugged. "I don't think we can wait for Miles, and Claire's lawyer friend cleared the contract. We may not get the answers we need, and he's threatening to pull the deal."

"I'm confused," Dane said. "You were the one who was so uncertain. What changed your mind?"

"I don't know," she said on a sigh. "I guess Miles."

He lifted a brow. "Miles?"

"Life's short."

"He's still alive, Aje."

"I know, but in a blink of an eye, everything changed. What if something like that happened to me? Who would take care of Zee? Every time I think of it, I worry. I don't even have life insurance, Dane."

"You can buy that." He put his hands on her shoulders. "I don't want you to make a mistake, is all."

"He doesn't have my hands tied, and what's the worst that could happen? He never gives me the money? I have the Termination signed and the lawyer has started the legal process to back it up. But if he does give me the money..." She stroked Zee's head. "This little guy will have security and I'll have peace of mind."

Dane sighed and nodded. "Okay, there aren't any more check-ins today and Deeley closed the cabana to go to the airport and get Miles's daughter. Let's go."

"Thank you," she said, so grateful he was the most dependable man she knew.

THEY PULLED into the parking lot of the Lighthouse Café a few minutes before the deadline Spencer had given her. Dane parked behind the ice cream shop, looking around at the few cars in the lot.

"Here's something you don't see much around here—a nearly deserted parking lot."

"The Lighthouse Café closes at three," she said, looking at her watch. "Which is in a few minutes. And I guess we're too early for the after-school ice cream rush."

"You think he planned it this way? So no one's around?"

Her heart kicked a little. "He's not evil, Dane. Made some poor decisions, strung me along and cheated on me, but I don't think he wishes me any ill." She hoped.

A white Ford SUV pulled in and cruised toward the back of the lot.

"That could be him," Dane said. "It's likely a rental."

"How can you tell?"

"That government contract work I did at Ambrosia was for the Department of Transportation, and we did this whole artificial intelligence program on rental cars, based on what people want most. Ford Edge is the top ten most common rental car, white is the number one color, and, in Florida, a rental car registration expires in June, so..." His voice trailed off as Spencer climbed out of the car. "Never mind, it's him."

She swallowed and gathered the envelope. "Um...he wanted to see Zee."

Dane whipped around to look at her. "What?"

"He asked me if I could bring him so he could..." She blew out a breath. "I can't deny the man a chance to hold his child for one minute."

Dane's lip curled. "He gave up that right when he married another woman."

"And he's officially giving up that right when he takes my signed papers. Please, I want to just end it on an amicable note."

"Of course. Do you want me to come with you?"

She squinted into the afternoon sun to see Spencer lean against the small SUV, hands in his pockets, calm as could be. Much calmer than she felt.

"No. I'll just walk over there with the baby and the papers. You stay here."

She climbed out and opened the back door, easing Zee out of his car seat, the movement waking him.

"Hey, little baby man," she cooed. "I'm sorry to wake you, bud. Just one minute, okay?"

He gurgled and smiled and fluttered his little lashes. Oh, God. Would Spencer tear up the agreement when he got a good look at this adorable baby? What was in his heart?

Guess she was about to find out.

She nestled Zee against her and shut the back door with her hip, then headed across the parking lot. As soon as he saw her, Spencer straightened and jutted his chin in greeting, walking toward her.

He met her halfway, in the middle of the parking lot, a wistful look on his face.

"Hey," he said as they reached each other. "Did you sign?"

"Yes, I did."

"Good, good. The minute I have that, I'll scan it to the bank and they'll change the account into your name. You'll get an email with access information, and you can go right in and change the password."

"Okay." She shifted Zee in her arms, handing the envelope to him. "And, uh, this is Zane." She turned the baby in her arms, and he obliged by looking directly at Spencer and sliding into a shy smile.

For a moment, time stood still while Spencer stared at Zee, silent and intent. Her heart fell with each passing second, wanting something from him—some reaction, some emotion, some connection.

"You can hold him if you want," she said.

Spencer took a deep breath, held it, then exhaled. "No, I shouldn't." He held up the envelope. "This is...the only thing I can give him as his father."

"Well, okay. Thanks, Spencer. You didn't have to do that, and I appreciate it. I won't...I won't bother you. Or your wife. I promise."

He gave the closest thing to a genuine smile she could remember, and reached out one hand to touch Zee's head. "See ya, kiddo," he whispered, then turned and headed back to the car.

She stood for a moment, awash in how anticlimactic the exchange had been.

Zee gave a soft shriek and a giggle, reaching for Asia's braids.

"That's right, you laugh, little millionaire. Come on, let's go back to Dane."

She rushed back and opened the front door, slipping into the passenger seat with the baby still tight in her arms. Dane was staring straight ahead, then finally turned.

"Not going to lie, Aje," he said. "I was so scared he was going to take that baby and run."

"I was scared, too, but..." She shrugged. "I guess there isn't a catch. He really wanted to do the right thing for Zee. And I'm grateful he's not so horrible after all."

They sat for a moment, then Spencer's SUV rumbled by, pulling out of the lot and disappearing onto Periwinkle.

"And he's gone," she said. She leaned in, a hand on Zee's head. "Thanks for coming with me, Dane."

He met her halfway with a kiss. "Anytime. Just don't scare me like that again. If anything ever happened to this kid...or you..."

A soft ding from her phone alerted her to an email. "That's either Toni wondering why I disappeared from my desk or..." She pulled out the phone and tapped the screen. "Oh! A notification from a bank in the Cayman Islands that I have full access to my account and that I can go in and change the password anytime."

"Really?"

She tapped a few more buttons and got to the account, scrolling toward the balance.

$1,000,000.00

"Wow." She angled the phone so he could see it. "He wasn't lying."

They both stared at the number and laughed a little, then kissed, giddier with each passing moment. She got out and put Zee in the baby seat, and then climbed back in the front.

"I don't want to go to work," she whispered, looking at the bank account again.

"Why would you? You're a millionaire, Asia Turner."

"Well, my son is. I won't touch that money. But today, no. I'm so relieved and so happy this is over, I just want to go home and let all the adrenaline fade away. Oh, and change this password."

Just then, she realized that she'd missed a few texts, all from Olivia. "Whoa, your sister has news. Or at least wants to tell me something. Maybe it's about Miles."

Dane tapped his pocket and grunted. "Shoot. I left my phone at Shellseeker Cottages," he said. "Call her back?"

"Okay, I will, but..." She dropped her head back. "He's gone. Can we just go home to the townhouse, put Zee in his own bed, and relax now that this is over? We'll call Livvie from there."

"Absolutely, Aje. Whatever you want."

As they drove, she tapped her phone to go back to that bank account and stare at the number again. "A million dollars...all in my name," she whispered, still a little in shock. "Oh, and there's my signature. He said something about scanning it. Man, he was serious about getting this done and fast."

"Change the password?"

She nodded, tapping the menu bar. "I'm going to right now. What's a good one? Allmymoney123?"

Laughing, he rolled his eyes. "Please don't be one of those people who use utterly hackable passwords. Especially for a million bucks."

"I won't." She entered a string of numbers and letters that were a combination of a few old addresses and added Zee's due date, which was not his birthday.

"Error message. That's weird."

"And *that's* weird," Dane said.

She looked up as Dane pulled into the parking lot of Tortoise Way Townhouses, following his gaze to their unit, where two men and a woman stood right outside their door.

"Who is that?" she asked, the first tendril of concern worming through her heart.

"I have no idea." He squinted at the trio, all in business-casual clothes, looking...official.

Dane parked and flipped off his seatbelt, climbing out of the car. She opened her door a small amount, but a protective instinct made her stay in the car with Zee. Almost immediately, one of the men started walking toward them, striding with purpose and no small amount of speed.

"Can I help you?" Dane called over the roof.

The man ignored the question, his full attention on the passenger side of the car. On *her*.

Suddenly, the world felt like it was moving in slow

motion as the man stopped inches from the door she'd just opened and yanked it wider.

"Hey!" Dane barked, but no sooner was the word out than one of the other two men hustled closer, right toward Dane. He said something, but Asia couldn't hear, because the blood was thumping so hard in her head.

"Asia Turner?" the first man demanded of her, widening his stance and holding the car door, effectively trapping her. "Step out of the car, please."

"Wha...why..."

"What the hell are you doing?" Dane demanded.

Ignoring him, the first man said, "I'm a U.S. Marshal, ma'am. Step away from the car with your hands visible."

Did he say...*U.S. Marshal?*

Her whole being vibrated as she stared into the hard-eyed gaze of a man she'd never seen before. Behind him, the woman had joined them, looking just as serious and intense.

"Do what he says," she heard Dane say, enough insistence in his voice that she somehow managed to get out of the car—but that meant she was away from Zee, who'd already started crying, as if even he sensed something was very, very wrong.

"There has to be a mistake, sir." She breathed the words.

"No mistake. Will you come willingly, or do we need to handcuff you?"

She stared at him, her mind blank. "Come for what?"

"Asia Turner, you're under arrest for criminal misappropriation of international property."

What?

He kept talking but she didn't hear anything. Her brain was swimming, the world was moving, and she felt like she might throw up.

She let out a soft cry as the man and woman flanked her and ushered her away from the car.

"Take the baby," she cried to Dane. "And help me!"

Chapter Twenty-one

Dane

On another day, in another life, without having witnessed the arrest of the woman he was falling in love with, Dane might have been able to hack Miles's computer. But he wasn't thinking straight, and hadn't been since the unreal and utterly unbelievable events had unfolded several agonizing hours earlier.

Olivia had called seconds after the U.S. Marshals had taken Asia away, and her news somehow fit the events, though he didn't really understand how. Prior to his accident, Miles had received a message from his friend, who they believed was a former British police investigator, but no one knew what it was about.

Possibly *criminal misappropriation of international property?*

All roads led to Spencer Keaton, who had to be at the heart of this, and maybe stole that money he'd just "given" to Asia. Dane was determined to find him, and this Scotland Yard associate was the first stop.

Dane had met his sister at Miles's house, and while she searched the boat for his cell phone, Dane went straight to the office to start looking for the contact's name and number. Nothing was visible on paper, so he'd have to hack Miles's email, desperate to find someone or something that could exonerate Asia.

He didn't even know where they'd taken her, which made him sick. A few Google searches showed that the U.S. Marshals investigated international crimes and arrested U.S. citizens involved in them, and that their closest office was in Fort Myers, in the county courthouse. He almost went straight there, but he knew he'd hit a brick wall, so he decided to come here and get information that could get her out.

But he'd hit a *technological* brick wall, and nothing frustrated Dane more.

"Come on, genius!" Olivia poked his shoulder in frustration after she returned from the boat emptyhanded. "I thought you could hack the NSA."

"I'm an AI software programmer, Liv, not a professional hacker. But I did see Miles type in a password..."

"And?"

"And all I was able to get was the name 'Eliza'—I missed the rest."

Olivia groaned. "Try Eliza and her birthday. The day they met. How about, 'I love Eliza' or, 'Eliza and Miles 4-ever.'" She cringed. "Too stupid for words?"

"Nah. I tried them already. And her address, his address, the zip code, everything. I even did Tinkerbellandeliza, all one word."

"His two best girls."

Dane huffed out a breath. "I know the word Eliza was in that password. You're sure you can't find his phone, because that I bet I could hack."

She shook her head. "I scoured the boat and this house. My guess is it's at the bottom of the Gulf."

Of course it was. "Well, I might be able to get into the guts of his software and find a back door. Gimme some time." He stretched and cracked his knuckles the way he did before he put his fingers on a piano, which only gave him an aching pang for Asia.

Would they ever write another song? What if that bastard Keaton set her up to take the fall for something he did? That seemed like the most obvious answer to why she would get arrested minutes—mere *minutes*—after he transferred a million dollars into her name.

He had to have orchestrated this somehow so that law enforcement would pounce on her while he got off Sanibel and out of the country. Disgust and fury and a low-key urge to strangle the guy rolled through him, but he shook it off and tried to concentrate.

"I'm going to search his physical files," Olivia said, yanking a drawer. "Maybe we'll find a list of, you know, all his Scotland Yard buddies." At Dane's look, she said, "Again, too stupid for words?"

"Liv. Give yourself some credit. It's brilliant. Search. Let me concentrate."

As he attempted to get into the operating system of Miles's main computer, he heard voices outside the office. He knew Roz and George had arrived a little while ago and were no doubt huddled with Claire, who'd contacted another attorney to develop a strategy for Asia.

Teddy was here, too, taking care of Zee, and probably

others coming and going if they weren't at the hospital holding vigil over Miles.

Not for the first time, the unity and support of this family that he'd once had the audacity to call his mother's "ragtag group of friends" stunned him.

He stabbed his fingers into his hair and dragged it back, his gaze scanning the three monitors, a laptop, a desktop, and a gaming station. Did he know Miles played video games like Dane did? God, did he know the man his mother loved at all?

Once more, he pushed the emotional, non-logical, unwanted thoughts from his brain and forced himself to focus on Miles's computer security, which was next level. Normally, that would be yet another reason to like the guy, but right now, he wished Miles hadn't been quite so thorough in protecting his data.

"It's like my brain won't work."

"You're in shock. Oh! Look what I found." She waved a piece of paper. "His cell phone records from...last year. Maybe there's a U.K. number on here that would be his Scotland Yard friend."

She started perusing as Dane closed his eyes and groaned at the thought of that beautiful woman and what the U.S. Marshals might put her through.

He cleared his head and peered at lines and lines of code swimming in front of him. It was little more than the guts of Miles's operating system, nothing that would give him the information he needed. He needed a different approach.

"Maybe I could just start calling rental car companies," he said. "And see if—"

"What was that?" Olivia's head shot up. "Is your phone vibrating?"

He lifted it off the desk next to him. "No."

"I heard a phone vibrate." She popped up, looking left and right.

"What did—"

"Quiet! Let me listen. What if it's Miles's phone? What if he—" Her eyes popped and Dane sat up when he, too, heard the faintest vibration in the air.

Olivia started flipping the cushions on the sofa. "I hear it. It's in this room! But why didn't I hear it hum when I called his number twenty times during my search?"

"Maybe we're hearing a second work-only phone," Dane said, jumping up to join her in the search. "His personal phone is in the Gulf, but this one—"

"Again!" she exclaimed. "I heard it again!"

Dane nodded as they both instinctively moved toward a bookshelf that lined a wall by the door.

"It's in there somewhere," Olivia said.

"Take every book down?" Dane suggested.

"Or find the one he hid it in."

They got closer and started reading the titles, which ranged from poetry to pop culture with a lot of law, military, boating, and a ton of classics in between.

"*War and Peace? The Odyssey?*" Olivia flipped out some fat titles. "*The Guns of August?*"

"Liv, there are—"

"Listen!" She held up both hands. "That's a different vibration. That's a call, not a text!"

He heard the staccato hum, each vibration lasting longer than what they heard before. Olivia pressed her ear to the bookshelf, moving as if she could find it, going lower, lower, lower until she was on the floor at the shelf.

"That sucker is in here," she announced, whipping out book after book until she'd emptied the bottom shelf. "Look in all of those!"

He started to flip through the titles when Olivia squealed. "There's a secret drawer! Miles, you sneaky private investigator."

In a flash, she'd popped the false bottom off the shelf, and they saw a flashing iPhone along with some papers and a strong box.

Olivia dove for the phone, but the screen went black.

"Oh, so close. But..." She tapped the screen and the familiar keyboard waiting for a password lit it up. "We are back to password guessing."

As Dane pushed up, he put a hand on Olivia's shoulder. "Man, I have spent my life underestimating you, Liv. You got Dad's relentless gene. It's impressive."

She smiled up at him. "Thanks. I will have to try every imaginable password on this phone."

"You'll get locked out for a while after six failed attempts. Then every time you try, the number of attempts gets lower. Don't overdo it or we'll never get in it. So, let's call Mom."

"You think she'll know the password to his work phone?"

"Maybe it's the same as his personal phone," Dane said.

"You think she knows that?"

"She might, or she might have seen his fingers move, and that could help us."

She nodded. "And you're a genius again. I'll call her. You call those rental car companies."

Before either of them could start the next task, Roz appeared in the open doorway, her face ravaged from a day of tears. "Asia called."

"Is she okay?" Dane asked.'

"We spoke for less than fifteen seconds. She's at the U.S. Marshal's office about forty minutes away. Claire is headed back to the hospital, but she has arranged for an excellent lawyer to meet us there. Do you want to come?"

Dane was up in a flash, then froze. "I think...I can do more here."

"What can you do here?" Roz asked.

"I *have* to find that guy before he leaves the country, which he said he was going to do. If he gets out of the U.S., we may never find him. But I know what he looks like, I know what he's driving, and I know he's on the move. I *have* to find him."

Roz came around the desk to hug him. "I think you're right, Dane. The lawyer Claire found is really smart. We've got this. George and I just have to get Asia's passport first, which the lawyer thinks we should bring so they can search her ID and prove she hasn't been in England."

"Is it in the townhouse?" Dane asked. "Do you need a key?"

"She left it in George's strong box," Roz said. With a softer expression, she added, "Look, we know she's not guilty, she's never broken a law in her life, and she doesn't know the meaning of criminal misappropriation. Neither do I, to be honest."

"Well, I know someone who does," Dane said. "And I'm going to find him and...and..."

"Just find him." Roz gave him a dark look. "Don't *you* do anything illegal or dangerous."

"No promises."

She eyed him. "Okay, don't take this personally, but if you're going to go after this guy on your own, please call Deeley. He was a Navy SEAL and..."

"I wasn't," Dane said dryly, making Roz laugh.

"Precisely."

"Yeah, I already called him," Olivia added.

Just as Roz left, Miles's secret phone rang again, and Olivia and Dane pounced on it.

The name Nigel Farnsworth flashed on the screen for a split second, replaced by the password keypad, making them both groan in frustration.

"That has to be him!" Olivia exclaimed. "Nobody in the U.S. is named Nigel Farnsworth! Oh, and now Mom's calling me."

He nodded, heading straight to his phone and Facebook. Old school? Yes, but it was still one of the fastest ways to find someone. He pounded the keys and groaned.

Of course, there were 114 Nigel Farnsworths on Facebook.

He narrowed the search to London and—

"I got it!"

His head popped up at Livvie's exclamation. "The phone?"

"Mom said his password was in the shape of an E, which is his nickname for her. Look!" She held up the phone and traced the numbers like someone would draw a capital E. It opened right up. "Oh, she thinks his computer password might be ElizabethMary1437. Which our mother tearfully informed me meant, 'Elizabeth Mary, I love you forever.' So, what do you know? We weren't *that* far off."

"About the password or the fact that he really loves her?" Dane asked with a wry smile.

"No kidding, dingbat. Here." She held the phone out. "Call Nigel and get us some help. Put him on speaker."

"First, let's read his email." Dane dropped to the desk, easily found his way to Miles's accounts using the slightly cheesy but very sweet password, and found the email from NFarnsworth to Miles. With Olivia next to him, they read it together.

Miles – I have a very interesting update on the chap you have me looking into. Too delicate a matter for email.

Let's chat. NF

After reading it, Dane took Miles's phone and called the man back, holding his breath until a British-accented man answered.

"I'm so sorry," Nigel said after Dane explained the

situation. "But surely you'll understand why I simply am not able to tell you anything at all, as I shall plead client privacy."

Dane refused to accept that. "What if you call the hospital and verify that Miles is truly in a coma?" he asked. "An innocent woman was arrested ten minutes after receiving unsolicited funds from Spencer Keaton, who you are investigating for her. Would you help us then?"

A long silence stretched across the ocean, then finally he said, "Give me the name of the hospital."

"I can give you the number."

"Just the name. I'll take it from there." With that, he clicked off, leaving them utterly and achingly frustrated as they tried to get over one more brick wall.

WHILE THEY WAITED, Deeley showed up with the report that he'd taken Janie and her husband, Brody, to the hospital. Miles's status remained the same, although there was some talk of bringing him out of the coma the next day.

When Olivia left the office with Deeley to get some coffee, Dane continued working. He went straight to Miles's files on the case and found the original travel information on S. M. Keaton. No outbound flight was listed, but that wasn't exactly a real problem.

Not for Dane, who had been the lead software engineer for his former company's large client, the Department of Transportation. He knew how to find passenger manifests.

He had, in fact, created an AI program that had ultimately been used for marketing purposes, tracking frequent flyers' preferences so the airlines could anticipate their needs and advertise accordingly.

The only catch? That knowledge was never meant to be used by him or for any...nefarious reason. And this? Whoa, this was pretty darn nefarious.

But...*Asia*.

Ignoring the guilt and fear that threatened, he typed so hard the keystrokes echoed in the room while Olivia and Deeley came in and out, with his sister naggingly asking if Nigel had called back yet.

He tried Delta. Nothing. United, Lufthansa, Air Canada, British Airways. None of them had a flight for Spencer Keaton.

Then he tried Virgin Atlantic and... "Bingo, baby!"

Olivia flew in, followed by Deeley. "Nigel?"

"No, but I have S. M. Keaton's return ticket on Virgin Atlantic from Orlando to London."

Deeley drew back, scowling. "How'd you get that information?"

Dane looked up at his brother-in-law, a former Navy SEAL and straight shooter. "Not sure you want to know that."

Deeley snorted. "When does he leave?"

"In..." Dane squinted at the screen and swore softly when he checked the current time. "Three hours."

"Orlando is four hours away," Olivia said, falling on the sofa with a groan.

Dane shifted in his seat, the ideas playing at the edge of his mind.

"Maybe his flight will be delayed?" Olivia said hopefully.

Dane met her gaze. "Yeah, uh...no maybe about it."

"And what does that mean?" Deeley asked. "Or don't I want to know that either?"

"Probably not," Dane admitted. "But I'll tell you. I can, um, actually delay that flight without a lot of effort."

They both stared at him. "That *can't* be legal," Olivia ground out.

The phone rang, saving him from answering.

"Sorry to doubt you," Nigel said in his thick English accent without preamble. "And even more sorry about Miles. And now I'll tell you what I wanted to tell him."

"I'm with my sister and brother-in-law, on speaker. Tell us all, please."

"All right, then. The Honorable Charlotte Simmons-Keaton, daughter of Dalton Simmons, Baron of Whittington, died in a motor accident three weeks ago."

Olivia gasped, slapping a hand over her mouth.

"She was under the influence and alone in the car, and for that reason, the family has managed to keep it out of the press. Lady Simmons-Keaton's husband, your chap Spencer Keaton, was so deep in mourning that he left the country. Currently, his whereabouts are unaccounted for."

"He's somewhere between Sanibel Island and Orlando," Dane said.

"Ah, well, that might be good for the authorities to know, since, in the past few minutes, I was in touch with my contact and have learned that Keaton is now under suspicion in his wife's accident. I can't say more than that, nor do I even know more than that."

All the color drained from Olivia's face as she stared at Dane.

"So they'd detain him if he tried to get on a plane?" Dane asked.

The other man chuckled. "If a lot of people are on top of their game, which I can tell you isn't always the case in these situations. More likely he could be apprehended and questioned when he lands in London. As I said, she was alone in the car and driving under the influence. Clearly, the accident was her own fault. However, there's more..."

Dane waited, hoping that whatever "more" he had, it could help Asia.

"I don't know for certain, and this is only speculation," Nigel said, "but there are whispers that a good bit of the young lady's trust fund has gone missing."

"How would anyone know that?" Dane asked.

"The baron is a very powerful man with deep connections. I think it is reasonable that his daughter's trust was digitally marked so that the baron would be alerted in the case funds were moved without his permission or knowledge."

"Which," Dane said, "would be criminal misappropriation."

"Indeed," the Brit said.

"But if Spencer took the money, why put it in his ex-girlfriend's name?"

"He likely had no idea the money was digitally marked and thought he was stashing it somewhere safe and not connected to him. My guess is that Ms. Turner could never have accessed it despite the fact that it was in her name."

Dane suddenly recalled Asia's words right before they saw the marshals.

Error message. That's weird.

"So, they think he killed his wife so he could steal her money?" Dane asked.

"At the moment," Nigel said slowly, "there is no evidence of the former, just a hint of suspicion, no doubt generated by the departed woman's father. As far as the money? It went directly from Charlotte's account to Ms. Turner's account, signed and accepted by her. Until a provable connection is made between Mr. Keaton and the disappearance of the money, Ms. Turner is in a very sticky situation."

"She has the paperwork to prove he gave it to her," Dane said.

"But they'll need to talk to him, and he is..." Nigel paused. "On his way to Orlando, you say?"

"I think so," Dane said. But who knew for sure? "Anything else?"

"Nothing," Nigel replied. "Except that I wish my

friend Miles a speedy recovery, and I hope you'll keep me in the loop as this progresses."

Dane promised he would and said goodbye, looking from Olivia to Deeley.

"So, big guy," his sister said. "What are the pros and cons of you illegally delaying a Virgin Atlantic flight and giving us a chance to get to Orlando to take this murdering thief down?"

"The con is simple," he said. "Prison time if I get caught. The pro?" He slid into a slow smile. "I could save the woman I love. Honestly, Liv, it's a no-brainer."

Chapter Twenty-two

Claire

It took tragedy to quiet Sophia, but Claire was grateful for the silence after the long and deeply stressful day she'd had. The normally boisterous, disruptive teenager had stayed in her room since the accident, or talked in hushed tones to DJ.

"Hey, Mom," Noah said as he came into the kitchen. "You look wiped out. Want me to get dinner?"

"I grabbed something at Teddy's house when I dropped off Eliza so Janie could sit with Miles, but thank you."

"How's Eliza doing? How's his daughter?"

"She's a rock. Eliza is a bit of a wreck, but I hope she sleeps tonight. They did another scan late today and his brain isn't swelling. If that holds, they'll bring him out of the coma."

"And then?"

She blew out a breath as she opened the fridge and looked longingly at an open bottle of Chardonnay. "Then we see how he is. He could be perfectly normal, he could have severe memory loss, he could be..." She didn't want to say the word "unresponsive" because it just hurt too much to think about it.

Instead, she just grabbed the bottle and poured a size-able glass for herself.

Noah nodded as if he understood both the wine and the rest of her unfinished sentence.

"Where's DJ?" she asked, settling at the counter.

"No clue. I've been at Katie's and just got back a few minutes ago."

"I'm right here," DJ's voice preceded him, but a second later he came through from the bedroom hallway, his hair mussed and his eyes hooded. "I crashed. But I heard the report on Miles." He closed his eyes as if saying the name hurt him. "God willing, he'll come out of this okay."

Claire eyed him as he poured himself a large glass of water and brought it to the kitchen peninsula, leaning against the counter to look at her.

"I'm not taking the job with Cornicione," he announced, making her draw back in surprise.

"No?"

He shook his head and gulped some water. "At least not for the first leg of the European tour."

"But you can join them after that?" Claire asked.

"Maybe, we'll see. I am, um..." He wet his lips and braced both big hands on the counter. "I am taking Sophia back to California, though."

"I imagined you might," she said, unfazed by the news.

"Yeah, she wants to stay until Miles is out of the woods or..."

Or *not*, Claire thought, but just looked at him, silent.

"Are you coming back to Sanibel?" Noah asked.

For a long time—long enough for Claire to know the answer—DJ didn't say a word. He looked from one to the other, then over their shoulders as Sophia walked into the room, her hair hanging sloppily over a tank top and sleep pants.

"He's not coming back," she answered for him. "My family needs him in California."

Claire flinched as a hundred different responses threatened to come out, but she easily kept them all to herself.

DJ cleared his throat. "This family needs me, too, but—"

"Actually," Noah said, "we're good."

They all looked at him, no one more taken aback by the statement than Claire.

"What? We are. We are our own family—Mom and me, plus Katie and Harper and everyone else." Noah took a slow breath and looked at DJ. "I'm glad I got to know you," he added. "I'm glad I don't have a hole in my heart wondering who my father is, and I mean that."

"Well, you know what Paulo says," DJ replied. "'Happiness is something that multiplies when it's divided.'"

Noah rolled his eyes—the first time Claire had ever seen him react that way to a quote from their favorite author.

"Quotes don't change reality, DJ," Noah said. "The fact is, you have a deep connection to your daughters and even your ex-wife. Sophia needs you much more than I ever would, and honestly?" He put a hand on Claire's back. "This woman right here? She's all the parent I will ever need. She's strong and smart and patient and caring. She's a fantastic listener, a brilliant lawyer, and just one of the best people I've ever known."

Claire blinked again, almost sending a tear down her cheek. "Oh, Noah."

"It's true, Mom. And you deserve a good man in your life. A solid, dependable man who lives for you, not the moment he's in."

Everyone was completely silent for a few achingly long heartbeats, the only sound the hum of the fridge.

"You know what?" DJ said. "You're right, Noah. And maybe I've known that all along."

"Well, I think you're a dimwit," Sophia interjected. "Because my dad—"

Noah spun around. "Shut up and grow up, Sophia."

She glared at him, silent, then bolted from the room, her slamming door punctuating her departure.

"She needed to hear that," DJ murmured as he put his glass in the sink. "I'm going to pack."

He walked back down the hall—no slamming door, though—leaving Noah and Claire next to each other.

"Wow," Claire said, lifting her wine glass to him. "My hero."

He smiled. "I meant every word, Mom. I had a lot of time to really think since Miles's accident, and I talked to Katie a lot."

"Did you ask her?"

He shook his head. "Not in the middle of all this." He made a face. "I lost the ring when I dove in after Miles."

"Noah! You're kidding! It was in your pocket?"

He swallowed hard. "It's why Miles jumped in instead of me."

Claire stared at him, processing that. "Oh, honey. Don't feel guilty about that."

He lifted a brow. "Too late."

"But you saved him!"

He nodded glumly.

"I'm so sorry about the ring. Did you insure it?"

He made a face. "Uh, I didn't see 'jump into Gulf of Mexico with ring in pocket' on my bingo card this year."

"Honey. I'm sure everyone would help you out. Was it expensive?"

He shrugged. "Small price to pay for Miles, honestly."

She put her arms around him. "Well, I've never been more proud of anyone than I am of you. You are a truly great man, Noah Hutchins. And I had nothing to do with that. I'm just in awe of you."

"You know the feeling is mutual, Mom. Please don't leave Sanibel. Please, whatever DJ decides, please stay here and make your life here. Start your law firm, be with your sister, and stay to be a grandmother to Harper and my kids—plural, God willing. We..." He tapped his heart and then hers. "We are family forever. I love you so much, I don't even want to imagine my life without you."

The tears spilled while he spoke, and an ache that had been around for twenty-six years literally disappeared like he'd shone a bright light on the old darkness in her heart.

"I love you, too, Noah. I told you once I'd be where you are, and I meant it. I cannot wait to watch the man you are grow into a father and husband."

"Thanks."

They hugged for a long time, both of them healing more with each second.

And when they were finished, she got up and tipped her head toward the bedroom.

"I have to say goodbye to him."

Noah looked at her. "You know what Paulo Coelho says."

She gave a soft laugh. "Something about the road to eternity being paved with crappy moments like this?"

He just smiled. "Not far off. He says, 'If you're brave enough to say goodbye, life will reward you with a new hello.'"

"That's hard to imagine right now, honey, but..." She leaned in and kissed his cheek. "I love you for hoping, and for all you said."

***

THE ROOM WAS dark when Claire stepped into it, squinting to find DJ on the bed, staring up at the ceiling.

"Hey," Claire said, coming close to the bed.

"Hey."

She dropped on the edge, letting her eyes adjust.

"Are you upset?" he asked.

She hesitated, considering how to answer the question. "There's a lot of upheaval in my life," she said carefully. "The man my sister loves is in a coma. My nephew's girlfriend got arrested for a crime she didn't commit. And you, the father of my child, just announced you're leaving me. Upset would be fair, don't you think?"

"Completely." He rolled over and put a hand on her leg. "Is that all I am to you? The father of your child?"

"Yes," she answered without hesitation, her eyes metaphorically opened with the admission. "I suppose I could have described you in other ways, but, bottom line..."

"Noah's the only thing truly keeping us together," he finished.

"I hate that that's true, DJ. But I'm afraid it is."

He blew out a noisy breath and they sat in silence for a few minutes.

"Sometimes I wonder," he finally said. "What would have happened if you'd have told me you were pregnant that summer graduation day at Fordham."

"Do you think you would have stayed and given up the chance to study architecture at Berkeley?"

"No," he said instantly, gaining points for real honesty. "Do you think you would have come with me, and that we'd have married and struggled through with a child?"

"No," she replied with the same speed he did.

"You wouldn't have come with me?" He pushed up on one elbow. "Claire, you surely would have dropped out of college and followed me to California."

She studied his face, not seeing the man in front of her, but the much younger version, the graduate who broke up with her on the steps of Keating Hall.

"You wouldn't have wanted that," she said. "You would have either assisted with adoption, or tried to convince me to go another route. You weren't going to stay in New York. You were destined to leave then, and you are now as well."

He nodded. "You're probably right. And I'm sorry for that."

"Don't be," she said. "It's who you are."

"Noah's right," he admitted, sounding sad. "You deserve more than that. You deserve better."

She lifted a shoulder. "Let's put it this way, DJ. I *want* more than that. Maybe, when I first got here and reunited with you, I was willing to settle for exactly what you offered, be it love or crumbs. But something's changed in my heart."

He sat all the way up, interest in his eyes. "What is it?"

"I never witnessed love the way I have here in Shellseeker Beach," she said. "The only real relationship I watched up close was my parents', and Dutch?" She chuckled. "Dutch loved Dutch more than anyone. He adored Camille, but he didn't love her. I was married briefly, and that was a huge mistake."

She thought about it for a minute, grateful that he was quiet and let her think this through.

"But now, I've seen the true power of love," she said with awe as the realization hit her. "I've connected with a sister, and that's a new kind of love I never knew existed. I've watched her fall in love, and watched my niece, Olivia, do the same. I've watched my mother blossom in true love with Buck, and I've had a front-row seat to Noah and Katie's discovery of what I believe will be a lifelong love for them."

"But..." He put a hand on her arm. "Not us.

She smiled. "We tried, DJ. We gave it the old college try, but now that I know what's possible, what selflessness can be involved, and how much joy that can bring? Well, I'll wait for it. I want it, I know what it is, and I will happily wait forever. In the meantime, I'm surrounded by family and I'm very, very happy."

She let out a long, slow sigh as she finished the speech, so deeply content with her situation and this break-up she could feel it in her chest.

"Claire." He took her hand. "I hope you find that love. I really, really do."

"Well," she laughed softly, thinking of Noah's pronouncement. Another hello? Another man in her future? God, she hoped so, but it wasn't going to be this one. "I guess I'll have a better chance with you gone."

He smiled at that, too, reaching for her with both arms to fold her into a hug.

They sat there like that for a long time, listening to each other's heartbeat, knowing that this was the best goodbye they could possibly have.

Chapter Twenty-three

Asia

"Dad, take I-75 North. The entrance is less than a mile. Take it."

George glanced into the back seat, his dark gaze reflected in the rear-view mirror. "We're going home, Asia."

"Actually, we're going to the Orlando International Airport as fast as you can possibly get me there."

Roz spun around in the front passenger seat. "Are you out of your ever-lovin' mind?"

She held up her cell phone, not really willing to go through the whole group text with Dane and Olivia, who were in a car on the way to Orlando with Deeley at the wheel.

She also wasn't willing to tell her mother that her boyfriend, who Roz thought was just a mild-mannered nerd-turned-musician, was literally breaking the law, illegally hacking into the Virgin Atlantic website to delay a flight.

Nope. Roz didn't need to know that.

She had told both her parents what Dane had heard from the former Scotland Yard man, and they'd agreed not to go back to the U.S. Marshals with this information, but to share it with her defense attorney tomorrow morning.

"Mom, if we get Spencer to admit what he's done before he's out of this country, we can end this whole thing. If he leaves, those marshals will be back for me. As you know, not a single person at that place believed me, with the possible exception of Deputy Marshal Stacey Feldman, who seemed to have a heart. We're going to confront him at the airport."

"We?" her mother demanded. "No, we are not."

"'We' is Dane and Deeley and Olivia, who are on their way to the airport."

"To do what?" George asked.

"Well..." She re-read Dane's lengthy text, her heart melting at the thought of such a rule-following, uber-logical man making a decision this wild and rash. For *her*. "Dane has a plan. But it won't work without me."

"What can you do?" Roz asked.

"I can get law enforcement, hopefully the marshals, there...at precisely the right moment."

"How?"

There was absolutely no way she'd tell her mother a single detail of what they were cooking up on this group text. "We got it figured out. Just get me to the airport, Dad, please."

"It's a big airport," George said, but his tone told her he was at least interested in helping her. "Where would you go?"

"Virgin Atlantic."

"That's the flight Spencer is on?" Roz asked. "Are you sure?"

She sure hoped so, since that was the flight that Dane had risked everything to delay for no reason any of the poor passengers or crew knew. All they could do was pray that Spencer didn't try to get on another flight, which would mean they'd lose him and this gamble.

But if he waited it out...this *could* work.

Wordlessly, George hit the turn signal to get into the interstate entry lane.

"No." Roz shifted in her seat like she had literal ants in her pants. "No, you cannot go along with this, George Turner!"

"Mom, stop!" Asia insisted. "You can't control this. I'm calling the shots. It's my life, my child, my ex, and my prison sentence if we fail."

Fortunately, that shut her up long enough for George to get on the highway and drive as fast as Asia ever remembered her father driving.

All the while, Asia texted Olivia and Dane and tracked their progress, about half an hour ahead of her. On her lap, she had Special Agent Feldman's card with a cell phone number. The woman had a hard edge, but confided that she was the mother of two, and seemed to feel Asia's pain.

Would she send out a team of local marshals to the Orlando airport on a chance? Would she believe it was a legitimate tip to arrest a man who'd stolen money from his wife's trust fund and tried to get his ex-girlfriend to take some level of blame?

She had no idea, but this was her chance to fool Spencer Keaton the way he'd fooled her, and she was taking it. Her phone buzzed with a text from Olivia, announcing that they'd arrived at the airport and were getting tickets on Spencer's flight, which was almost full. She gave Asia all the information, including the gate number.

Thank God her parents had needed her passport, which was now safely tucked into her bag.

She waited a bit longer, and when she saw the last sign to the airport and knew they'd be there soon, she texted the number on the card.

I can prove I'm innocent and deliver the real thief to you in less than an hour. MCO. Terminal A. Gate 120. You can arrest him there. Just answer your phone when I call you. And you may want to get local marshals to the airport now because Spencer Keaton may also be responsible for his wife's death.

She hit Send and closed her eyes.

Would that work? She had no idea. But if it was true, she wanted him to pay for that crime, and hopefully, Deputy Marshal Feldman agreed.

When they got to the airport, her father dropped her off outside of Terminal A, and agreed to continue circling the airport until he heard from her—over the protestations of her mother, of course. With a quick goodbye, Asia walked into the crowded terminal hearing nothing but the hammer of her heart.

According to Olivia's last text, they were at the front of the line now. She couldn't find them in the melee, but the line for First Class ticket holders to get boarding passes was much shorter than the others. And without bags, she moved quickly, reaching the kiosk as her phone dinged with a text. Not Deputy Marshal Stacey Feldman, but Dane.

We're through security and getting on a tram shuttle to the gates. Meet Olivia in the closest bathroom to Gate 120. We don't want you visible or anywhere near me in case he sees us. Must have element of surprise on our side.

He closed the message with a fingers-crossed emoji and a heart that almost made Asia smile, but right now all she could do was concentrate on getting a ticket.

She snaked her way to a kiosk, scanned her passport, inserted her credit card, and got the last seat on the delayed flight. A First Class ticket set her back a mere $3,048, which was pushing her limit for sure.

She prayed her card cleared and breathed a sigh of relief when a boarding pass slipped out with her name on it. Clutching it in one hand, her phone in the other, and a handbag on her shoulder, she hurried to security, Dane's message echoing in her head.

Must have the element of surprise on our side.

Well, she was about to surprise the heck out of Spencer Keaton. The trick would be making him admit what he'd done.

By the time she got through security, Asia was sweating. When she got on the tram to the terminals, she had a hard time breathing. And by the time she saw the gate number, she needed the nearest bathroom for more than just a rendezvous with Olivia. The last meal she'd eaten threatened to make a reappearance.

She managed to keep it down, but washed her face and hands in ice-cold water.

The moment she tossed the paper towel in the trash bin, the door popped open and Asia looked up, crying out at the sight of Olivia.

"Oh my God," they both muttered in unison, coming to each other for a supportive hug.

"Is Dane out there?" Asia asked, aching to hold him.

"Yes, but he's keeping an eye on Spencer."

"You found him?" she asked on a gasp, her knees nearly buckling with relief. "Seriously? He's here? He hasn't gotten on another flight?"

"He's sitting at a bar a little bit away from the gate," Olivia said. "He hasn't seen Dane and doesn't know me or Deeley." She inched back and pulled Asia to an area where no one was in line or listening. "Did you contact the marshal?"

Asia nodded. "But she hasn't replied."

"She will if you do your job and get the entire conversation into your phone with her on the line. Can you do that?"

"I'm going to try, but I'd also like to tell Deputy Marshal Feldman where he is right now."

"You talked to her?"

Asia shook her head. "Left a text, but I'm hoping. What's the name of the bar?"

"JR—Johnny Rivers, I think. It's not far from here, with some tables and a long bar. He's sitting at the bar with his back to the concourse, so unless he turns around, he won't see you. It's all packed, though, thanks to the, ahem, unexplained flight delay."

Her eyes shuttered. "I hope Dane doesn't get caught."

"He's got his laptop, and the very second we're done, he's going to wipe out any proof he did this. I hope. The man would do anything for you, Asia."

That made her smile. "Then I better do something for him." She looked down at her phone and texted the marshal again, repeating the gate number and dropping a GPS pin, then she hit "share my location" on the message thread. "And now the U.S. Marshals can find me easily," she whispered, looking up. "So I better get to Spencer fast."

"Asia." Olivia squeezed her shoulders. "Be careful."

Asia nodded, they hugged again, hard, and stepped outside.

Taking a deep breath, Asia looked around the crowded terminal, zeroing in on the neon sign to a small and wildly crowded restaurant and bar. Right outside of it, behind a thick column, Dane waited.

For a moment, they both just stared at each other, then Asia couldn't help herself from running toward him. She tried to walk, tried to be cool, certainly didn't want to attract attention, but she couldn't wait to feel that man's arms around her.

"I can still go with you," he said as he pulled her into an embrace.

"No, no. If he sees you, he won't say a thing. I know him. I can make him talk." She might have to get under his skin, but if there was one thing she knew how to do, it was get way under Spencer's skin...and then he snapped. That much couldn't have changed.

"Asia."

"Please. I can—"

He pulled her into him and kissed her on the mouth, long enough to make her dizzy. And determined.

"I'm going in," she whispered, pulling away toward the neon sign.

She spotted Spencer immediately, alone at a bar that was two or three deep with people waiting for drinks. He had a seat, though, and a beer, and was clicking through his phone.

Her throat was so dry she could hardly speak when a harried-looking hostess greeted her.

"The wait is an hour or more," the woman said with emotionless rote, as if she'd uttered the words four thousand times in the last hour.

"I'll go to the bar."

"Good luck getting a seat there, too."

"Thanks. I hope I don't need luck." She threaded the tables full of diners to head straight to the broad shoulders she still recognized from the back. As she walked, she pulled out her phone and called Stacey, who *thankfully* answered on the first ring.

"Asia, if you—"

"Just listen to the conversation I'm about to have, okay? And do not say a word, you're on speaker and if he hears you, he won't confess a thing." Still holding the phone, she smiled at two men blocking her access to Spencer, and they separated.

Then she was close enough to smell his cologne, count the unshaven whiskers on his face, and deliver her greeting.

"I was so, so sad to hear about your wife," she said, making him jerk as he turned to her.

Silent, he stared, his nostrils flaring for a second.

She clasped the phone in two hands pressed to her chest, the bottom up so the microphone could pick up the entire conversation.

"What the hell are you doing here, Asia?"

"Why didn't you tell me she passed away?"

"You didn't ask." He narrowed his eyes. "How'd you find out?"

"I did a little digging. People's deaths do get announced, you know."

"What do you want?" he asked gruffly, glancing behind her for a quick second.

Answers, she thought. *I want answers that will incriminate you and save me.*

"Where did you get the money, Spencer?"

"Does it matter?"

"Yes, it matters very much. Is it your wife's money?" she asked.

"What's hers is mine."

"Even her trust fund? Was that yours, too? Did you just help yourself to that money to take care of me, or did you take more for yourself?"

He searched her face, as shocked and surprised as she wanted him to be. "Shut up, Asia," he finally said, a sure sign that he couldn't find the composure he so desperately needed. *Good.*

"Just tell me the truth, Spencer. Then I'll leave you alone forever. But I have to know the truth."

"The truth is I did want to help you. I felt like crap for what I did, and when I found out you had a baby, I wanted to do something for him. And as far as the money?" He shrugged. "We were married. That money was...*is*...it doesn't matter. It's mine...or should have been."

"So you're admitting it, right here in this Orlando bar, that you stole her money after she died."

His gaze flickered for a moment, then he narrowed his eyes, and...there it was. That look of fury that came right before he snapped or yelled or demanded or controlled. Right before he lost it, which was what she needed him to do.

She just had to push him right over the edge, then get it all in Stacey's ear.

Leaning in, she whispered, "Did you help her into the car, Spencer?"

His eyes flashed, dark and furious. "What?"

"Did you give her whatever made her intoxicated? A little something in her drink, maybe?"

All color drained from his face as he straightened and looked around, slightly frantic that someone may have heard.

"You did, didn't you?"

"You are going somewhere you do not want to go, Asia Turner."

"Why? Are you going to help me die, too? Then take your one million dollars back from my Cayman account?"

He stared at her for a long time, slowly exhaling a noisy breath. "You want more?"

"Of course I do. *Is* there more?"

He answered by turning back to the bar, but she nestled closer, the phone still there. Surely the marshal who was listening would send back up now. Unless she couldn't hear over Asia's pounding heart.

"I'm not giving you any more, Asia."

"But there is more," she said—a statement, not a question—lifting the phone imperceptibly, pretending to clutch it nervously.

"You think you're going to get it from me?" he scoffed. "Think again."

"Maybe I will. Because I know you so well, Spencer Keaton. I know what you're capable of when you want to control a woman."

He narrowed his eyes at her, leaning down. "Whatever I did, you benefited greatly from it. So take the crumbs I'm giving you and get the hell out of my life forever."

"Is it blood money? Did you kill her?"

"She drove into a tree, Asia. I wasn't at the wheel."

"She was intoxicated. Did you make sure of that?"

"Stop it!" he ground out. "She insisted she was perfectly fine to drive, so I let her." Once again, his eyes tapered to brown slits, pinning her. "You should watch what you say to me, Asia, or you'll have a convenient accident, too."

Her eyes popped and suddenly, he shot out of the seat, grabbing the phone from her hand with a furious flash in his eyes. He took one look at the screen and threw it on the floor, lifting his foot to smash his heel into it. But she was too fast, kicking it under the bar.

Swearing, he pushed her aside and bolted from the bar, moving insanely fast for how crowded it was.

"Spencer!" she called, grunting when the two guys behind him blocked her as one of them dove for the free seat.

"You lose this, ma'am?" The bartender held her phone out to her.

"Yes! Thank you!" She grabbed it and spun around in time to see Spencer whiz past the hostess stand.

"Spencer Keaton!" she called at the top of her lungs, praying the call was still connected. "Don't you dare leave this bar!"

He vaulted toward the concourse and started to run, but Dane popped out from behind the column, throwing himself at Spencer. They tussled, but Spencer was so much stronger. He grabbed Dane by the arm, then slammed his fist right into Dane's jaw.

Asia screamed as she ran out, practically colliding with Olivia as they both stumbled toward Dane.

He pushed up, putting his hand over his nose as blood rushed out.

A small group gathered around, but Olivia dove in

and scooped up Dane's backpack. "He's fine," she hollered. "He's fine. Back away."

Asia stood helpless then peered down the crowded concourse, catching sight of Spencer the very moment a great big, muscular Connor Deeley pounced and took him down to the ground.

"Go!" Olivia pushed her in that direction. "Stay with him so they can track you. Let me handle Dane."

She was right, of course, so Asia ran toward another group of people trying to break up a fight. Someone was trying to pull Deeley back, but he was too strong and broke free, getting hold of Spencer again.

Where was airport security? The U.S. Marshals? Anyone at all?

Air screamed in her ears as she ran to them, nearly knocking two old ladies over in the process.

"Don't you dare go after him, Asia!"

It took a second to realize the voice was Stacey and coming from her phone. "Too late. Where are your people?"

"Stay back and stay safe!"

Ignoring the order, she reached Deeley, who had Spencer on the ground with a knee, holding up one hand to the crowd.

Just then, three uniformed security guards and three more men barreled into the concourse, yelling orders, making all the bystanders scatter like cockroaches. Someone screamed, another person fell to the ground, and fifty phones came out to record the whole thing.

"United States Marshals! Back away!" Two new men

arrived at full speed, hollering at Deeley, who instantly jumped off. A third officer grabbed him by the arm.

"Here's the guy you want," he said, kicking a foot in Spencer's direction. "I'm just doing your dirty work."

Asia tapped the phone again and brought up Face-Time, getting a blurry image of Stacey's face.

"Wanna see?" Asia asked, hitting the button to switch the view. She focused the phone on Spencer, who was being cuffed. "That's your man," she said. "He did a lot more than steal money."

"I heard," Stacey muttered. "Let me talk to a marshal."

Asia handed the phone to the man who'd come next to her, not even bothering to read the ID he showed her.

Just as she did, she heard her name being called from behind. Whipping around, she spotted Dane and Olivia running through the crowd, smeared blood on his face.

As they reached her, Dane threw both arms around her, hugging her with all his might.

"Oh my God, Asia, you're okay." He squeezed her tighter, as if he didn't really believe it. "You're okay."

Adrenaline dumped through her body like a water-fall, mixing with pure joy and true love as she fell against him in relief. "You are my hero."

"Hardly a hero. That clown clocked me."

She pressed her hand on his cheek, moaning at the swelling and blood. "But you beat him with your brains, baby. And I love that. I love *you*."

He smiled through the injury and leaned into her. "Then that punch was worth it."

Chapter Twenty-four

Eliza

The neurologists wanted to speak privately with Janie to discuss the next move. They'd hoped Henry would be here, too, but he was still traveling from an undisclosed military base. During the blur of time that passed, Eliza got to know Miles's daughter, who was so much like him in looks and spirit that Eliza couldn't help but the love the woman instantly. She also had time to mull over all that she'd heard about the stunning drama that had unfolded at the Orlando Airport.

And of course, she had plenty of time to think about Miles, to look at his sleeping body when Janie needed a break, and to know that whatever happened at the other end of this ordeal, she would not leave his side.

But, oh how she longed for him to wake up so she could tell him that.

While the nurses tended to Miles and Janie talked to the doctors, Eliza waited in the undersized family area when Olivia came in with coffee and a bright smile.

"Oh, I didn't expect you here this early," Eliza said, giving her a kiss and accepting the coffee.

"With a three-year-old? Please. He never sleeps past

sunrise." She sat down and took the lid off her own coffee. "Status on Miles?"

"Janie's meeting with the doctors about the next step and I'm..." She didn't even know how to explain it all to Olivia. "You know."

"I know." Olivia put her head on Eliza's shoulder, proving she did know, and didn't require an explanation.

"Tell me more about what's going on at home."

"Well, let's see." Olivia straightened her head and took a sip. "Jadyn's taken over the Bash babysitting duties. God love that woman and her amazing childcare. Oh! She has Tinkerbell, too, while Noah and Katie are working. So, no worries about your favorite furbaby."

Eliza's heart folded at the thought of how bereft sweet Tink must be, having no idea where Miles was all this time. "Miles will be so grateful when...when..." She swallowed, not ready to talk about what would happen when he woke. "And Teddy?

"Teddy stayed on at the resort to handle some check-ins, Dane and Asia are meeting again with the marshals, then probably headed home to their townhouse."

Eliza sipped the hot coffee and shook her head. "I still can't believe all that happened. I can't believe what the four of you did."

"We did it, but I have to tell you, your son master-minded the whole thing, using his powers for good, including bending the rules a little more than I ever expected from Dane Whitney."

"But they have Spencer in custody, right?"

"Yes, they do, and Asia is free but might have to go to

London to testify or be deposed or something. Nothing immediate."

"And Dane? Do the authorities know he was behind that flight delay?"

"Nope. He erased his digital fingerprints like a pro." She snorted. "He should stick to computing because, dang, he got sucker-punched."

Eliza winced. "Poor guy."

"Ah, he's fine. Let's just be clear..." She grinned. "*My* man took the baddie down."

"And how is Asia in all this?"

"Well, not a million dollars richer, it seems."

"But she got Dane," Eliza said. "And he's worth that and more."

"Aww." Olivia cooed. "Spoken like a true mother. What do you think the pow wow with the doctors is all about?"

"If and when to bring him out of the medically induced coma." She shuddered with a sigh. "I'd like to get him out as soon as possible, but I'm not his wife. Janie's next of kin."

"You like her though, don't you?"

"Very much. She's solid and so is Brody, her husband."

"We're due the same month," Olivia said. "So we are truly like sisters."

"Miles would like that," Eliza said wistfully.

"Just think..." Olivia leaned back and put her hand on a still-almost-flat stomach. "If you marry him, our babies will be cousins."

If you marry him...

The words bounced around Eliza's chest, landing heavy on her heart. "I should have said yes," she whispered. "Before he had this accident...before I lost the chance."

Olivia looked at her. "Did he actually propose?"

"Not really. Although he's said he intended to, I think he knew that I wouldn't have even entertained the idea. He said he loved me."

"And you?"

"Did not say it back."

"Well, there's still time."

Eliza shot her a look. "I hope so, because I'm...pretty sure I'd roll up in a ball and cry forever if I had to live without him."

"Oh, Mom." Olivia put her hand on Eliza's arm. "You know now?"

"I guess. I was a fool, waiting for a 'moment of clarity.' I wasted way too many moments waiting for that elusive one."

Olivia eyed her for a long time. "You know, when he comes out, he could be..."

"Another man to nurse," Eliza said bluntly. "I've thought about that."

"Could you do it again? Taking care of Dad all those years really took it out of you, Mom. I'm not sure you could do it again."

But Eliza was. "I only want to see him open his eyes. That's all I want."

"But if he does, will you marry him?"

Eliza smiled. "I guess I'll have to wait for him to ask, won't I?"

"Eliza?" A nurse, one Eliza recognized, stepped into the waiting room.

"Oh, hi, Pamela. Are you finished doing his morning assist?"

"We are, and I thought I might find you in here." She gave a broad smile. "You can go and see him now. But, I'm sorry, only one at a time."

"It's fine." Eliza pushed up. "Oh, and Pamela? Miles's daughter is talking to the neurologist. When you see her, please let her come into the ICU. I'll leave and let her be with her father."

"You bet."

Before she left, she put a hand on Olivia's shoulder. "I'll be back in a bit, Liv. Can you wait?"

"Of course. But only if you do me a favor, Mom."

"Anything."

"I know he's in a coma, but tell him what you just told me. You don't know for sure if he can hear you or not and...it might help."

She gave a bittersweet smile. "Okay, I'll tell him."

A few minutes later, she stepped into the room, the unnatural lighting casting everything in a milky glow she'd come to hate. Miles slept in the same position, even though she knew the nurses had turned him, bathed him, and taken care of all his needs.

Would Eliza have to do some—or all—of that when he woke?

Maybe. But she would. With all the love she had in her heart.

"Oh, Miles." She sighed his name and dropped into the hard leather chair that had been home to her for a few days now. "I'm here with you, darling."

She'd never called him darling. Never called anyone darling that she could remember, but it seemed right. She put a hand on his, always surprised that his skin was warm when it was so cold in this room. It cheered her to feel his warm, smooth skin and the big hands that made hers feel small when he held them.

"Janie is meeting with the doctors!" she said brightly, trying with everything she had to believe he could hear her. "Can I tell you how much I like her? I guess I knew I would. She reminds me of you, so smart and capable. Henry will be here any minute, too. Anyway, we're praying the doctors are telling her that they'll be bringing you out of this darn coma state soon."

She waited a beat, as if he might answer or flutter his eyelashes or even give her hand a nearly imperceptible squeeze. None of that happened.

"Oh, and you certainly have missed the most excitement we've had in a long time. It turns out Asia's baby daddy is a murdering thief who wanted her to take the fall for his crimes. But Dane swooped in and solved the crime with his computer genius and truly unexpected bravery." She could hear the smile of pride in her voice. "I'm sure they can't wait to tell you the whole story."

She powered on with her one-sided conversation, the

most she'd talked to him since he arrived in the room. The more she said, the more she wanted to say.

"Oh, and DJ is leaving," she continued. "He and Claire have officially broken up, which is so sad. She's handling it like a trooper, and so is Noah, who still hasn't proposed to Katie. I think he's waiting for you to wake up. You can say, 'I told you so,' since he did lose the ring when he jumped into the Gulf, but it was worth it. So worth it. When you wake up, you and I should buy another for him to give to Katie, don't you think?"

But whatever he was thinking—if anything at all— there was no reaction. Maybe he just couldn't dig deep enough to react to any of that news. Maybe he needed to hear...

Olivia's words teased her. *Tell him what you told me...*

Would that be enough?

She took a breath and threaded her fingers through his, getting closer. "And speaking of rings, Miles Anderson..." She swallowed as her throat thickened. "Ever since I've been sitting here next to you, I've been, uh, thinking. I know I always told you that I was a 'one time down the aisle' kind of girl, and that ship had sailed, but..."

She wet her lips and blinked back some mist in her eyes, staring hard at him as she waited and prayed and hoped and...nothing.

"But...but...I've really been thinking about that," she announced, a little louder, as if that had to wake him up.

It didn't.

"I have never said the three most important words in

the world to you, and I...I want to. I want you to know that you're The One. Not the *second* one, but...the *only* one." She leaned very close, putting her lips to his ear as if that little bit of breath and warmth might be enough to wake him. "I love you, Miles Anderson. I love you with my whole heart and soul."

She closed her eyes and waited, but he remained unmoving. A tear fell down her cheek and landed on his pillow, so she drew back to continue, aching for a response.

"I love you so much that I can confidently say that I want to spend the rest of my life with you." She held her breath and watched his chest rise and fall with no hitch, no reaction. "Miles Anderson..."

She brought their joined hands to her lips and kissed his knuckles, realizing that the moment of clarity had been every minute she ever experienced with this man. That moment had been this whole year with a man who patiently waited for her to grieve. It was the future and today and forever and ever. It was *now*.

How could she not have realized that?

She rose off the chair to get as close to him as she could, wishing she could get on one knee, but the bed was too high. She just leaned in to say the rest.

"I think it's going to have to be me asking you, Miles."

She laid her head on his shoulder, the tears falling.

"Miles Anderson, will you do me the honor of becoming my husband? I'm ready, darling. I'm ready for richer and poorer, in sickness and health. And I mean that part, Miles. No matter what happens to you. No matter who you are when you wake up, I will be your wife. I've never wanted anything so much in my life. I love you, no matter what happens..."

The words caught in the next sob, shaking her so hard, she couldn't speak.

And neither did he, she realized after a few heartbeats had passed.

Could he have heard anything? Unlikely. But that was fine. She'd ask again. If only she had the chance.

"Eliza?"

She turned to see Pamela, with Janie right behind her. "Oh, yes, of course." Eliza wiped her tears as she stood, gathering herself. "I'll step out so Janie can be with him."

She picked up her bag with shaky hands and took a few steps to the door. Janie stepped in and took Eliza's hands, compassion and warmth in her sweet green eyes.

"Eliza."

Not trusting her voice, Eliza just smiled.

"They're bringing him out of the coma today. They'll start soon, and it will take some time."

"Really?" She felt her heart lift. "That's fantastic!"

Janie nodded, her expression serious. "It is, but...it's tricky. There's a chance he might not come out, so I wanted to spend a few minutes with him."

A chance he might not come out.

Eliza felt her heart stutter with the impact. "Of course," she managed to say, gesturing toward the bed. "I'm sure that...he'd love that."

A flicker of confusion played over Janie's features,

but then she softened into a smile. "I know what he'd love," she said softly. "And that is to see your face when he wakes up. He adores you, Eliza. This past year has been the happiest I can remember for my father. Don't go far."

"I won't," Eliza promised, giving her a spontaneous hug. "I love him too much to go anywhere."

COMING out of a medically induced coma, Eliza learned, wasn't like turning on a light switch. The process took the better part of the entire day, during which no one was allowed to see Miles.

That didn't stop everyone from gathering in an over-sized waiting room that the hospital arranged just for this family. As the day wore on, everyone from Teddy to Harper arrived, and all those in between. Camille and Buck had returned from their honeymoon and Deeley closed his businesses and brought Bash, who was under Jadyn's care but managed to spend time entertaining every one of them.

Katie and Noah came, and, of course, Claire, who sat with Eliza in a corner for hours and told her all about the tearful goodbye to DJ and Sophia.

Roz and George showed up, then Dane—sporting a black eye he was pretty darn proud of—and Asia with the baby. They fascinated everyone with the story of how they'd brought down a criminal.

Janie was there with Brody, and, before long, they

were finally joined by an exhausted-looking Henry, Miles's son, who was stoic and strong. He stayed close to Janie and Brody, grateful for the local support but clearly needing familiar family connection to get through what felt like an endless day of small talk, worry, coffee, stress, more chatting, more worry, and so much waiting.

Several of Miles's friends arrived, mostly waiting downstairs, but some came up a few at a time, just to hug Janie and Eliza, to leave flowers or say a prayer.

Through it all, Eliza was in a fog so thick there were times she literally couldn't see. But maybe those were tears blurring her eyes, because she'd certainly shed a few today.

It was getting into evening when Eliza felt her lids get heavy and she let her head fall back, her body pressed into the seat with Olivia on one side and Claire on the other. She was almost asleep when she heard Olivia say, "Oh, look, it's Jonathan MacGregor."

Eliza wanted to open her eyes and greet the judge who'd come to their aid on more than one occasion over the past year, but the stress and exhaustion pressed so hard, she simply couldn't.

Next to her, she felt Claire sit up straighter. "How sweet of him to stop by," she murmured. "I should go say hello. You stay with your mother, Liv."

"Thank you," Eliza whispered under her breath, giving Claire's hand a squeeze as she caught sight of the handsome judge through the glass window to the hall. "I don't think I have another conversation in me."

Claire rose and walked out to the hall to talk to the

judge and Eliza pulled herself from the sleepy daze, blinking at Olivia.

"I told him," she said softly. "I confessed my love. It didn't bring him out of the coma."

"He'll be awake soon, Mom," Olivia assured her. "You can tell him again. What did you say?"

"I told him I loved him." Eliza felt a smile pull. "And I proposed."

"Oh." Her eyes widened, then filled. "You're the best, Mom. And who knows? Maybe deep in his subconscious, he heard you. They say some coma patients can hear but can't respond. Also, can I be in your wedding?"

"Yeah." She smiled again, closing her eyes but holding Olivia's hand. "You and Teddy and Claire, I think. We'll marry on the beach and have a party with everyone there."

Please, God, please. Give me that dream. Give Miles a life. Give us a future and a chance to love again.

"Harper can sing," Olivia said, unaware of Eliza's silent, fervent prayers as she planned a wedding they both knew might never happen.

"And I'll sing, too," Eliza said. "Remember when I came here? I couldn't sing."

"You were in deep pain, Mom."

"It's...gone." She put her hand on her chest and realized that she had different worries and concerns, but the hole in her heart that had been left by the death of her husband had healed, filled by love and laughter and shellseeking and tea and... "Where's Teddy?" she asked, sitting up and looking around.

"Right here." Teddy slid into the chair left vacant by Claire and took Eliza's hand. "Just watching those two and thinking perhaps we overlooked that possible romance?"

"What are you talking about?" Eliza looked around, following Teddy's gaze to the window that framed Claire and Jonathan. Her sister looked up at the tall, good-looking man of about fifty, who was clearly riveted by every word she said. "Ohhh," Eliza dragged out the word with a smile. "The lawyer and the judge. I like it."

"Very much," Olivia agreed. "They're kind of perfect together."

"Even through the glass I'm picking up a good aura," Teddy said, still staring at the couple.

"We should invite him to the wedding," Olivia leaned in to say. "In fact, he should officiate."

"What wedding?" Teddy asked.

"Miles and Mom," Olivia said without missing a beat.

"Oh?" Teddy gave a smug look. "Now that's a wedding I won't miss."

Eliza looked from one to the other, her heart smothered in affection for these two generations of amazing, funny, loving women. "From your lips to God's ears, girls."

Just then, the doors to the ICU opened and two doctors in scrubs came out, one that Eliza instantly recognized as Miles's neurologist, Dr. Cooke.

"Mrs. McCann?" he called, scanning the room for Janie.

She popped up immediately, flanked by her brother and husband.

"You can see him now," the doctor said.

"He's awake?" Janie asked.

The doctor nodded. "He is. He's lucid, he's conscious, and he's asking for...E?"

Next to her, Olivia let out a soft cry, but the light cheer that went up in the room drowned it out.

"E?" Janie turned to Eliza. "Please come with us," she said, beckoning her with one hand. "He's asking for you."

Eliza pushed up on shaky hands, taking a breath. "Yes, yes, I'd like that."

"This way," the doctor said, leading them through the doors. Eliza hung back as Janie and Henry peppered him with questions, her head light and dizzy as the words played in her head.

"He's asking for E."

Oh, Miles. I'm coming. Your E is on the way. Her heart walloped her ribs as they turned the corner to his room, and she gasped as the door opened and she saw Miles—awake and sitting up, a Styrofoam cup in his hand.

"Dad!" Janie launched toward him, then caught herself before she pounced on him, and Henry followed, with Janie's husband behind.

Eliza stayed by the door, wanting to give this family a moment, and taking that time to study Miles. He looked good! There was some color in his cheeks and his eyes seemed bright. Best of all, he was talking, smiling, and... looking past them for her.

"Oh!" Janie exclaimed. "Eliza's been here every minute, Dad. She's never left your side. Come here, Eliza."

She approached slowly, feeling like she was in a dream—the *best* dream—and didn't want to wake up. But with each step, Miles's smile grew and he put down the cup, reaching a hand to her.

"E." It was all he said, but it was enough to bring another flood of tears.

"Oh, Miles." She pressed one hand to her lips and took his with the other. "I'm so happy to see you."

"Same," he said on a dry laugh, then caught his breath. "I can't laugh," he said. "The ventilator ripped my throat to shreds."

"And the anchor did a number on your head," Eliza whispered, coming closer to the side of the bed and vaguely aware that the others had given her space.

"It's okay," he said in a raspy voice. "I'm okay."

"Are you? Do you remember anything?"

He looked at her for a long time. "On the boat? Or... here, in my dreams?"

She straightened and searched his face. "You had dreams?"

"I did." He took her hands, his skin warm, his grip surprisingly strong. "I dreamed that the woman I love said words I longed to hear and asked a question that I thought I was supposed to ask."

Her heart soared. "You heard me?"

"Or...it was a dream." He held her gaze, his green eyes bright and so beautifully alive and clear.

He looked at her for a long time, eased her as close as she could get to the bed, and sat up in invitation. She came close to his lips, brushed them with a gentle kiss, then he turned his head so he could whisper in her ear.

"Yes, my sweet, sweet E. I will marry you and make you the happiest woman on Earth."

"On Earth?" She laughed. "I'm already the happiest woman on Sanibel Island. And that, my darling man, is all anyone ever needs."

Epilogue

Teddy

One *ne Year Later*
	As she dressed for yet another spectacular beach celebration, Theodora Blessing sensed some discord in her universe. It wasn't the first time she'd felt it, and by now, she knew what was calling her. Or rather, *who*.

Turning from the full-length mirror, she eyed the blue lapis lazuli box on her dresser, the current and temporary home of Aloysius "Dutch" Vanderveen. She took a moment to inhale the faintest salty air that flowed in through the balcony, bringing the delicate fragrance of her garden and the fresh scents of a Sanibel evening into her room.

"I know, Dutch," she breathed out his name. "You want out. You want to be free. You want...peace."

She closed her eyes and imagined what he'd say, since she didn't really hear voices, not even Dutch's, and she was happy about that. She felt the messages, though. And his spirit, yearning to be part of the universe and no longer trapped in the box he'd been in for nearly two years.

She walked to the dresser and put a hand on the box.

"You asked me to put you in the sky, Dutch. But I have not figured out a way to do that short of renting a hot air balloon or going up in a parasail which, by the way, you can now rent from Deeley on the beach."

Something had stopped her from either of those adventures, sensing that her late lover's request that his ashes go "in the sky" meant something more personal. Of course, being a former pilot who loved nothing more than going off into the wild blue yonder, he meant something like *a plane*. The conundrum—and her busy, happy life— had kept her from making a decision or taking action.

But Teddy sensed she couldn't put it off any longer.

"I'll talk to everyone about it tonight," she promised him. "We're having a big party to celebrate Bash's official adoption into the Deeley family, and everyone will be there. All the people who..."

She thought about how she'd describe her found family to Dutch. He knew some of them, friends from before his death, like Roz and George, or Deeley. And Katie, of course.

But so many new arrivals and connections and relationships had bloomed in Shellseeker Beach in the nearly two years since that blustery morning when Dutch slipped into the next life. In some ways, it was a different place altogether.

Yet, she owed him a final rest. And she owed herself closure.

"Tonight," she promised again. "When I gather the great minds and big hearts of all the people who have become my family, we'll have an answer for you."

She opened her jewelry box and selected a simple crystal pendant, sliding it over her head to let it dangle on her chest. When she looked up to the mirror, though, she saw Dutch's face, with his own beloved crystal, the one he'd believed helped him live far longer than the doctors predicted.

She could see his face, his gray-blue eyes and outsized smile, hear his booming voice and endless opinions. A man who made a thousand mistakes in life, but still managed to touch so many hearts...and in his death, he'd brought so many people to her.

"I owe us both some closure," she told that remembered face on a ragged whisper. "I have carried around a lot of mixed emotions for you, but any that weren't bright and loving have been erased like that Gulf of Mexico washes away the shells each day and brings something different."

Swallowing, she looked down at the box and put her hand on it again. "I will find a way to get you out of this box and into the sky, dear Dutch. I'm not alone anymore, and my family will help me."

Many hours later, around eleven that night, she hadn't found the perfect moment to ask everyone for ideas, but only because the Beach Bash for Bash, as they'd called the celebration, had been non-stop fun from the time it started to now.

But the sun had long ago set, leaving Shellseeker Beach bathed in moonlight, and just the core of her closest friends and family gathered around a grouping of tables near the tea hut.

The music on the sound system had been lowered to something conducive to quiet, easy conversation, and the vineyard lights Noah had strung around the tea hut sparkled with promise and privacy.

There were only a few still partying hard—like the guest of honor, who had discovered the cake *and* cookies. Bash was currently zooming around the sand with Tinkerbell, the tireless pooch who was too sweet to rest until the little boy did.

"Get that kid a dog," Miles said to Olivia as Bash whizzed by and Tink kicked sand on a few of them.

Olivia looked up from where she sat like a queen, holding her precious baby Benjamin—or Bennie, as everyone called him—the six-month-old light of her life. And, based on the way her husband was looking at the child, the light of his, too.

"A dog's a great idea, Liv," Deeley said. "What's one more in the crazy house anyway?"

She laughed and looked at Eliza. "Can't we just borrow Tink from you and Miles, Mom, when we need a dog? I have a new house, a new baby, and I'm still attempting to run a business."

"I don't know. You'd have to ask my husband. Miles? Can you part with Tinkerbell once in a while?"

He leaned back and crossed his ankles. "Yes, because that's the only way we can go island hopping for a month, E."

Eliza looked skeptical. "I know you love that idea, but a month on a boat? I don't know."

He leaned closer to her. "You know, there was a time

when I thought I could never step foot on the deck of *Miles Away* ever again. You changed that." He took her hand. "Nothing like a wedding ceremony on the bow to make me seaworthy again. And now, I want to go. With you, my sweet wife."

Teddy sat quietly and watched the exchange, as the others did. Miles's recovery was nothing short of miraculous, at least that's what all the doctors said. With only a sizeable scar on his temple, he'd suffered no brain damage from the accident, and had fully recovered his memory. His first month or so required a tremendous amount of physical and psychological therapy, but Eliza never left his side.

Once he was able, she eased him back onto the boat, knowing that was his happiest place. And when she arranged for them to marry on board in a ceremony officiated by Judge Jonathan MacGregor and attended by this small group of family and friends? Miles was healed inside and out.

That very judge sat a few feet away, also listening as he clasped Claire's hand in his. They'd been dating since Eliza's wedding, and Jonathan had been by her side when Claire took—and passed—the bar, then opened up her small law practice. He'd become part of this found family, most especially because his presence brought a glow to Claire that none of them had ever seen before.

Dane put his elbows on the table in front of him. "If you two want to go island hopping for a month and Liv and Deeley can't take Tinkerbell, Asia and I certainly can. Our new place has plenty of space, and with Zee walking so much, we've gated off stairs and doors and the pool."

"Yes!" Asia said, shifting the sleeping boy in her arms. "We'll take her."

"How is the new house?" Deeley asked. "Or do you miss your little townhouse?"

Asia and Dane shared a look, laughing because their newfound success as a songwriting team had afforded them the chance to buy a place on Sanibel.

"We like it," Dane said. "Especially the music room, which is home to my family's grand piano."

"I love that," Eliza said. "That piano is exactly where it belongs."

"Thank you, Fletch McBain," Dane said, lifting his glass to Asia to toast the country artist who'd recorded "Guts and Glory" and had then gone to Number One with their catchy tune "You're My Ex and I Know Why."

It had provided a windfall of cash for the young couple, especially welcome because it meant they didn't have to touch the reward money Baron Simmons had given them after Spencer Keaton was arrested for criminal negligence and embezzlement. To celebrate, they'd gotten engaged a few months ago, and Roz was in her glory planning the wedding of the century.

"We can always take the dog," Camille chimed in from a chaise Noah always set up just for his *grandmère*. "Can't we, Abner?"

Buck Underwood ambled over to the group with a fresh glass of tea, settling in next to Camille and taking her hand. "Whatever you want, sweet lady."

She gave a smug smile. "My favorite words."

They all laughed, knowing that as much as Camille pretended her billionaire husband spoiled her, everyone knew it was the other way around. Camille's heart had been cracked wide open not by her heart attack, but by true love after a lifetime of an unorthodox and frequently unstable marriage to Dutch.

At the thought of the man, Teddy shifted in her chair and let out a soft sigh, wishing she could bring up the uncomfortable topic of Dutch's ashes without bringing down the beautiful contentment of a moonlit night on the beach.

"You okay, Teddy?" Next to her, Katie was close enough to sense Teddy's low-key stress.

"Me? Oh, of course, sweetheart. I'm good." She glanced around. "Where are Noah and Harper?"

"On the beach. She wanted to go down to the darkest section and see if there were any turtles on the sand."

"Uh-oh," Olivia cracked. "Knowing Noah, he'll come back with one, name it Tommy, and have it star in his next book."

Everyone laughed, no one more than Katie, who also beamed with pride over her fiancé's success.

"The book comes out in two months," she said, referring to Noah's first children's novel, being released in hardcover by a large New York publisher. *The Adventures of Iggy*, a "security iguana" at the Ding Darling Refuge, promised to be quite a hit, if his book tour and healthy advance meant anything at all.

"Now that will be cause for another party," Teddy

said. And maybe by then, she'd have figured out what to do about Dutch.

"That and"—Katie flashed her diamond ring—"a wedding a month after that."

"It feels like you've been engaged forever," Jadyn, Katie's sister, said. "I'm dying to be a maid of honor already."

"He had a book to write, an agent to obtain, and a publishing contract to sign," Katie said. "And you had a second daycare facility to open."

"And I need time to plan perfection," Claire chimed in. "Unless you two want a surprise wedding like *some* people around here had."

Olivia laughed and put her head on Deeley's shoulder, while Camille lifted her champagne glass.

"Three cheers for surprises. We need more of them around here."

"There's one right now," Olivia said, pointing to another chaise a few feet away where Bash had crashed. "Our son finally sleeps."

Everyone breathed a sigh of happiness, including Tinkerbell, who could finally settle at Eliza's feet, her favorite resting place.

Teddy took a deep breath, sensing that this had to be it. This was her chance.

"Well, my friends," she said. "Speaking of surprises, I have one."

A squeal came from the sand as Harper ran closer. "Surprises? I love them! What is it, Aunt Teddy?"

Noah was right behind her, laughing. "We managed

to not see a single turtle," he announced. "Which is good, because she really wanted to pet one. What's the surprise?"

He dropped into a seat next to Katie, letting Harper climb on his lap, completing the group.

Teddy took a moment to look around—at Camille and Buck, Eliza and Miles. Of course, there was Deeley and Olivia with their sons, and Asia and Dane fussing over Zee, who had just been transferred to Dane's arms. She glanced at Claire and her newfound love, and Noah, Katie, Harper, Jadyn, and Roz and George.

She loved them all so much. And she needed them.

"The surprise is that I have a problem with Dutch, and I need you all to help me solve it."

"Dutch?"

"What's the matter?"

"Whatever you need, Teddy!"

The chorus of support encouraged her more than she realized it would, bringing tears to her eyes.

"Well, it's not that big a problem, but the thing is... he's not buried."

They all looked at her, quiet and, yes, surprised.

"I have his ashes," she explained. "Which he asked be put 'in the sky,' and I have no idea how to do that."

"Parasail over the water?" Deeley suggested. "I can take you or anyone else out anytime."

"I actually thought of that, but it just doesn't feel right," she admitted. "Also not...what he'd want."

"Sanibel has some hot air balloon companies," Asia suggested. "Would you go up in one?"

"I'd hate the idea, but you know who else would hate it?" Teddy asked, laughing softly. "Dutch. He called them a sissy's way to fly."

George snorted. "That sounds like Dutch, right?"

"Yeah," Deeley agreed. "If it doesn't have a motor, wings, and a flight plan, it's not really worth considering."

Teddy nodded, chuckling at how well some of them knew the man in question.

"What was his exact request?" Camille asked. "Maybe he already had an idea."

Teddy closed her eyes and slipped back to the day they'd had the conversation.

"It was shortly before he died," she told them. "We were walking the beach on a night very much like this one. He'd drawn a heart in the sand and said something about the end being near."

They were all quiet, no doubt lost in their own memories or impressions of a man as large in death as he was in life.

"I asked him if he wanted to be buried there, on the shores of Shellseeker Beach, and he said, no, in the sky, where he belongs. He wanted people to look up and feel something."

"Something like what?" Olivia asked.

"He didn't say, but I guess everyone might look up at a cloud or a plane and feel something...different. Inspired or wishful or awed or even sad. Something."

"I know," Camille said suddenly. "I know exactly where you can put him in the air and people would look up and feel something. And it's also where he belongs."

All eyes were on her but she didn't answer, and Teddy gasped as she instantly knew, picking up the idea like it had floated over on the salt-scented air.

"Yes! That's it!"

"What's it?" several of them asked.

"Oh, I know," Miles said on a chuckle. "It's perfect."

"Yes!" Deeley clapped. "I love it."

"All right, some of us are dying here," Olivia whined. "Where? What?"

"Actually," Noah said, leaning forward. "The question is *how*."

At the slight outburst of questions and laughter, Teddy held up her hand, like they were playing a game of charades and she had to end the guessing. "The answer is the lighthouse on Sanibel Island."

"What?"

"That's brilliant!"

"The closest thing to heaven on Sanibel Island," Miles added.

"And utterly illegal," Claire called out. "Only a representative from the city can go to the top."

"But it's so small," Jadyn exclaimed. "It looks like it would be relatively easy to climb."

"I could do it," Noah said. "In fact, I'd love to, if you trust me, Teddy. I won't drop the box."

That got a groan and a few laughs.

"Well, like Claire said." Teddy shrugged. "We'd need permission and..."

Buck just started laughing. "Not with me, you don't. I used to own the land that lighthouse is on, the city council is pretty much in my pocket, and..." He looked over at Jonathan. "I know a high-powered judge in the county."

Jonathan lifted his beer. "Not so high-powered, but I can pull a string or two."

Everyone started to buzz and laugh, getting up and walking around, pouring more drinks and joking about how they all could make history and memories.

"And break the law," Claire reminded them on a laugh. "So if you need a good lawyer..."

Teddy leaned back and watched the controlled chaos she'd somehow set into motion, and a few minutes later, she and Camille were up in her room, getting the box.

"You know," Teddy said to Camille. "He was your husband, not mine. Did he give you any other ideas about his final resting place?"

Camille smiled and lifted the box, wrapping her fingers around it. "No, Teddy. We never talked about anything like that. We never..." She sighed. "I never knew what love was until now. I actually think you loved Dutch more than I did. And he loved you very, very much."

Teddy put an arm around the other woman and drew her closer. "I love him most for what he gave me, and that includes you."

With another hug, the two of them went back down to the beach with their treasure box and followed Noah, who'd become the de facto leader of the Lighthouse Farewell to Dutch party as they designated the drivers, piled into cars, and made the short trip to Lighthouse Beach Park.

The whole area was deserted and lit only by the dim light at the top of the iconic, if understated, lighthouse. They parked and gathered, talking in hushed tones with the occasional giggle from one of the kids, and low, excited laughter from the adults.

As a group, they walked toward the iron skeleton tower that stood no more than one hundred feet in the air. Did that qualify as "the sky"?

Teddy wasn't sure, but she knew one thing: Dutch would *love* this.

Around them, the beach was dim, and close enough to hear the waves splash on the sand as the tide came in.

The air crackled with adventure and fun as Teddy clutched Dutch's box to her chest and looked around the group of a dozen or so faces that she loved more than life itself.

Noah had jogged closer to the lighthouse with a flashlight, then came back to report.

"No one around anywhere. There's a spiral staircase around the middle, but I don't think you can do it, Teddy. It's a climb. I'll go."

She nodded, not willing to risk life and limb for this.

"I'd like to go, too," Dane said. "We're the grandsons, connected to him by two different mothers. We could do it together."

"I love that idea," Teddy said, holding the box out to Noah. "You two go up there and we'll watch."

"It's close enough that you can talk to us," Noah said. "We'll sprinkle and everyone can say their goodbyes."

They all loved the plan and sent them off, huddled together at the base of the lighthouse as they watched Noah and Dane climb.

Flanked by Camille on one side, who had her other arm around Claire, and Eliza on her right, who also clung to Olivia, they all grew very quiet, with only the sound of a breeze in the palm trees and the steady clunk of feet on metal as Noah and Dane made their way to the top.

This was truly perfect, Teddy thought. A fitting goodbye to Dutch.

"Okay," Noah called down, keeping his voice soft, but they could easily hear him.

"We made it," Dane added. "I'm removing the ashes."

"He did this for Ben," Eliza whispered. "He knows what to expect in that box."

Comforted by that, they all waited in silence.

"I'll start," Dane said. "May you rest in peace, Dutch Vanderveen. I am honored and humbled to come from your line. Thank you for giving the world my mother."

"Aww." Eliza sighed and looked up at the lighthouse. "We had our ups and downs, Dad," she whispered. "But in the end, you managed to guide me to exactly where I needed to be. Thank you."

"I never met you, Grandfather Dutch," Noah said after a few seconds of silence, his voice easily reaching them on the ground. "But someday I will write your story, and I will do it justice, you have my word." After a moment, he added, "We're fluttering ashes, everyone. Say what you'd like to say to send him off."

There was a moment of silence, then Olivia lifted her face to the lighthouse. "Once, when I was about five, you made a rare visit to our home. You made me a paper airplane and told me that whatever I did, I should touch the sky. I've never forgotten that, and I'll never forget you. Goodbye, Dutch. I will always attempt to touch the sky."

"You were the most exhilarating father a girl could have," Claire said next. "Maddening and hilarious and never dull. Thank you for giving me life."

"And thank you for flirting with the stewardess in First Class," Camille added. "I was never bored with you, Dutch. You made me crazy, you made me laugh, and you made me who I am today. *Au revoir, mon ami.*" Camille's French hung in the air for a moment, as everyone let out a collective sigh.

"You were a father when I needed one," Katie whispered. "And a grandfather to my baby, Harper."

"You were a friend when *I* needed one," Deeley added. "I will never forget how you helped me out of dark days."

"You welcomed Roz and me to Shellseeker Beach like we belonged here," George said. "You made the second half of our life so special."

"You gave me complete control of the shell shop," Roz added. "Because you knew I needed it."

"I remember you made me laugh, Uncle Dutch!" Harper sang out.

With each brief tribute, even from those who didn't know him, Teddy felt her throat thicken. Emotions rolled through her as she listened to the words, remembered the man, and acknowledged his impact on so many people.

Finally, when everyone was done, she took a slow, deep breath and looked at the stars and moon as she spoke.

"Dutch Vanderveen," she said softly. "You might have been a flawed man. No, no," she added on a laugh. "You were most *definitely* a flawed man. A sinner, some would say, living on the hairy edge of right and wrong. You broke some hearts, you healed some others. You learned your lessons, and you taught a few. You loved with every bone in your body and never met a stranger. But most of all, Dutch...most of all..."

Her voice cracked and she felt both Eliza and Camille squeeze her hands.

"Most of all," she continued, "you brought these people to me. From all over the globe, a collection of rare shells that, when put together on a canvas, creates the most beautiful picture of a family. You gave me sisters, brothers, daughters, sons, and grandchildren. Me! A woman who never married or had a child. When I met you, I was lonely, old, and expecting to die alone. But you gave me the miracle of a family and for that, I am eternally grateful."

As she finished, they all shared a teary, emotional hug.

Teddy looked to the sky one more time. "Goodbye,

my dearest Dutch," she whispered. "Fly into the night, across the horizon, and find your peace."

She wiped a tear, closed her eyes, and held tight to the family she'd never dreamed she'd have but would never again live without.

WOULD you like to read more sun-drenched stores full of family drama, wholesome romance, and fresh starts on new beaches? Good news! There will be another Hope Holloway series to sweep you away very soon! Visit www.hopeholloway.com for news on the next series!

The Coconut Key Series

While you're waiting, have you read Coconut Key, Hope Holloway's first, now completed, series set on the sun-kissed sands of the Florida Keys? With a cast of unforgettable characters, and stories that touch every woman's heart, these seven delightful novels will make you laugh out loud, wipe a happy tear, and believe in all the hope and happiness of a second chance at life.

A Secret in the Keys – Book 1
A Reunion in the Keys – Book 2
A Season in the Keys – Book 3
A Haven in the Keys – Book 4
A Return to the Keys – Book 5
A Wedding in the Keys – Book 6
A Promise in the Keys – Book 7

The Shellseeker Beach Series

Come to Shellseeker Beach and fall in love with a cast of unforgettable characters who face life's challenges with humor, heart, and hope. For lovers of riveting and inspirational sagas about sisters, secrets, romance, mothers, and daughters...and the moments that make life worth living.

About the Author

Hope Holloway is the author of charming, heartwarming women's fiction featuring unforgettable families and friends, and the emotional challenges they conquer. After more than twenty years in marketing, she launched a new career as an author of beach reads and feel-good fiction. A mother of two adult children, Hope and her husband of thirty years live in Florida. When not writing, she can be found walking the beach with her two rescue dogs, who beg her to include animals in every book. Visit her site at www.hopeholloway.com.

Made in the USA
Columbia, SC
10 December 2024

48905508R00207